ALI

CARA MIA DELGATTO MYSTERY SERIES

Joanna Campbell Slan

~Spot On Publishing~

All Washed Up: Book #3 in the Cara Mia Delgatto Mystery Series -- Copyright © 2016 by Joanna Campbell Slan

All rights reserved. No part of this publication may be reproduced, distributed or transmitted in any form or by any means, without prior written permission.

Joanna Campbell Slan/Spot On Publishing
9307 SE Olympus Street
Hobe Sound /FL 33455 USA
http://www.SpotOnPublishing.org

Publisher's Note: This is a work of fiction. Names, characters, places, and incidents are a product of the author's imagination. Locales and public names are sometimes used for atmospheric purposes. Any resemblance to actual people, living or dead, or to businesses, companies, events, institutions, or locales is completely coincidental.

Book Layout © 2016
http://www.BookDesignTemplates.com
Covers by Dar Albert, Wicked Smart Designs
http://www.WickedSmartDesigns.com
Editing by Wendy Green.

All Washed Up: Book #3 in the Cara Mia Delgatto Mystery Series—
Joanna Campbell Slan. – 2nd ed.
ISBN: **1545322651**
ISBN 13: 9781545322659
Revised 07/11/2017

ALL WASHED UP

BOOK #3 IN THE
CARA MIA DELGATTO MYSTERY SERIES

CHAPTER 1

Last week in January
Jupiter Island, Florida

~Cara Mia~

Morning dawned gray and indistinct on Jupiter Island. Locking my front door behind me and gathering my Chihuahua's leash in my hand, I pointed us toward the narrow road that led to the Hobe Sound Beach Park. The gloomy weather disappointed me, but Jack didn't mind at all. Waving his tiny tail, Jack threw his weight (all two pounds of it!) against the leash so that he leaned away from me as he scampered down the street.

The fog sent a chill through me, but Jack's merry attitude brought a smile to my face. Okay, so this gloomy weather wasn't what I'd expected of sunny Florida. This was the best time of day for walking on the beach, right before the fisherman dragged their gear to the water's edge. Long before the sunbathers would spread their colorful towels and pop the tops on their soft drinks. This quiet island would reveal its secrets to me while I watched the sun pop up on the horizon like a ripe orange being squeezed out of a grocery bag.

Jack and I turned left where Bridge Road dead-ended at Hobe Sound Park. The gloom muted the colors of larger-than-life sculptures of sea turtles, a vivid reminder of our fragile ecosystem. A sign on a plinth reminded visitors of the turtles' lifecycle. I noted that nesting season was a full two months away. I tightened my grip on Jack's leash, rather than let him roam the dunes. Raccoons, possums, and cane toads could all pose a danger to my small companion.

The wood of the boardwalk was old and bounced under my well-worn tennis shoes. Since finding a stray fishhook in the sand, I've learned that being barefoot can be hazardous. Especially early in the morning, when you can't see clearly. At the crest of the boardwalk, I paused, taking in the magnificent view. An overcast sky touched the concrete-colored water, creating a seamless, endless ribbon of dull nothingness. A wave of vertigo made me dizzy as the band of dull, lifeless color stretched out in front of me, arched up and over me. One word popped into my head: Dead.

A shiver ran down my spine. I was being silly. Jack sensed my reticence. Rearing up on his back legs, he plonked his front paws against my calf muscles, urging me onward.

Determined to master my emotions, I shook my head and got my bearings. On either side of the boardwalk, sea oats rustled in the breeze. Their golden serrated heads created a spot of metallic color against the glum vista. Impatiently, Jack yanked me forward. Following his lead, my feet touched the wet sand. The pungent smell of seaweed greeted me. Last night's storm had left a wrack line dark with dense mounds of Sargasso. Jack lunged to the right, sniffing eagerly at a knot of sand sporting a halo of wet feathers.

"Get away from that," I urged him.

A handful of seabirds died in every storm. Riding the winds exhausted them. Eventually, the high winds would fling their bodies into the surf so that they littered the beach the next day. While Jack fought me to sniff and explore, adorable sandpipers ignored the carnage. Their tiny legs moved double-time as they raced to pick up yummy delicacies before the crustaceans burrowed too deeply in the sand, making their escape.

"Knock it off, buddy," I chided Jack as he fought the leash and pulled me forward. He lunged toward a huge clump of seaweed, shaped like a person.

So I wasn't alone on the beach this morning! Someone had gotten here before me. Jack tugged relentlessly toward the sand sculpture. Thanks to our walks, I'd discovered that beachgoers showed endless creativity. I'd found messages in bottles, seashells spelling out love notes, sandcastles of all sizes, and now someone had crafted a mermaid, half in and half out of the water.

"Huh. Somebody must have been working in the dark," I muttered. "Weird."

In the distance, the roar of an ATV signaled that the beach patrol had started its day, making the rounds. When the wind changed, a whiff of diesel made my nose prickle even though the ATV was a football field away.

I had rescued Jack after a truck driver tossed him out the window of his pickup. Not surprisingly, the little dog gets spooked by loud engines. But this morning, he didn't notice the ATV. Despite the noise of the approaching vehicle, Jack dragged me toward the lumps in the sand. He pitched his entire weight against the leash as he strained toward the mermaid. Closer inspection showed a remarkably realistic creature with dark brown hair, presumably a clump of seaweed. Her arms were thrown up over her head. Her face was turned toward the water. The advancing tide nipped at the tip of her tail.

Jack's toenails threw up sand as he struggled to get closer to her.

"Come on, buddy. If you get wet, you'll need a bath." I tugged at his leash.

The *put-put-put* of the ATV's motor roared louder and louder. The driver's faded blue cap bobbed up and down, appearing and disappearing, as the vehicle climbed low hills and descended into dips. Usually our beach is perfectly flat, but last night's rough tides had caused escarpments, jagged chunks carved from the friable surface. As the ATV got closer, Jack started to get nervous. He backed away from the water's edge, growling at the mermaid.

"Come on," I urged him. "It's just a pile of sand, Jack! There's nothing to be scared of!"

He froze in his tracks.

I nearly tripped over my own feet, rather than step on him. An ear-piercing howl splintered the morning quiet.

"Buddy, it's okay!" I bent low to scoop Jack into my arms. My eyes followed the direction of his stare.

The mermaid lifted her head and groaned.

CHAPTER 2

"Help! Over here!" I screamed and waved down the ATV driver. The man in the vehicle roared up, stopping a foot from the prone figure.

"S-s-she's alive," I said, pointing to the mermaid. "Help me get her away from the water!"

"Jumping Jehoshaphat!" The man turned off his motor, grabbed at a first aid kit, and hopped down from his seat.

Quickly tying Jack's leash to the handlebars of the ATV, I waded into the surf. The driver was ahead of me, but not by much. Together we lifted the soggy figure and moved her up to the dry sand. As light as she was, I figured she must have weighed less than a hundred pounds. Maybe even more like seventy-five. Wiping the sand from her face exposed a sagging neckline, crow's feet around her eyes, and gray streaks in the hair that framed her face.

"A-B-C. Airway cleared, breathing established, circulation resumed," he said. "That's the order."

"Right. We need to roll her on her side," I said.

"One, two, three." With a nod, he signaled for us to flip her onto her side. I pried open her mouth, stuck my fingers in, and hauled out a wodge of sand and seaweed. She gurgled and puked up more seawater. The smell was weakly acidic. I held her head until she was done. She went limp. The driver positioned her so that her neck was straight and her airway was open. I lightly tapped her face and tried to bring her around to consciousness. "Stay with us!"

"Did you call for help?" The driver put his head to her chest and ran his fingers along her throat, feeling for a pulse. "Of course, it might not matter. Cell coverage is spotty on the island."

"No," I said. "I don't have my phone with me. I'm Cara Mia Delgatto."

"Lucas," he said. "Lucas Petruski. I can't tell if she's breathing or not."

He quickly called for help. At one point, he told the dispatcher my name. After he ended the call, he said, "Okay. We'd better start CPR."

His first aid kit produced plastic bellows that he used to force air into the woman's lungs. I measured down the proper distance and began doing compressions on her chest. As we worked, I debated the wisdom of our actions. The woman drooped like a limp dish rag. Although the surface of her dark skin was reddish-tan, the color of a brick, the undertone was a dull, lifeless gray.

"She might have been without air for too long," said Lucas. "Might be a mercy if she doesn't come around. I've seen drowning victims before. They come back only to die later. Pneumonia kills most of them."

"But that's not our choice to make," I said.

"True enough."

As I rocked back and forth, shifting my weight to compress her chest, I sent up prayers, although I was unsure what to ask for.

Her face was swollen, exaggerating her features, and blistered, making the shapes hard to discern. She was emaciated, without the normal padding most women accumulate. Watery bubbles covered her cheekbones, the tops of her ears, and her shoulders. Thin sheets of white skin were peeling off her nose and neck. Despite the dunking she'd obviously endured, she smelled strongly of urine. Tattered flags of fabric clung to her torso and legs. Bits of bark brown seaweed tangled in her hair.

Sirens sounded in the distance and grew ever closer until they stopped.

Medics raced along the boardwalk, their heavy footfalls causing the weathered wood to shake.

"We'll take it from here," one of them commanded us, as the other quickly straddled the mermaid and took over for Lucas.

Lucas and I did as told. I untethered Jack. He'd been solemnly watching Lucas and me. Some canine instinct told him the situation was serious.

The screech of brakes and slamming of doors suggested more official helpers had arrived. Crackling voices and radio static mixed with terse comments from the EMTs.

I retreated as far onto the dunes as possible without stepping on sea oats, a protected part of the environment. Jack came along reluctantly.

While the EMTs checked our mermaid's vital signs, the cops spoke into radio units hooked to the shoulders of their shirts.

A tech ripped open a foil pack, swabbed the mermaid's inner arm with an alcohol rub, and inserted a needle leading to a plastic bag of clear liquid. There was a low murmur of discussion among the medics as they triaged the woman. It didn't sound good. Not at all. In short order, they had the woman on a gurney, one guy continuing to work on her, and they were racing her toward the ambulance. With sirens and lights blazing, they went tearing out of the parking lot.

"Copy that," said one of the cops to his buddy. "The boss is on the way."

The ATV guy shook his head as he took his place at my side. "What a mess. Second one this morning. Heard about it on my radio. Over at Blowing

Rocks."

Jupiter Island is rich with nature preserves, thanks to the farsightedness of the Reed family, one of the earliest landowners. There's one north, one south, and a park in the middle of the island where we were standing. This beach is the most convenient to local highways. The admission and parking are both free, although the number of spaces is limited—and with good reason. Our island is part of a fragile ecosystem, one of the world's prime nesting areas for endangered sea turtles.

"Does that mean a boat capsized?"

Lucas gave me a speculative look. "Maybe."

I opened my mouth to ask another question, but he had turned his back on me. The set of his shoulders suggested all conversation was over.

Why? What wasn't he saying?

I was so intent on watching the cops comb the area that I jumped in surprise when Detective Lou Murray tapped me on the shoulder.

CHAPTER 3

"What's with you and dead bodies?" The big detective frowned down at me. Lou has a craggy face and eyes that tell you he's seen a lot of misery in his life. He also has hands the size of small footballs. As he rested one palm on my arm, I realized this was a man who could pack one whale of a punch.

The blood rushed to my face. "Excuse me? You can't possibly be blaming me for this, Lou. Even you aren't that stupid. Not my fault that I found this person."

I sounded defensive because I was upset. Less than two weeks ago, I'd stumbled onto a body and gotten involved in a murder investigation. Moving to the little house that my grandfather owned on Jupiter Island had seemed like a guarantee that such gruesome discoveries were behind me.

Evidently not.

"Whoa. Calm down. Didn't say you were to blame. Just noticing you're a human cadaver dog. When it comes to dead bodies, you seem to sniff them out. That's not good, Cara. You need to stay away from situations like this."

Jack and I had been standing around for nearly half an hour, as the sun burned off the fog and shooed away the last vestiges of the night. However, the air was still chilly, so I hugged Jack closer to keep myself warm. My wet shoes and soggy hemline on my pants added to my general discomfort.

Reaching across me to pat my dog, Lou looked into Jack's eyes and said, "How's Jack, huh? Is Cara your human familiar? Maybe you're the cadaver dog and she's just your handler?"

The little dog's tail wagged aggressively.

"Traitor," I growled at my dog. Jack used to be afraid of Lou, but the big man has won him over. With a wriggle of joy, the little rascal tried to climb out of my arms. He loves getting his ears rubbed.

"How come you're here?" I asked Lou. "This isn't your patch." He's a detective with the Stuart PD, ten miles north of here. Jupiter Island employs its own public safety workers, AKA cops.

"I was having breakfast with a friend from the Martin County Sheriff's Office. He took the call. I overheard your name. Skye would never forgive me if I didn't make sure you were okay."

He and my part-time employee and full-time friend, Skye Blue, have become quite the item. Although their romance is moving along at a glacial pace, they're definitely a twosome. I have a hunch that since I moved out of the apartment next door to Skye's, Lou might have started spending the night with her, but I can't say for sure. I've thought about asking her, but I can't figure out a pretext for being so nosy. They're both grown-ups and what they do is their business, after all.

Beyond us, the sun had parted the dark clouds. Its golden reflection looked like a handful of coins bouncing off the surface of the water and chasing shadows out of the nooks and crannies of the dunes. Despite the bleak scene before us, this was shaping up to be another perfect day in Paradise.

"How'd you happen on her?" Lou asked. "What's your secret? This is your third dead body in, what, less than nine months?"

"She isn't dead. Or didn't you hear?" I shaded my eyes as I turned toward Lou.

Lucas overheard me. He sighed and clucked his tongue. "Might as well be. No telling what kind of condition she'll be in."

The biologist shifted his weight and glanced at his watch. His canvas sun hat dangled limply around his neck. Something about the shared experience of finding the woman caused Lucas and me to stand shoulder-to-shoulder in solidarity. We drew comfort from each other's presence. Lucas continued, his words echoing my earlier thoughts. "Given the shape she was in, I don't know that we did her any favors."

Jack burrowed deeper into my arms. The flurry of activity was making him nervous. His tiny body shivered.

"It's okay. Sh, sh," I murmured as I stroked him.

"Cara?" A familiar figure jangled his way down the boardwalk.

"Poppy! Am I ever glad to see you!" I threw my free arm around my grandfather's neck and breathed in the scent of Aqua Velva. Jack didn't like being caught between us, so he struggled to get loose, but I wasn't ready to let Poppy go. A sense of vulnerability struck me hard.

"How's Sid?" I was asking about my eighteen-year-old computer whiz who'd just moved in with my grandfather.

"Sound asleep. We can talk about him later."

Lucas stared at my grandfather, as if trying to place him.

"Dick Potter." Poppy offered his hand to my new friend. "I'm this here girl's granddaddy."

"Yeah, yeah, yeah." Luke nodded. "That's right. I remember. You owned the Gas E Bait. In Stuart. Downtown. Used to bring this ATV in for a yearly tune up."

"Yup." Poppy jerked his chin. His gas station had been closed for months now, but a place like that was sure to linger in the minds of the locals. When a cheap sign painter confused the squiggle (technically called an ampersand) with the letter "E," the pit stop and bait shop became the "Gas E Bait." The quirky name appealed to Poppy's sense of humor, so he kept it. "How's your ATV running?"

"Could use a tune-up."

"Bring it by my house. I'll get it humming like a sewing machine," said Poppy, reaching into the pocket of his jeans for a business card. He'd added his home address in an untidy scrawl. "Of course, that's only a temporary address. You heard about that new Fill Up and Go? I'm going to be in charge of the garage there. Have a whole crew of mechanics working for me." Poppy puffed up with pride.

"Why're you here?" I whispered to my grandfather. "Can't be to drum up business."

"I phoned him when I pulled up," Lou said, leaning close to us. "Figured you might need somebody to hang around after I check the house for you."

"Check my house?" I repeated slowly. "I locked the door behind me when we took off for our walk. I should be fine."

Little known fact: Jupiter Island has the largest ratio of cops to citizens of any municipality in the U.S. Not only do they have *To Serve and Protect* painted on their cars, but I'd bet you a hundred bucks it's tattooed prominently somewhere on their hot little bodies. When we dial 911, they come double-quick.

In the distance, more sirens wailed, but they sounded like they were headed away from us.

Lou and Poppy exchanged knowing looks.

Then it hit me. "Lucas said there was someone else. At Blowing Rocks. Two people in one morning? Who goes out into the ocean at night in a small boat? No one. And it can't have been a big boat or they would have sent out a distress call. But the Coast Guard doesn't seem to be involved. So, there's something else happening here, right? Something more…involved."

"Let's get you home, Granddaughter." Poppy took my elbow. "You make a statement, yet?"

"Nope."

"I'll ask that young pup over there if he's ready to take it." Lou stalked off in the direction of a cop who looked barely old enough to shave.

"There's something going on, isn't there? More than…this poor half-drowned woman." I scowled at my grandfather. "Poppy? Are you listening?"

"Yup."

Lucas had edged his way toward the older of the two Jupiter Island policemen. After a brief confab, he hopped back on his ATV, while Lou talked to the young cop. In short order, the officer came over, introduced himself, and took my statement. I didn't have much to say, except that I'd been walking my dog and stumbled over a mermaid.

While we were finishing up, Lucas turned over the engine and drove past.

Lou and the JI cop exchanged business cards.

"This is like an ad hoc Chamber of Commerce event," I said. "Everyone passing around business cards. Everyone except me."

"Cara?" Lou ambled toward me. "Meet you at your place." He pointed his chin at his police cruiser.

Poppy slung his arm around my shoulders and twirled me so I was pointed at his Toyota truck. He whispered in my ear, "Hold your tongue, Granddaughter."

We were walking through the parking lot when more of the pieces clicked into place. "This isn't the first time, is it? There was that group that washed up two weeks ago. That family. All dead. From the Bahamas, right? There's a pattern here."

Poppy's eyes turned flinty. "We can talk at your house."

CHAPTER 4

After Poppy keyed the engine, I said, "Someone is bringing people to this island, isn't he? Or she? Or them? Because we keep it dark for the turtles."

"That can wait for Lou. We got other things to discuss. You and me."

"But—"

The glare he sent me shut me up. Fast. My grandfather could be as stubborn as a barnacle. While I mustered up the energy to complain, he snarled, "Before Lou gets to your place, you and me need to have a little powwow of our own. What in the blue blazes were you doing on that beach?"

"Taking a walk. What else would I be doing at this hour?"

"Have you lost your pea-picking mind? You got no business being all alone out there. Did you have your cell phone on you?"

"No. What good would that do me? Coverage is spotty on the island. I certainly wouldn't have called you."

"Why not? You know I'm up at crack of dawn. I'm here, ain't I?" He jerked the steering wheel as he made the right turn into my driveway. "I expected you to use your brain, Granddaughter. This house is your'n, and I won't go back on my word, but I never expected you to act like a witless fool. Running around in the dark? By yourself?"

"A witless fool?" I couldn't believe what I was hearing. "I had my dog with me."

He threw his hands up. "Dog? You could walk a hamster and be better protected."

"Are you kidding me? Can you hear yourself? Poppy, I couldn't be any safer! This is Jupiter Island. There are security cameras following on every vehicle that comes over the bridges."

"Fat lot of good that'll do you if someone rolls up in a boat. Did you even think about that, smarty? What if they dragged you to a house and held you captive? Or stuffed you into the trunk of a car? No, missy, you didn't think about that, did ya? I thought not! You got no business walking on the beach in the dark, especially without your cell phone. I thought you were smarter than that. I guess I thought wrong!"

Before I could spit back a response, he had already hopped out of the truck. Although Poppy is nearly eighty and suffers from diabetes, he's as nimble as a teenager. Probably because he's stayed active. If he isn't working on motors, he's fishing or kayaking or hiking or puttering around in my store, The

Treasure Chest, a shop featuring recycled, upcycled, and repurposed products with a beachy theme. We've developed our own funky coastal style, a unique look that's all ours.

I unlocked the front door. Poppy pushed past me and into the house. Soundlessly, he walked from room to room, before announcing, "Okay. Glad to see that at least you're locking the front door."

"It's not like anyone is liable to break in. I don't have anything worth stealing."

"It ain't your possessions I'm worried about." He crossed his arms over his chest and waited at the kitchen window until Lou pulled up. "What you really need is a bigger dog. A Dobie or a Shepherd."

A rap on the door cut our conversation short. I ducked into the kitchen while Poppy let Lou in. From the half-wall that divided my dining area from my living room, I watched as the men took seats on opposite ends of my sofa.

"Kinda Spartan, isn't this? You slumming it here on Jupiter Island?" Lou looked pleased with himself.

"How come you ain't dragged any of that there furniture from your store over here?" Poppy scratched his head.

"I only make money when I sell it. Not when I sit on it. Until you two came along, no one complained," I said. That wasn't strictly true. Skye and MJ (my ace full-time employee) had also made fun of my meager belongings.

"When are you going to tell me more about Sid?"

"When I know more. I picked him up from the hospital yesterday, and he's been sleeping most of the time. He and I ain't had much chance to visit. Iff'n he's up to it, I plan to bring him into your store later today. Matter of fact, I was on my way to buy him an Egg McMuffin for breakfast when Lou called."

"I'll put the kettle on and make us all coffee. There's fresh banana bread. I can send you home with half a loaf of it, Poppy." Thinking of Sid's accident, and how he'd been hit by a car, caused me to shiver. While I puttered around in the kitchen, the men were quiet. They perked up when I handed Lou and Poppy each a plate. "What's so hush-hush that you wouldn't talk about it back at the beach?"

"When you fly over Florida, there's a dark patch along our coast." Poppy spat out the words. He put a lot of violence behind what seemed like a simple statement of fact.

"Okay. Got it. That patch is Jupiter Island. We keep it dark for the sea turtles, right? To encourage their nesting." I parked my backside on a Styrofoam cooler that I brought home to turn into an ottoman. Styrofoam is a modern scourge. It doesn't break down. It's deadly to sea creatures, but useful for packaging items that must remain cool, like Poppy's insulin. I was determined to find a way to reuse these coolers, although I knew it would be tricky. A lot of glue eats right through Styrofoam, melting it. Covering up this ugly white box might prove a challenge.

Lou swallowed a big chunk of his banana bread. "Imagine you're piloting a boat full of illegal immigrants. You got your choice. Steer toward the bright lights of Miami or Palm Beach. Point your bow toward the Jupiter lighthouse. Or go toward a dark patch. Totally black. Where would you put into shore?"

"Jupiter Island." I hopped up before the kettle whistled its way to an ear-splitting decibel. As I poured water into the French press, I asked, "But why come to this side of the island? There's the Intracoastal on the other side, and it's got all those docks. Wouldn't that make disembarkation easier? Did my mermaid fall overboard? Or did a tender tip over?"

Poppy chortled. "Not likely."

"Are you suggesting that she jumped? In these waters? With sharks and jellyfish and coral reefs? I wouldn't have. I'd have waited until we docked."

"Not if someone held a gun to your head," said Lou.

"You're kidding!"

"Nope. The trafficker gets his money on the front end. He doesn't care about delivery. In fact, he probably gets a bonus if he makes it home with the boat in one piece." Lou brushed the crumbs from his hands and watched Jack eagerly lick them up off my tile floor. "The people who make it to shore want to get away as fast as possible and blend into the population. Often there's a person waiting to pick them up and drive them away. In fact, they're keeping an eye out for that person right now. Needless to say, JI's public safety department has its hands busy. Have you given any thought to getting your concealed carry license? Keeping a gun on the premises?"

That was the longest speech I'd ever heard from Lou. In response, I laughed. "Why? So I could shoot myself in the foot?"

"How about getting a bigger dog?" Lou raised a thick eyebrow.

"That's what I told her." Poppy sighed. "This mutt's a yapper. Good dog, but not bigger than a minute. Granddaughter, you need a dog that'll make an intruder think twice."

"Right. I'm already supporting Jack and Luna, my cat. Two rescues. Why not add another mouth to feed?"

I scooted my ersatz ottoman closer to Poppy and Lou so they could rest their coffee cups on the Styrofoam before picking up their empty plates and walking back into the kitchen to refill them.

"Ah," said Lou, slurping his coffee. "You make a good brew, Cara. I like the banana bread, too. I was hoping there was more."

More.

That word struck a chord. This wasn't the first time undocumented immigrants had washed up on the shores of Jupiter Island. A handful had been found last week, wandering up and down Bridge Road. Poor people had nothing but the clothes on their backs.

Lucas had spoken about another body at Blowing Rocks. At least, that was what I thought he was saying. Had I gotten it wrong?

And…MJ! She had mentioned a home visit she'd made, here on the island. When was it? A week ago? A resident had called asking if we wanted to buy a few vintage Florida pieces. The woman had shown MJ her furnishings and a raft made of small trees, little more than saplings, all lashed together with twine. The sort of twisted hemp you'd use to tie up packages. According to the resident, her gardener had discovered it, hidden under a stand of sea oats at the edge of her lawn. The property owner thought it hilarious. MJ reported how the woman had laughed and offered to sell us the raft for fifty bucks. She thought we could use it in our display window.

"Gross." MJ had shaken her head in disgust. "Think of it. Clinging onto those toothpicks for dear life. The desperation. But Mrs. Norland thought it a hoot. A real chuckle. Ugh."

Three separate sightings. Four, if you counted my mermaid. People were washing up on a regular basis. But how did they know to point their boats toward Jupiter Island? Sure, if you had the money to hire a plane and fly over, you'd notice we were dark, but we were talking about illegal immigrants. If they had access to airfare, they wouldn't be clinging to homemade rafts or paying dodgy captains. They'd be working with immigration attorneys.

Instead, they were tumbling along in our surf. Rolling up on our sand. Heading for an alleged dark spot some three hours north of Miami.

Why here?

Suddenly, the answer came to me. "You two are thinking that someone on this island is behind all this, right? Someone is pointing the traffickers here? Maybe even involved in human trafficking? Offering the boat captains a place to dock? Financing the whole shebang?"

Lou became intensely interested in his shoes.

But Poppy stared straight ahead. For a long, long time, he said nothing.

And then finally, "Yup."

CHAPTER 5

~Lou~

Since Cara hadn't been living on the island more than a couple of weeks, George Fernandez, Director of Public Safety for Jupiter Island, needed to know that she was "good people." As a courtesy, Lou dropped by at George's office to speak on her behalf.

Lou and Fernandez had known each other for years; Fernandez had worked for the Stuart police before getting the job on Jupiter Island.

But there was another reason that Lou stopped by the white clapboard building that housed the Jupiter Island law enforcement officials. He, too, was curious. Did Fernandez think a resident was welcoming the illegals? If so, what was he planning to do? Every time a boat spewed out more undocumented immigrants, the entire area had cause to worry. The illegals coming ashore could be mentally unstable, could be violent, or have terrorist links. Since they hadn't been vetted, no one knew what the tides were turning up.

And that made Lou concerned, both for Cara and for the city of Stuart, his turf.

Fernandez seemed to have expected Lou. He stood, greeted his old colleague, and nodded toward the vacant chair across from his desk. The other chair was occupied by Brandon Mashler, the young first responder who had taken Cara's statement out on the beach.

"Glad you dropped by," said Fernandez. "Had things turned out differently we might have needed your help. As it stands, the town's cameras and license identification system helped us identify the pick-up vehicle. A suspect has been apprehended."

"That's good. Thought you might be wondering about Cara Mia Delgatto. She's a solid citizen, even if she does have a habit of showing up at the wrong place and the wrong time. She's Dick Potter's granddaughter. One of them, at least."

"I'd heard rumors that she's all right, but confirmation is nice to have. If she's A-OK in your book, that's something."

"She is. But I am concerned about her on another front. She's living in Dick's cottage all alone. Her dog's a little yappy thing. Not sure if anyone filled you in on her situation."

"Noted. I'll tell our crew to keep an eye out for her. As you know," Fernandez said, as he leaned forward to steeple his fingers, "we've had a rash of these undocumented immigrant landings. We're working with state and federal agencies to figure out what gives. They've increased the number of patrol boats along our coast. The boats' presence has encouraged a lot of the smugglers to turn back. But not all of them. A few are, well, ruthless. Ms. Delgatto got lucky this morning. If she had happened upon the captain of the boat that brought this group in or if she'd seen the pick-up vehicle, things could have gotten…"

Lou didn't need Fernandez to finish his sentence. He knew full well that a coyote would not have hesitated to shoot Cara. Human traffickers were brutal, driven only by the promise of rich rewards. A young woman and her dog were unwanted complications, easily disposed of.

Fernandez let the implications hang in the air. Officer Mashler shuffled his feet.

"Maybe you can speak to her, Lou. Suggest she confine her walks to areas where we have lifeguards."

"I'm not sure that Cara will listen to me. She's very strong-willed."

Fernandez gave Lou a crooked smile. "I should have guessed as much. Especially after you confirmed that she's Dick Potter's granddaughter. Does she have any idea about Dick's past?"

"No. At least, none that I know of. I doubt that he's told her…all of it."

Brandon had been sitting as quietly as a lizard watching for gnats, but now he sprang to life. "What past?"

"Later," said Fernandez with a wave of his hand. "Brandon, you're new here, so right now, what I want you to understand is that this stretch offers an ideal spot to bring criminals, drugs, and undocumented immigrants to our country. Or human cargo. Even foreign nationals. And Lou? That's what we think we have here. Someone who is bringing warm bodies to our shores. Sure, it's possible these are random landings. But I doubt it. We've had more than our fair share lately."

"Why?" Brandon leaned forward in his seat. His eyes snapped with interest. "I mean, isn't it possible these are random groups of desperate people? They don't act like anyone among them is in charge. Why don't you think their landings are accidental?"

"Your average undocumented immigrant can't afford a 25-foot boat," Lou said. "No way. Someone is behind this operation. Think about it. As a rule of thumb, people pay $1,000 per foot for a boat. That doesn't include a trailer, maintenance, insurance, gas, or the captain. In fact, a captain is often paid $1,000 per foot. Of course, that's a captain with experience who plans on bringing the souls on board and the boat back in one piece."

Fernandez nodded. "The Coast Guard stopped a 32-foot Chris-Craft speeding away from Peanut Island last week. They weren't out for a midnight cruise. No, these boats are too big, too fast, and too well navigated. This smacks of organization."

"Usually there's no season to these landings," Lou directed his remarks to Brandon. "The smugglers wait until they get enough people to make the crossing worthwhile and then go. They don't worry about the weather, because frankly, they don't care whether the cargo makes it or not. But we've had so many landings recently it sure looks like an organized effort. And the vessels they're using are primo."

"In Season, we have 668 residents," Fernandez said. "Half of our residents live here part-time. They come down to go to the club, see their old friends, and play golf or tennis. Sure, they love the beach, but we aren't really a tourist destination. Not like Daytona or Delray or even Fort Lauderdale. So our beaches are sparsely populated, compared to some."

"Got it." Brandon's scowl deepened. "But Ms. Delgatto is a full-time resident, right? She has a business in Stuart."

"That's right." George Fernandez nodded. "She's young, attractive, and—here's another problem—she's single. At least from what I've heard. No one might notice she was missing for hours. That's why I want her to stay off our beaches in the pre-dawn hours. At least until we figure out who's behind this. It's not safe for her to wander around."

"Then you're thinking it might be a local behind this?" Lou asked. "A person familiar with the area. Someone would have the money for the boat, who knows the island is barely occupied, and maybe someone who's squatting on a dock on the Intracoastal side of the island."

"That's right. Our population skews toward the elderly. A few residents are infirm, living out their last years here where it's warm with caregivers in charge. They might not even know that their dock is being used. In fact, they might not know if someone is using their property. Couple of years ago, we discovered a homeless man squatting in a guest house. The place had been unlocked, so he moved in. Might have been there two or three months."

"Whether it's a local who's behind these landings or not, he or she isn't going to take kindly to Cara's interference," Lou said. With a sigh, he added,

"The tough part will be convincing Cara that she's in danger. She's a spitfire."

"Yes, well, that's why I need your help," said Fernandez. "Lou, I want you to be the one to warn Ms. Delgatto. At least convince her to stick close to the areas frequented by the public and to contain her wanderings to daylight hours."

Lou chuckled. "That's going to go over about as well as wearing a fur coat down here in August."

CHAPTER 6

~ Cara Mia~

"What is an ATV guy? I have no idea what you're talking about," said MJ Austin, fluttering eyelashes thick with mascara. Her blond hair was caught up in a plastic clip that allowed tendrils to frame her face.

"Is it a kid who rides a three-wheeler on the sand?" asked Skye Blue, as she pushed a stray curl away from her eyes. Her hair isn't as blond as MJ's, but it has honey-colored sunstreaks.

Me, I'm the dark-haired one of the trio, harking back to my Italian heritage.

"An ATV guy? That's the person who rides the beach on his ATV," I said.

"What?" MJ stared at me. "Is that his hobby? Or is he a nut?"

I'd forgotten that the ATV rider/biologist on duty was yet another Jupiter Island anomaly. "The ATV guy? Jupiter Island employs people who ride an ATV up and down the beach each morning during nesting season to count and keep track of the number of turtle nests. There's a man and a woman, both biologists, and they can actually tell from the tracks, shape, and location what species of turtle made each particular nest. I've run into the scientists on the beach before," I said as I poured myself a cup of coffee. "But since this isn't nesting season, Lucas was there to do a survey in preparation for beach renourishment. Adding more sand. They'll keep him busy making sure the giant pipes don't suck up turtles as they move the sand around."

We were sitting in the back room of The Treasure Chest. Although we'd been open for less than a year, my employees and I had already formed ironclad habits. Each morning before the store's opening, MJ, Skye, and I gathered in the back. Over our preferred hot beverages, we shared trivialities and eventually our lives. Skye was the first person I had met when I moved to Stuart, Florida. She's naturally outgoing with a fresh, open way about her. When she's not working for me part-time, she's a server across the street at Pumpernickel's Deli. I wish I could afford to hire her full-time, but she's so good at her job as a waitress that she makes more in tips than I can pay. Right now at least. Maybe someday.

In contrast to Skye, MJ can seem aloof, and she is, sort of. Her va-va-voom figure and sultry ways have made her an easy target for other women's jealousies, so she's learned to be guarded around other females. Slowly, she's let down her metaphorical hair. The three of us are very different in our looks, our styles, and our backgrounds, but all three of us care about each other.

MJ used to work for Essie Feldman, the original owner of The Treasure Chest. She has scads of experience with retail sales and vintage décor items.

"As you might guess, Jupiter Island employs all sorts of experts for all sorts of reasons. Thank goodness, because on this particular morning, I was thrilled not to be out there alone." I wouldn't have said this to Poppy or Lou, but I could be honest with my pals.

"Human traffickers have no regard for human life. I saw a true crime show where they locked people into a railway car and left them there to die. There has to be a special punishment for people like that. They call them coyotes for a reason," said MJ, as she sipped her black coffee. "They're predators. Vicious flesh eaters."

"Coyotes?" I stirred Stevia into my coffee. Skye has us all being very conscious of sugar in our diet. She's into health food in a big way.

"Coyotes. That's what they call human traffickers." Skye sighed over her cup of peppermint tea.

From his crate, Jack whimpered in response to our mood. I got up and offered him a yummy. He, too, was suffering from the stressful events of our walkies. Usually he's ready for a nap when we get to the store. Not this morning. His ears were pricked up and his eyes watchful, mournful even. From the sales floor, Kookie the Cockatoo sang a sailing ditty. Like the rest of our pets, she—or he, we don't know which it is—is a rescue animal.

"Human trafficking? It's all news to me. I know nothing about it," I said. "That poor woman had washed up like a piece of trash. She must have been out in the sun for a long time. You should have seen how blistered her skin was. It came peeling off her in big white sheets."

"I've read about human traffickers. They promise people a better life and take their money in exchange for getting them into the U.S. People really believe the streets here are paved with gold." Skye shrugged. "I guess they are compared to the lack of opportunities in other countries. These creeps who bring people here really exploit the weak and helpless."

"And criminals," MJ said. "We have no idea who's coming over our borders. Sure, maybe some are good people, but others might be the worst of the worst. What a great racket. All you have to do is load them on the boat and head out for deep waters. If things get dicey, you toss them over the side. Who's left to complain?"

"That woman you found probably paid the coyote a king's ransom," Skye said. "Everything her family could scrounge up. It was all riding on her and their hopes that she could make a new life for herself here in Paradise."

"We need to stop illegal immigration," MJ said. "We need to build a fence. A giant wall. Patrol our seas better. They're taking our jobs. Putting pressure on our services. Here in Florida, our school systems can't support the number of kids these undocumented immigrants are having. It's a stress on our economy."

"But you're talking about kids." Skye's voice rose a notch. "Helpless children. What kind of lives will they have in Haiti or in Cuba? Even in Guatemala? What kind of opportunity? Your family came here from somewhere else, MJ. Mine did, too. So did Cara's. Who are we to say, Stay home?"

It was an old argument. One that MJ and Skye had often. They could really get mad at each other. Lately, I'd considered buying a black and white striped blouse so I could play the part of referee.

"Come on, guys." I patted the air. "No fights this morning. Please? Give me a break."

Fortunately, fate intervened.

CHAPTER 7

"Just your size," said Danielle Cronin. "I wanted to bring this dress over before your store got busy."

A wire coat hanger was hooked over one hand. With the other, Danielle lifted the garment, so I could see the fabric more clearly through the plastic drycleaner's bag. Paramount Cleaners on Jupiter Island. I passed it on my way home each day.

"The moment my client pulled it out of her closet, I knew you had to have it, Cara. Got your name all over it. Figuratively speaking, of course. Actually, it has Lilly's name all over it. It's a vintage Lilly Pulitzer. In fact, it was one of the first fabric patterns she commissioned. You certainly won't see yourself coming and going in this. But people will recognize the style of print. Especially since Target did that big Lilly promotion. People who'd never heard of her now are lusting for Lilly Pulitzer items like never before. See, Lilly used to be like a code word among the wealthy who spent season in Palm Beach. When they wore Lilly, it was a way of saying, 'I'm rich enough to have a second home in Florida.'"

"You just got this?" I stroked the fabric under the plastic sleeve. I was trying to temper my enthusiasm. The key is buying anything at a good price is not to act like you care, one way or another. Once the seller knows you covet the item, the price goes up.

With an exaggerated glance at her vintage Cartier tank watch, Danielle said, "It has been in my possession for less than an hour. I brought it directly to you. Didn't even bother to take off the drycleaner's bag."

Danielle was a fabulous salesperson. Furthermore, she knew exactly what I wanted, and her taste was exquisite. Since coming to Florida, I'd abandoned my St. Louis wardrobe. The LBDs (Little Black Dresses) that I'd worn while working at my family's Italian restaurant were far too somber and dull for this climate. Although I tried wearing them when I first opened The Treasure Chest, I'd shuddered when I caught a glimpse of my reflection in one of our big display windows. Among the bright tropical colors of my merchandise, I stuck out like a blotch. A moving ink blot. A crow in a bouquet of flowers.

Then I discovered Lilly and her bright tropical colors.

Wearing Lilly Pulitzer matched the vibe I hoped to project. She'd been a staple of east coast Floridian society.

"That's going to look terrific on you," said Skye. "With your dark hair,

Cara, those colors will really pop."

MJ stood up to check out the dress. "Too bad it isn't cut lower in the front. I suppose you could have it altered to show a bit of cleavage."

"No way," I said.

"You are such a Puritan," MJ said.

"Let's look for Lilly's name," suggested Danielle, as she draped the plastic bag over the back of an empty chair.

On cue our heads bent to examine the images of big pink nautilus shells. Sure enough, I spotted the cursive writing next to one of the shells. The true test of a Lilly was her hidden signature. Her "John Hancock" was a playful nod of individualism that never failed to bring a smile to my face.

Through the plastic wrapper, I fingered the white rickrack along the top border of one of the pockets. Pockets were a useful commodity to me. Every time I turned around, I was tucking away an index card with a note to myself or a receipt or change. A pocket made life much easier.

"How much?"

"One hundred."

"That's a steal," said MJ.

Skye only smiled. She's on a really tight budget, paying off old debts. To her, a hundred bucks was probably a fortune.

As if she knew what I was thinking, Skye chimed in. "Cara, it'll look wonderful on you."

"For anyone else it would be one hundred and twenty, but for you there's a discount. After all, we are neighbors." Danielle adjusted her designer eyeglasses.

Her shop, Vintage Threads, occupied the space immediately next to mine. Although I suspected she wasn't a good businesswoman—and I based that opinion on comments she'd made about her inability to read a profit and loss statement—she certainly was an expert when it came to women's fashion. As I understood it, Danielle had dropped out of University of Miami to sell women's clothes. With her height (5'10"), her slender frame (MJ thought she was a cokehead), and her long red hair (Skye was sure she wore extensions), Danielle showed off what she sold to best advantage. But she was also chronically short of cash. MJ thought it was because Danielle snorted her profits. Skye figured she was spending too much on upkeep. I knew it was partially because Danielle was a real party animal. She often bragged about bar-hopping in Miami.

But for all that, she was a kindred spirit because she was an entrepreneur.

"I get three types of clothes in here," she had explained to me as she walked me around her store. Pointing to one rack and then the other, she said, "First there's a garden variety, mass-produced designers. Next, there are those high-end designers that are few and far between."

She paused and walked me to an alcove in the back with spotlights and a set of display hooks set up high. "And finally, here I keep my unicorns."

"Unicorns?" I couldn't imagine what that might mean.

"That's what I call my ultra-unique goods. One of a kind, thrilling, museum quality finds. Like a 1980s dress by Yves Saint Laurent that was shown on the runway at one of his shows. It's a black pouf silhouette. Very chic. Never made it into regular production. However, it's stunning, isn't it?"

Danielle seemed to be reading my mind as I fingered the hem of the dress she'd brought me. She said, "In case you're wondering, Cara, this is a unicorn from when Lilly began her career. This dress came from a woman on Jupiter Island who knew Lilly very, very well. In fact, I'm sort of shocked that she gave this one up. I picked it up today with a lot of other stuff that's plug ugly."

After adjusting her glasses, Danielle continued, "If you don't buy it, I can sell it just like that." She snapped her fingers. "It reminds me of the dress that sent Lilly's business into orbit. Jackie Kennedy wore it on the cover of Life Magazine in 1961."

"Grab it," suggested MJ. "You'll find a place to wear it. In fact, why don't you wear it tonight? You're going out to eat with Jason, aren't you?"

"He's taking you to Ian's, isn't he? That dress will be perfect," said Skye.

"Okay, okay," I said. "I'll take it on one condition. Can I pay you next week?"

Danielle tilted her head to the left and tapped a midnight blue fingernail against her cheek as if thinking hard. "No, really I can't."

"It'll have to be Saturday or I can't do it," I said, stepping away from the dress. "That's the soonest I can get you the money. It's just not in my budget. Not for this week. Much as I love it."

"All right. It's yours." Handing the coat hanger to me, Danielle said, "I'm leaving for Orlando in an hour, but I'll be back late Friday night. I want to work on my books Saturday afternoon and settle my accounts. Could you bring the money by my house on Saturday? Say around eleven?"

"Sure. Why not?"

After scribbling on a business card, she handed it to me. "That's my home address in Port Saint Lucie. I would like the money sooner, but if that's the best you can do..."

"It is. I can drop off the money Saturday after I make my bank deposit and cash my paycheck." I didn't want to pull money out of savings. Not for a dress, at least. Moving into the house on Jupiter Island was turning out to be a costly endeavor. The interior needed painting. The exterior needed work. Each of my paychecks had funds earmarked for home improvements that simply could not wait. The dress hadn't been figured in. To make ends meet, next week I'd be eating a lot of tuna fish, but I didn't care.

"Fine, as long as you promise to bring me the cash on Saturday. I'd like the money before I reconcile my books." With a toodle-loo of her fingers, Danielle swished out the front door.

CHAPTER 8

I carried the dress upstairs to my empty apartment, a mirror image of the place that Skye rents from me. My old apartment has been vacant since I'd moved to Jupiter Island. I intend to fix it up and rent it out, but that might take a while.

My footsteps echoed in the empty rooms in a sad sort of way, repeating the nostalgia that tapped me on the shoulder each time I visited the second floor. The upstairs area over The Treasure Chest held fond memories for me. My parents and I had stayed here each summer when we drove down to visit Poppy. Back then it had been one big apartment. That was before Essie Feldman had the space upstairs split in two so she could double her rental income.

Somehow, this old/new apartment has never felt "right" to me. While Skye decorated her place beautifully, I had been content to sit on folding chairs pulled up to a battered card table. Apart from a new mattress and a sofa bed that I bought so that Tommy, my eighteen-year-old son, would have a place to sleep when he was on break from University of Miami, I hadn't added a thing to these rooms.

Something had held me back.

The fact that my grandfather owned property on Jupiter Island had come as a surprise to me. The widow Fingersmith had left it to my grandfather in her will, as a way of thanking Poppy for taking care of her. Or so Poppy had told me. His eyes had gotten all shifty when he told me his version of how he came to own pricey JI property. When he got to the part about serving in the Navy with Mrs. Fingersmith's son, my grandfather had acted evasive.

I had a hunch there was more to the story. But I'd filed my curiosity away in a place reserved for "to be continued," and on a whim, I made the drive to Jupiter Island.

One look was all it took. I saw Seaspray and fell madly in love. To me, the place was—and is—perfect. A tiny white cottage with clapboard siding. Pecky cypress paneling in the kitchen. Two bedrooms with adjoining baths and a laundry room in between. Stairs leading to a second floor room. An upstairs full bath. And a view of the ocean from every room in the house.

Best of all, Seaspray is secluded.

The house is nearly invisible from the road. The first owner had gone a little nuts, planting trees and shrubs on the one-acre lot. The second let the plants run riot. So did Poppy. Overgrown foliage obscures the tiny cottage. From the beach side, the dunes keep the house a secret. I love the cozy feeling of having no visible neighbors.

Downtown Stuart is twenty minutes away from my place on Jupiter Island. I don't mind the drive, but to make life easier, I keep a change of clothes and toilette articles in my "old" apartment above the store. That's where I tucked my new dress into a closet. I didn't even need to try it on. I knew it would fit. After wearing other garments by Lilly Pulitzer, I knew how her sizes ran. MJ's suggestion had been a good one; I planned to wear the dress when I went out with Jason.

We'd met because he was overseeing the crew working on the new Fill Up and Go gas station that would replace Poppy's old Gas E Bait. Jason's a goodlooking man built like a weight-lifter. But he's also eight years younger than I am. Sure he's sweet. Considerate. Protective. Smart but not brilliant. And kind. There's a lot to like about him.

"But he's too, too young for me," I muttered to myself.

I had told my friends as much last week right after he invited me out for dinner.

In her typically opinionated way, MJ had said, "Don't be ridiculous. Women live longer. We stay young longer. You're a youthful thirty-eight. He's an old soul."

"It's not his soul that worries me. He has other body parts that have a lot of get up and go," I grumbled.

"To the marriage of true minds, let me not admit impediments." Skye shook her spoon at me. A drop of yogurt landed on the table. The fragrance of strawberries perfumed the air.

"Huh?" Using my napkin, I wiped up the mess.

"Shakespeare." She sighed. "I've been reading his sonnets to educate myself."

A pause suggested she was debating how much to share. Finally, she gave in and added, "I dropped out of high school after my freshman year. Sid helped me go online and find a list of what people read for college prep."

I struggled not to react. MJ's mouth quivered, too. We both wanted to tell Skye she was being silly. She has absolutely no reason to feel self-conscious about her lack of education. None. Skye is wicked smart. She's a crafting genius. People love her, because she's so authentic.

"If you're right for each other," Skye continued, "you're right for each other, no matter what stands in your way."

"I don't think we're right for each other."

"Why not?" Skye persisted. Her pretty face puckered up with curiosity. Skye's such a romantic. I hated to burst her bubble, but she asked and so I answered, "It's not that I have a daddy complex or anything like that, but I enjoy older men. Worldly men."

"Captain Nathan Davidson fills the bill admirably," said Skye, with a brisk salute. "Lou tells me he's really interested in you. When was the last time you two went out?"

"Last weekend. We have a date for this Friday night." I liked the police captain. He was smart, kind, and incredibly masculine. But something held me back. I couldn't put my finger on it, and Nathan had been blunt. He wanted to take our relationship to the next level.

"How about Jay Boehner?" MJ leaned closer. "He's one hot father-figure. Major league eye candy, if you ask me. Rich, too."

"She's right. What a hunk," said Skye. "Reminds me of Cary Grant. I love the way he dresses, too. Sort of old-school elegant. Nice manners."

"Have you heard from him lately?" MJ asked.

"No." I bit back a sigh of disappointment. "You're right. Jay Boehner reminds me of Cary Grant, too. He's exactly the kind of man I had in mind. Too bad he doesn't seem all that interested in me."

"Valentine's Day is right around the corner," said MJ. "If I were you, I wouldn't dump any of the three of them. Not yet. At least wait and see what they give you."

Skye rolled her eyes.

Mentally, I did, too.

CHAPTER 9

The back door squealed open, and Honora McAfee arrived in a fluster. Her straw boater tilted perilously to one side as she lugged a slow cooker toward the counter. Skye jumped up to help our friend with her burden, while MJ close the door behind our friend.

"EveLynn should have helped you with that." I shook my head as I took the slow cooker from Skye and set it on the counter. Honora's adult daughter, EveLynn, has Asperger's Syndrome. Okay, so she's not wired to think of other people. I get that. But Honora should have insisted that she offer assistance. At seventy-six, Honora is too old to take a chance on falling. From the off-balance way she lurched into the back room, a face-plant seemed pre-ordained.

"I'm fine!" she protested. The scent of lavender followed her like a shadow. "A little stiff this morning. That's all."

"What's in the slow cooker?" Skye asked.

"Tex Mex Spaghetti Squash," said Honora. "Found the recipe online and couldn't resist. Unfortunately, EveLynn won't try anything new. Every Wednesday is pasta night, and I tried to explain that this was exactly like pasta except—"

"Except it isn't," I said.

"A fine point." Honora waved away my objection. "Rather than waste the leftovers, I brought them here. That child is going to drive me into an early grave." After removing her hat, setting the hatpin in the antique pin cushion that MJ had found expressly for this purpose, Honora patted the knob of gray hair at the back of her neck. "Well, now, I'm glad we're all here because I have something I wish to discuss. Let me pour myself a cup of tea. Anyone else want one?"

Skye asked for a second cup of tea. I poured coffee for me and for MJ while Honora bustled around with the kettle. While the water heated, she took a seat and perked up at our willing audience. "There's a yearly contest held by one of the prominent vendors of miniature items. It's called the Creatin' Contest. I'd like to enter this year, but I need your permission, Cara, darling, to work on the project here at the store."

There had to be more to her question. I've never thought of myself as a whip-cracking overseer, so why was she asking my permission so formally?

Honora continued, "Before he had his accident, Sid suggested we start a store blog. If I enter this contest, I could share my plans for the project, any problems I encounter, and how I solve them. I believe my efforts would be of interest to miniaturists around the globe. Since we have such a lovely online store, we might even be able to attract new customers as a result. Of course, you could also display the finished product in the front window."

I leaned back and thought about what she was proposing.

"As for the theme," Honora said, "I've never seen a dollhouse that reflects the sensibilities of the Treasure Coast. This part of our peninsula is special. Really special. We aren't as commercialized as Sanibel or the Gulf coast. Nor do we have as much of the surfer culture as Daytona Beach. We're not as Latin as Miami. Nor as touristy as Orlando. Or as funky as the Keys. That said, we have our own style here, don't we? So many of my neighbors live off what they catch. They go fishing once a week. They eat Key Limes, lemons, oranges, and tangerines that grow on trees in pots in their yards. We all share any extras. In fact, when someone comes back from the Keys with ice coolers full of lobster, we all sit down and have a feast."

Seeing what she meant, I nodded. "How about the murals? I've never seen murals like we have down here. Wherever you turn, they are a part of the landscape."

"So are paddleboards, kayaks, fishermen, and surfers," said Skye. "But we're not like Daytona, because our surfers work during the day. The folks around here keep their day jobs and surf when they can."

"There's the way we all love our sea turtles," agreed MJ. "Even the burliest man at the Elks Club goes all giddy when he talks about seeing hatchlings crawl out of the sand. There's a magic to our coastline. I've watched perfect strangers stop to chat about pelicans or sandpipers."

"We work to live here," I said, "unlike some places where you live there only because you work there. There's a rhythm to our lives."

"That changes with hurricane season," said Skye. "When a storm heads this way, everyone pitches in, nailing up plywood, starting generators, and sharing resources like D batteries."

"Don't even talk to me about D batteries," said Honora. "The last time we had a storm scare I couldn't buy D batteries anywhere! They were snapped up right away."

MJ and Skye nodded in agreement.

"My goal is to be 'green' by incorporating as many locally sourced materials as possible," Honora said. "All of us care so much about the environment. Living here, we get a first-hand glimpse of how waste impacts our ecosystem. MJ, I was wondering if you could give me guidance about vintage Florida pieces representative of the Treasure Coast. Skye, I know how good you are at crafts. I'll probably need help making some of the furnishings and decorating the place. I'd like to use a lot of sea shells and local botanicals. Of course," and Honora looked at me shrewdly, "all of this is contingent upon Cara's approval. What do you say, Cara, darling?"

"Go for it."

CHAPTER 10

On that particular day, the back door was magically transformed into a revolving door, of sorts. Shortly after Honora announced her grand plans, Poppy arrived.

"Guess who was rip-roaring ready to git back to work?" my grandfather asked, as he cocked an eyebrow and held open the door.

"Sid!" We all squealed with joy.

It was good to see Sid, although it saddened me to watch him struggle along on his crutches. MJ and Skye both jumped up to hug him. Honora waited her turn before bestowing a kiss on his cheek. Jack about went nuts, trying to get out of his crate so he could lick Sid's hand. I waited until everyone else had settled down before giving him a hug and peck on the forehead.

Poppy guided the young man to a chair while I grabbed Jack. Once he was in Sid's lap, the love fest began between boy and dog. Watching them brought a smile to all our faces, but worry hung over us, like a brewing thunderstorm.

Sid was incredibly pale. Dark circles rimmed his eyes. In a word, he looked feeble. Long days in a hospital bed had not been good for his health. After making light conversation with all my employees, I beckoned to my grandfather. "Poppy? Do you have a moment? I've got questions about Seaspray. Will you come into my office so we can talk?"

"Be right back," I told the others.

After closing the door behind us, I asked Poppy, "How's Sid really doing? He looks awful. I didn't expect you to bring him in so early."

Poppy put his feet up on my desk. Normally, I would have barked at him to take his shoes down, but I wanted to encourage my grandfather to get chatty and Poppy is usually economical with words. Chewing on his lower lip, he said, "That boy's got a lot of healing to do. Clumsy as all get out. You'd have to expect that. Broken arm. Broken bones in his foot. He's lucky to be alive."

"Tell me something I don't know."

My grandfather removed his red St. Louis Cardinals baseball cap and scratched his crown. "You probably ain't heard that his no-good mother ain't been by to see him once. Not even once! As for that old bird that hit him, she's all lawyered up. I heard that through the grapevine over at the deli."

Pumpernickel's Deli was where Skye worked. The little restaurant across the street was one of the area's favorite places for a quick bite. Everyone stopped by sooner or later. When they did, the good food loosened their lips.

I wasn't surprised to hear that the woman who'd hit Sid had gotten counsel. She probably shouldn't have been driving at all, especially not on a rainy night when it's hard to see clearly. After making a right turn on red at an intersection, she'd sent Sid flying through the air. She'd driven away, but others had seen the accident and called for help. Sid had landed against a Bank of America building, hitting his head hard. His bicycle had been crushed into a wad of metal the size of a can of peas. All in all, he'd been lucky to survive.

At the emergency room, they'd phoned his stepmother and gotten a recorded answer. As a result, Sid had given them my name and number. I made a mad dash to Jupiter Medical Center.

When Amberlee finally returned my call, well after the crisis was over, I couldn't hear her for the music in the background.

"So? What do you expect me to do about it? He's not mine, you know."

I had literally gnashed my teeth, an action I'd read about but never performed. The dentist later confirmed that I'd chipped a back molar rather than snap at her. Instead, I'd responded in a perfectly civil tone. "I understand he isn't yours. However, you were married to Harvey Heckman for twelve years. Sid's only eighteen. You've known him since he was six. Surely you feel some—"

She cut me off. "Look, I gotta go. I've got company."

I learned later that she still claimed Sid on her taxes as a dependent.

"That no good she-cat had Harvey tied up in knots," said my grandfather as he worried the edge of the baseball cap. "Getting him to leave her all his money. That fool."

"MJ says that Amberlee promised Harvey she'd look after his son. I guess he wanted to believe her. Especially when he learned he had Stage 4 lung cancer."

"All that asbestos. He worked on boats his whole life. That's how come he could leave her with so much money; it was a settlement. Harvey was smart as they come. That's where Sid gets his brains. They tell me Harvey could do anything with a boat. Anything. He understood exactly what adjustments to make in how they was built. All a matter of math, I 'spect." Poppy turned bleary eyes to me. "Men like that, you call 'em geeks, right? What with those plastic pen protectors in their pockets? One look at Amberlee with her fancy ways and old Harvey took on water. She swamped his boat. That was it."

"How much does Sid owe the hospital?"

"A passel of money for his deductible. And you ain't heard the worst of it yet."

"Hit me with it. Give it to me all at once. Don't hold anything back."

Poppy's feet clattered to the floor. He leaned across the desk to whisper, "That kid's gonna need all sorts of therapy. That break in his arm? It'll have an effect on how he does computer work. Moving around that moose?"

"Mouse."

"Mouse? That's the gizmo he uses? The doctor says it'll be hard for him to get back to normal. He's also gonna need physical therapy for his foot. That fool woman crushed it good. Once that surgical boot comes off, he'll need help flexing his toes. They're gonna be stiff as all get out. Gotta get it mobile again or he'll limp for the rest of his life."

"Is that it? The worst of it?"

"Nope. Thanks to that there blow to his head, he'll probably be moody. Might have trouble remembering stuff. Could have personality changes. And get this. Yesterday, I stopped by the trailer to pick up his computer? So he could have it at my place? That tin box he called home was wide open and empty. Those other kids done moved out."

"Why were you looking for his computer? It should have been there with him at the hospital. He had it with him when he left the store the night he was hit."

"Yup, but he told me this morning that he ain't got it."

"Let me get this straight," I said. "You're telling me that we don't know where Sid's computer is."

"Right, and his brain is addled. I ain't completely sure he can tell us what happened to it."

How on earth was Sid going to live without his computer? It was more than a portal for entertainment. To him, it was his virtual workplace. I'd hired him to computerize my business. That involved creating a website, a shopping cart, and moving all our accounting onto QuickBooks.

Then it hit me: Did the thief have access to my financial records?

Surely not. They'd have to get past Sid's password.

But what if his friends were as talented with computers as he was? Then a password wouldn't provide much, if any, protection at all.

CHAPTER 11

"Sid," I pulled up a chair next to him at the table in the back room. "Do you have any idea where your computer is?"

"In my backpack."

"All right, and where's your backpack?" I did my best not to sound as panicky as I felt.

"Next to my, um, desk." He frowned and winced. Although most of his bruises were fading, the ER doc had sewn up his lip with two stitches. Talking was difficult, and the grimace had been painful. Moving carefully, he rotated in the chair and tried to look over at his desk, which was next to where MJ sat working on a delivery ticket.

"Your desk?" I'd just walked past his desk on my way out of my office, and the floor was clear.

Sid closed his eyes. "No. That's not right."

Honora raised her head from her work. Her expression was one of regret. I knew exactly how she felt. I hated having this conversation with Sid. Especially today, his first day back. But what else could I do? Nothing. It was my responsibility to track down his computer because if my financial information got in the wrong hands, my business would be in jeopardy.

"When did you have it last?" I asked.

"I had my backpack with me when I was riding my bike before I got…hit. That's how I carry my computer around. There's a padded pouch in the backpack. My paycheck was in the small pocket, because I'd just gotten paid. But my computer wasn't in the bag last night. I looked because I wanted to see how you file for bankruptcy."

"Bankruptcy?" I repeated.

"What else can I do if they slam me with the hospital bill? It's bound to be huge! More than I'll make all year. Maybe in a lifetime. They'll come after me. I know they will." Despite the multiple piercings and the need for a shave, Sid looked like he was all of five years old and ready to have a melt-down.

"Let's take this one step at a time," I said. "Bankruptcy is a long way off. Remember the other driver hit you, so her insurance should cover your injuries. There are lawyers who can help you. Trust me on this, okay? Good. Let's go back to your computer. When was the last time you saw it?"

He screwed up his face, winced again and said, "In my room. At the hospital. I emailed you."

That was right; he had.

Sid twisted in his chair to stare up at my grandfather. "Poppy, you carried my things to your truck. They made me ride in that wheelchair. Said it was hospital policy. Remember?"

Somewhere along the line, Sid had begun calling my grandfather "Poppy." The endearment brought a tender smile to the old man's face. That signaled good news about their relationship. Sid badly needed more loving adults in his life. My grandfather needed more responsibility and a reason to get up in the morning.

"Yup," Poppy said. "I got you into the house and then went back and carried the backpack and that there sack of your clothes into your room. But that backpack felt lighter than a seagull's feather."

"My computer is a notebook. It's small," Sid said.

"It has to be at the house, right? Somewhere," I said. Knowing how messy Poppy's place was, the computer could be well hidden.

"It sure wasn't at his old trailer, but I coulda sworn that there bag was nearly empty. It was awful lightweight."

MJ shook her head ever so slightly in a motion of sympathy. Honora sighed. Skye picked up the sugar bowl and pointed it at my grandfather. I understood instantly what she was saying. Poppy isn't always as compliant about his diet as he should be. Like most diabetics, he's prone to fuzzy thinking when his blood sugar is out of whack. I had to wonder how cogent he'd been when he took Sid home.

"Poppy did you happen to look inside the backpack when you put it in your truck?" I asked.

"Nope. I'll look for it when I leave. Maybe the computer fell out in the truck," Poppy said. "Could be under one of the seats."

Time to move on. "I'm sure we'll find it. Sid? I just want to tell you again, how happy I am to see you. I'm glad you're okay."

"But you're worried about your paperwork. Your accounting stuff." His eyes blazed with anger.

"Of course I'm worried about that and about your computer, but I'm also worried about you. You come first. You know that. Cut me some slack."

"Right." Sid lifted his chin defiantly. This was a boy who didn't trust adults. He especially didn't trust adult women. And why should he?

"Hang on, buddy." I rested light fingers on his wrist, the one that wasn't covered in plaster. "Let's back up a bit. I care about you. If you'll recall, I was the first person at the hospital. The minute you had them phone me from the ER, I raced to your side. Since then, I've visited you every day. Poppy asked you to move in with him because I suggested you could keep each other company. I've told you that you've still got your job. No matter what. In fact, I've told you repeatedly that you don't have to come in until you feel better. Sure, I'm worried about the computer and my financial statements, but that doesn't mean I didn't think about you first."

It wasn't until I shut up that I remembered one of the side effects of a hard hit to the head: emotionalism. Would this be the new normal for Sid?

"Yeah." His voice cracked. "Cara, I'd never, ever, never let anything happen to your business. Swear on a stack of Bibles. Ever."

I wanted to believe him, but I also reminded myself, He's an eighteen-year-old boy with a head injury.

"I know you've done everything in your power to protect my business." I gave him a hug that he accepted stiffly.

I also knew Stuff happens. For years, we struggled to keep our family restaurant afloat after my ex-husband, Dom, had gone to the media and suggested my father had taken advantage of his creativity when he was working as a poorly paid intern in our kitchen. Meanwhile, Dom opened his own restaurant with a menu very similar to ours. As it turned out, my father's non-compete contracts with his staff weren't worth the paper they had been written on, much less worth the amount he'd paid a fancy attorney to draw up the agreements. Consequently, I had learned the hard way that even vigilant entrepreneurs can get tripped up. My father had been cautious, prudent, and honest as George Washington's face on a dollar bill. He'd also been taken for a fool.

MJ went over and stood next to Skye. Honora rose from her stool and bookended MJ. Forming a line of solidarity, my three friends faced me. MJ gave a tiny thumbs up, Skye offered a slight head bob of approval, and Honora winked at me. In their own quiet ways, they were trying to reassure me. I'd done right by Sid. He'd been worried, rightly so, and I'd been crystal clear about my affection for him.

Poppy cleared his throat. "Granddaughter? I'll go rustle up that there computer. It's bound to be at the hospital, in my house, or in my truck."

I only hoped he was right.

CHAPTER 12

To celebrate my son's sixth birthday, my parents and I took him to Disney World. My son's favorite part of the park was Mr. Toad's Wild Ride. We would stand in line, hop on, ride the ride, and get back in line to do it all over again.

In the hours that followed, I mentally nicknamed this day, "Cara Mia's Wild Ride." Visions of my new dress brought a smile to my face, but that didn't last long. The smile was turned upside down when I considered the possibility that somewhere, out there, my financial information might be floating around. If someone got into Sid's computer, they would know I was living on a shoestring that had been stretched tight. I had faith I could make a go of this business, but I'll admit that the numbers did not look promising.

Here we were in January, a few weeks out from Valentine's Day with little to boost our sales. Sure, Skye had decorated our front window in winsome colors of baby blue with dark red hearts and pink touches. Yes, customers were walking through the front door. But could we make enough now, during Season, to last through the doldrums that would inevitably come after our snowbirds went home?

I sure hoped so.

But as it happened, things started to look pretty good as the day wore on. Customers came in and bought one big piece after another. Mentally, I totted up the sales and decided we were doing very well indeed. In fact, we were selling home furnishings at such a clip that I needed to apply my best thinking to another problem, our lack of space. We needed a workshop and staging area where we could prep used furniture, paint it, and get it ready to sell. With all those challenges buzzing around in my head, time moved along swiftly. Because Skye was working across the street at Pumpernickel's, the task of waiting on customers fell largely to me.

As usual, I handled a multitude of problems when I wasn't busy ringing up sales. A delivery truck had run over a customer's new grass. A woman, who had ordered placemats made by EveLynn, wanted matching napkins and a table runner. A client who had seen Honora's work on our website hoped to commission a room box for her daughter who was graduating from high school. A vendor wanted credit references. Bills had to be paid.

A little after one, my stomach grumbled. There seemed to be a lull, so I took the chance to walk into the back and see how Jack was doing. One hand was on the latch of his crate when my dog went totally bonkers.

"Cara?" The soft male voice behind me caused my stomach to take an elevator ride to my toes. Steeling myself for the encounter, I counted to ten before answering with a wobbly, "Yes?"

But I could barely hear myself over Jack's raucous barking. He hopped up and down, banging away at the crate walls.

I didn't turn around right away. Facing Cooper Rivers, my first love, is always hard. If I expect to see him, I give myself a little pep talk so I'm prepared. But a chance meeting such as this is always unsettling.

"Cara?" the voice repeated.

There was no help for it. After crossing my arms over my chest in a gesture that any psychologist would label "defensive," I faced Cooper and stared up into his warm brown eyes. The periphery of my vision picked up a fuzzy yellow blur. A big yellow dog stood at Cooper's side. One of the mutt's ears was folded over while the other stood straight up. His brown eyes studied me intently. Normally, I would have introduced myself to the pooch and tried to make him my friend, but I was frozen into position, like the tin woodsman in The Wonderful Wizard of Oz. My legs had turned to gelatin as I zeroed in on Cooper. "What do you want?"

It came out more harshly than I intended. The mutt sniffed Jack's crate, and that little Chihuahua of mine wiggled his tail with joy. A loud hiss from under MJ's desk signaled that Luna, my cat, was not as enthusiastic about the visitor as Jack.

"Could we talk?" Cooper asked. "It's about Dick. I thought maybe we could go into your office."

"Honora?" I went over and tapped her on the shoulder. She often became so engrossed in her work that she blocked out all activity around her. "Would you go keep tabs on the sales floor for me?"

"Of course, dear." With a nod, she toddled off.

Jack quit barking and started whining.

Without a backwards glance at Cooper, I headed for my office where Sid was working on my computer. "Sid? Could you give me a minute here?"

"Sure."

He clattered around with his crutches but managed to limp out. I somehow managed not to look at Cooper as I sank down into the chair behind my desk.

"Ooph!" I had come face to face with a cold wet nose. The yellow mutt was leaning over me with one paw on each shoulder.

"Down," said Cooper, as he tried to get a purchase on the leash. "Gerard, get down."

But Gerard wasn't cooperating. A pink tongue curled out to caress my face. The pooch stared into my eyes. To my amazement, he smiled, exposing doggy teeth and a sliver of pink gum. He looked so comical that I giggled. "Gerard? What a stupid name for a dog."

The mutt slurped my ear. I hugged him and stroked his head. "You're a good boy, aren't you? I can tell. What is he?"

"A Bahamian Potcake dog."

"Oh. Never heard of them."

"I hadn't either until we got him."

Gerard's tail did a slow rhythmic wag.

"Yup. You're a darling. Now you have to get down because you're blocking my way." Carefully I gathered his paws and guided them toward the floor. Gerard pivoted to take his place at my side. Backing up, he eased his butt into my lap.

"Okay, fine," I said.

"Down," said Cooper.

Gerard ignored him.

"Come." Cooper tugged on the leash. Gerard's collar popped off and flew past Coop.

"Hand it over," I said. When he did, I slipped it around the dog's neck. "Seriously, Cooper. The dog is fine."

"But you'll get his hair all over you."

"Big deal. Don't sweat the small stuff."

Cooper reached behind his chair and closed the office door. Gerard sighed with contentment as I scratched his ears.

"As you know, I had offered Dick a job as head mechanic at our new Fill Up and Go station. He agreed to come and work for us. Unfortunately, the folks in charge of hiring have told me that Dick can't pass our physical."

"What?" I couldn't believe what I'd just heard. "My grandfather is as spry and agile as the day is long. He's not sick. Sure, he's got diabetes, but we've gotten that under control."

I crossed my fingers where Coop couldn't see them. Mostly we had Poppy's diabetes under control.

Cooper looked down at the floor. "I know. Believe me, Cara, I've been over and over this with the HR department. I even told them that I can't see how this could be legal, but they're insisting that he's too big of a risk. They won't let me name him head of the department."

"Okay, so don't give him a title. Just let him work for you. He's capable, but the title would be icing on the cake, right? Why not hire a newbie to be the chief mechanic but let Poppy be his right hand person? Wouldn't that work?"

"Um, no." Cooper avoided my glance. "Unfortunately not. I made the same suggestion."

"You have to be kidding me." I sounded stressed because I was. Poppy had been counting on that job. It was a matter of pride to him. How would he be able to face his former customers? What about the people he'd told about his new position at the Fill Up and Go?

And wasn't a problem like this exactly what I'd hoped to avoid by snapping up this building?

Yes, it was.

I fought it, but the news hit me like a blow to the gut.

A soft whimper escaped from Gerard. He watched me intently, taking in every word. For a mute animal, his sympathetic gaze spoke volumes. Gerard was clearly worried.

"It's okay, puppy," I said as I reached up to rub his soft, floppy ears. "Look, Cooper, Poppy's been counting on that position. He's been talking up the new gas station to all his old customers. This will be a crushing blow. Isn't there some way you can convince them to reconsider? Sounds like age-ism to me."

"I know. I pointed that out to them."

"So can you do anything? Yes or no. Be straight with me."

"I have serious doubts that they'll change their minds. The young woman who runs their HR Department is just out of college. I don't think she puts any value on Dick's years of experience. In fact, I don't think she believes he's a viable job candidate, period. She mentioned how all the cars today are run by computers. I get the feeling she's dead set against hiring your grandfather."

"Crud. I should have insisted we get this in writing when I sold you the old Gas E Bait. Or I should have demanded that the new people keep Poppy on a retainer until the building is completed."

"I'm not sure that it would have made any difference. Given her attitude, she would find a way to force him out. Do you remember what you were like in your mid-twenties? A little taste of power goes a long way. She's the type who'd drag this thing out until..."

He didn't have to complete the sentence. I knew what he was getting at. Poppy couldn't live forever.

"Let's be frank," Cooper said. "If you've got enough of a legal department working for you, you can hassle other people into doing what you want. If we did convince them to hire Dick, I'm a hundred percent certain they'd find a reason to dump him."

I sighed. "Does Poppy know?"

"No."

"Thank heavens for small favors."

"I can tell him," said Cooper.

"No way. It has to come from me. This is going to kill him."

It had been difficult for my grandfather to give up his old gas station, even after he discovered the underground fuel tanks were leaking. Rather than shut his doors, he'd simply let the tanks run dry. After the oxygen system gave out on the shiners' tank, he quit carrying the minnows he had been selling as bait. But he had never, ever given up working on people's engines. My grandfather loved fixing cars. He enjoyed any sort of tinkering, problem solving, and repair work. A steady stream of vehicles had passed through his shop. He woke up each day excited about getting to work. His business had kept him mentally agile.

How was I going to break this bad news to him? How would he react when he found out that he'd been shoved aside by a business that had taken over the corner lot where his gas station had been a fixture for so long? I shuddered to think about it.

"The folks at the Fill Up and Go home office think that Dick is all washed up. That he has no value. I've tried and tried to explain otherwise, to get them to review his records, to interview people who know him, or even talk to his doctor. All to no avail. This young woman has dug in her heels. She's not even taking my calls anymore. I can't change her mind." Cooper spread his fingers wide in a gesture of submission. "I give up, Cara. I'll see if I can find another place for Dick to work, but I don't see any way for him to get involved with the new gas station."

"Don't you dare say a word to him."

"I'm involved in this up to my eyeballs. I worked to help get the franchise to come here. But of course, I didn't realize what would happen when this new HR person came onboard. It's the law of unintended consequences in action. So it is my problem."

"But he's my grandfather. My family. I'll handle it."

Reluctantly he said, "If you insist."

"I do. I repeat, don't you dare tell him. I'll be the one to do it."

CHAPTER 13

As I locked the back door behind Cooper, Honora glanced up from her workspace. "Are you all right, Cara, darling?"

"I'll be fine," I said. "Thank you for asking."

No way was I going to burst into tears, even though they threatened. Instead, I compartmentalized my conversation with Cooper. His concerns went into a little brown box that sat next to my worries about Sid's computer.

"How's the contest entry coming?" I was struggling to sound interested although really, I wasn't. Not right then.

Honora's laugh reminds me of wind chimes. "It's not coming along at all, yet."

"Why not?" I went over to her work table, expecting to see what the matter was.

"First I have to order the kit."

"Kit?" I repeated.

"Every Creatin' Contest begins with a kit. That's the basis of the project. After you buy the kit, you can build it as per the instructions or bash it."

"Bash it?" That didn't sound good. Not at all.

Again, Honora laughed. "In the miniatures world, we call it 'kit bashing,' and it means that you rework a kit to turn it into something new. Something beyond the original plans."

"Okay," but I sounded dubious.

"Let me show you." She tapped the screen of the iPad that Santa had brought her for Christmas. "This is the original kit from last year."

A tiny garage appeared, complete with rolling door.

"Here are the kit-bashed versions. Variations on a theme, as it were. So first I have to order the basic kit. While they are shipping it, I'll brainstorm ways to make the kit unique. I'll also survey what I own, so I can see what I'll need to buy, if anything. I'll also plan out what I can do in advance so it's ready to go when I get to work. For example, if I want the project to have a tile roof, I should start making the tiles because they take time."

I scrolled through the finished Creatin' Contest projects from the year before. Most of them bore no resemblance to the original kit. A few did if you concentrated on the bare bones of the structures, but even those had been thoroughly transformed.

"Magical, isn't it? Like so much of life, we tend to pigeonhole what we see and assign it certain properties. But each miniaturist approached the kit with a different vision. It's wonderfully creative, isn't it?" A sharp intake of breath preceded her next comment. "Cara? I overheard your discussion with Cooper. I'm a shameless eavesdropper. What will you do?"

I didn't know what to say, so I hesitated while Honora barreled on ahead.

"People look at us, the elderly, and make assumptions. It's true that none of us are as active as we once were. I have friends who have become childlike and cruel. Others who have mellowed with time. Of course, we didn't know as much about taking care of our health as your generation does. Why, goodness me, I recall how they passed out cigarettes to me and my fellow students, urging us to smoke."

"You have to be kidding!"

"No, I'm not. See, I grew up near Pinehurst in North Carolina, where tobacco farming was a typical form of employment. Getting us to become smokers was a way to support the industry. They didn't want to believe that cigarettes were harmful, so the tobacco company executives lied to themselves. I know that because my uncle worked for one of them. Until the day he was diagnosed with lung cancer, he challenged the notion that smoking was harmful."

"Then what did he do?"

Honora plucked at a strand of twine that she was turning into a basket. "At first, Uncle Floyd insisted that the diagnosis was wrong. He went for the chemo and the radiation, but he refused to give up cigarettes. Aunt Rose went along with the deception. She told my mother, 'There's no reason to make Floyd feel worse about his situation by pointing out he's been wrong all these years. Or that other people died because he refused to accept the new information about causation.' While he was being treated, Uncle Floyd continued to attend board meetings. Aunt Rose told my mother in confidence that he was afraid that if he put up a fuss, he'd be fired. Then they would have to fight for his medical benefits and for his pension."

I didn't want to hear the end of the story. The churning in my gut told me there was no "happily ever after" involved. But I couldn't tell Honora to stop. The train wreck was going to happen, and I was trapped in the role of spectator.

"Uncle Floyd did everything he could to pretend he was getting well. He insisted on working, mowing the yard, and acting like life was normal. Aunt Rose told us that he refused to discuss what might happen if he died. One evening she heard a loud thump and found him on the floor in the bathroom.

He was in and out of a coma for a month and a half."

"I'm so sorry."

Her smile was weak. "Yes, well, that was such a long, long time ago. I don't know why I bothered you with such a sad story. To circle back to the beginning, Dick has a lot of life left in him. Going to work kept my uncle alive much longer than the doctors had predicted. Your grandfather is comparatively healthy. His diabetes is under control. You need to find something for Dick to do or he'll..." and she quit talking.

"He'll curl up and die," I finished for her.

"Yes, I believe so."

CHAPTER 14

The rest of the day, I worried about Poppy. How would I tell him that his dream job had evaporated, poof? I marveled at the way my good intentions had gone wrong. Six months ago I'd impetuously sunk all my savings into this shop, in an effort to protect my grandfather's gas station. It seemed like a simple, straightforward plan.

But it had backfired.

The old gas station had since been torn down. My grandfather had been deemed unemployable. I was now the proud owner of a fledgling business that required careful nurturing. Along the way, I'd insisted on paying him a token amount for a beach cottage on Jupiter Island, even though he'd offered it as a gift. I'd taken in two stray animals as pets. (Three if you counted Kookie, the cockatoo, but Skye had kinda-sorta adopted the bird.) I'm also responsible for five people on my payroll: MJ, Skye, Sid, Honora, and EveLynn.

Actually I have seven dependents, if you count my staff, plus the cat and the dog. Eight if you include my son down in Miami at the university. (Since my ex can't be trusted, there's always the chance he'll quit paying for Tommy's education—as promised—and that I'll have to pick up the slack.)

How could I have made such a mess of things? What was wrong with me? And how could I fix everything? Make it all right?

A crushing sensation in my chest left me breathless. The edges of my vision darkened as stars danced in front of my eyes. I gripped the cash station counter hard and forced myself to calm down.

I knew the symptoms of a panic attack.

I'd had them before.

My therapist back in St. Louis would have scolded me for "awful-izing." According to Dr. Prengo, "awful-izing" happens when negativity overrules good sense. When you "awful-ize," you conjure up the worst possible outcome as the result of a seriously skewed—and flawed—perspective.

"Most of our worries will never come to pass," said Dr. Prengo, as she adjusted her designer glasses. "When we awful-ize, we quit living in the moment. Seriously, Cara, have you noticed that you're only hurting yourself by thinking such extreme thoughts? It's an indulgence, and an unhealthy one at that. Remember the chicken who ran around screaming that the sky was falling? You've adopted her as a role model."

With Dr. Prengo's voice echoing in my brain, I gave myself a good mental face-slap. I was healthy, so were my son and grandfather. Everything would work out. All I could do was my best. "They can't kill me and they can't eat me," I said, under my breath, reprising a funny little motto that Dr. Prengo had shared.

I plastered a fake smile on my face and waited on customers as they walked in. Putting my heart into my spiel, I cheerfully explained our philosophy: "Everything and everyone deserves a second chance." I tried to sound upbeat as I interacted with employees.

Mainly I succeeded.

A little after five, after flipping the sign to CLOSED, I changed into my new Lilly Pulitzer dress. My spirits brightened right away. The dress fit as though Lilly had sewn it just for me. The colors brought out my eyes. The pink heightened the slight tan I'd gained from my beach walks. Finishing my toilette, I sprayed on perfume and freshened my makeup. I was halfway down the stairs when MJ beckoned to me.

"Hey, that looks terrific on you. The news is on. I think you'll want to come and listen." With a twist of the wrist, she cranked the volume up on the tiny TV sitting on her desk in the back room.

A solemn faced reporter stood in front of the sign designating the Hobe Sound Beach Park and said, "Earlier this morning, a half dozen people washed up on the shores of Jupiter Island. One woman was discovered by a local resident. A second victim was found dead at Blowing Rocks Reserve. Authorities aren't saying whether the two illegals came ashore together or not, but locals are being cautioned to keep an eye out for more sightings. This is the third landing of undocumented immigrants since the beginning of the year."

The camera switched to a horse-faced woman seated behind a desk and saying, "Human trafficking is a $32-billion industry. The tightening of security at our land borders has encouraged more illegals to come by water. As evidenced by today's tragedies, their choice often has deadly results."

We stood there, stunned for a moment as the numbers sank in. Thirty-two billion dollars? Wow.

As MJ turned down the volume, I glanced at my phone. It had been vibrating in my pocket. "Lou wants me to know that the woman I found is in critical condition. She's not out of the woods, but at least she's alive."

"She might have brain damage." Honora didn't look up from her work. "Especially if she was without oxygen for long."

"You're right," I agreed. "That's been nagging at me all day. The ATV guy and I even discussed that as a possible outcome when we administered CPR. The alternative was to do nothing and let her die before our eyes."

"Not much of a choice." Honora was using a needleless syringe to apply a thin line of glue to a piece of furniture.

"I'll always wonder if we did the right thing. That is, unless I hear that she's made a full recovery," I said.

Honora finished with her piece and put it to one side. Only now would she look our way. "Cara, that dress!"

"Like it? Danielle brought it in for me today." Sticking my hands in my pockets, I unfurled the skirt and did a quick twirl. I felt very pretty in my new frock.

But the look on Honora's face was not admiring. She stared at me with a slack jaw and said, "Why are you wearing Binky's dress?"

CHAPTER 15

"What do you mean? Who or what is a Binky?" I asked.

"Binky," repeated Honora. "That's her dress."

"I have no idea what you're talking about," I said.

MJ's eyes went from me, to Honora, and then to me again. "Binky? You mean Mrs. Rutherford? The one who lives on Jupiter Island on that huge estate? That dress was hers?"

"I'm almost positive." Honora came over and examined my hem. "That's blind hemstitching, and it was done by hand. This has to be Binky's. I watched her hem this myself. This couldn't belong to anyone else. But how? Why? Binky would never let this dress go."

Her tone implied that I'd stolen the frock—and that irked me. "I bought this from Danielle who owns the consignment store."

Honora pored over the dress. Reaching out, she crushed a corner of the skirt in her palm. Upon release, she studied the wrinkled mass. "Same hand."

"Hand?"

"A tailor's term for the weight of the fabric." Honora was talking to herself rather than to me.

"Who or what is a Binky Rutherford?" I repeated my question to MJ.

"She's a contemporary of your grandfather. Very much a part of the Palm Beach social scene. Used to read about her all the time in the Palm Beach Post." MJ studied me. More correctly, she studied Honora while she studied my dress. MJ continued, "Binky's folks were early residents on the island. Their land never left the family."

"Is Binky dead? No one told me that she was." Honora sounded as if she might faint.

"She isn't. At last she wasn't this morning. According to Danielle, the owner pulled the dress out of her closet earlier today."

"And Danielle brought it directly to you?"

"As far as I know. Danielle said that the minute she saw this dress, she decided it was perfect for me so she brought it right over. In fact, the drycleaner's bag was still intact. I left it upstairs."

Honora rubbed her eyes. "Why would Binky let that dress go?"

My good mood had been nibbled away. "Why would anyone on Jupiter Island give up anything? Because they have too much stuff and not enough room? Same reason the rest of us pare down."

"Darling girl, that's not what I'm saying. Let me explain. This is a Lilly Pulitzer like none other."

Crossing my arms over my chest, I said, "So I heard. From Danielle."

"Yes," Honora said, "I'm sure she gave you the dress's provenance in a nutshell, but did she tell you it's a prototype? Lilly and Binky were best friends. Devoted to each other. So much so, that when Lilly decided to expand, to make clothes for other people, Binky was her first model."

"I went to an exhibit at the Museum of Lifestyle and Fashion History down in the Boynton Beach Mall," said MJ. "The placards explained that Lilly commissioned her fabrics. She directed what the artists painted, didn't she? Because she couldn't find exactly what she wanted off the racks. Her first patterns were designed to cover up splashes of orange juice. The family sold juice to tourists, and Lilly was in charge of the juice stand. But she was a bit of a klutz. Always staining her clothes. Hated how aprons looked."

"Exactly," said Honora. "Lilly came up with the brilliant idea that vibrant prints would hide the stains. She knew that an A-line form would be flattering to her figure. Without a waistband, the dresses would be cooler and perfect for our hot climate. First she ran up a few dresses for herself. Binky thought they were adorable and volunteered to give Lilly's early pieces a test run. She helped to popularize Lilly's apparel."

"Including this dress," I said.

"That's how Lilly's work caught on." Honora nodded. "The two friends discussed each piece, judging what looked good and what didn't. This style in particular was a huge hit. However, Lilly only had one dress made from this particular fabric. The artist wasn't interested in working on textiles. She created just enough of this to make up one shift, and it went to Binky. Later Lilly commissioned copies in a similar pattern, but the colors were a little different, and the print slightly altered."

"So Binky's had this dress since, what? Nineteen sixty-something? What's the big deal? She was probably paring down. Doing spring cleaning."

Honora took off the magnifying headband she usually wore when she worked and picked up her regular glasses. Wiping them carefully on the hem of her blouse, she studied the dress and me for what seemed like a long time.

"Well, no. That can't be what happened. You see, Binky had other plans for this dress."

"The museum in Boynton Beach Mall. I bet she was going to give it away," said MJ.

"No," said Honora. "Absolutely not. Don't get me wrong, Binky has given away scads and scads of clothing to charity shops. No one could be more generous. That's not the point."

She inched around me, taking in the dress more slowly. Her eyes were bright with concentration. "Binky always swore that this was the dress she'd be buried in."

"Gross," I said. "Maybe there was a misunderstanding. Danielle is a saleswoman, and she loves a good deal. Maybe Binky didn't mean to hand over this particular dress. I'll put this aside until we find out."

I hated what I was about to do, because the dress was particularly becoming. It had been a long day, and it had started off with a sad occurrence. Now I felt unreasonably put out and defeated. "I'll go upstairs and change out of this while you call Binky."

"I shall phone her later tonight. She's usually puttering around in her garden until six. Cara? You are doing the right thing," Honora said.

Then why didn't I feel good about it?

CHAPTER 16

When he arrived to pick me up, Jason brought a large bouquet of red roses. They seemed a bit overtly romantic, but I certainly didn't complain. Instead, I stuck my nose into the cool petals and inhaled deeply.

"Gorgeous."

"So are you," he responded.

I didn't feel as feminine in my dark-wash jeans and sheer boho blouse, but at least I knew these clothes were mine. We actually matched better than if I'd worn my Lilly because Jason was wearing a tight pair of jeans and a Guy Harvey tee shirt.

"Cara needs to let her hair down," said MJ, after she volunteered to trim the stems on the roses and put them in a vase.

"Why?" asked Jason.

I explained about finding the undocumented immigrant.

"You found the live one, I hope. Not the woman who turned up dead."

"No. Not the dead one."

MJ shooed us out the door with a little brushing motion of her fingertips. "Don't worry about your pets, Cara. I'll make sure they're fed and watered. You two kids go and have a good time."

Easy for her to say. She's been married six times and dated almost every man on the Treasure Coast. Somehow, she manages to glide from man to man without any involvement. Me? I'm a "marry in haste and repent for the rest of your life" type of girl. I'd been all of eighteen when I eloped to Chicago with Dominic Petrocelli. Eight months and a big baby bump later, I walked in on Dom while he was ramming his tongue down the throat of a waitress in the back of my parents' restaurant. When she laughed at the expression on my face, and he joined in, I grabbed a cast-iron skillet and hit him. Dom went down and hit his head, hard. Fortunately, he regained consciousness. Unfortunately, he decided to press charges against me for attempted murder. Just for laughs, he also did his best to ruin my parents' business.

Suffice it to say, I've been a wee bit skittish around men ever since. Jason was hoping to have an exclusive relationship. But I didn't have any experience with intimacy except for my brief marriage—and to call me "scared" was a vast understatement.

I was petrified.

My marriage not only cost me my self-esteem, but the resultant legal fees and impact on my parents' business cost me my freedom. Guilt compelled me to keep working at the restaurant and doing exactly what my parents asked of me. To the outside world, it looked like I had tremendous freedom, but in actuality I had none. Year after year, my only goal was to be a good daughter, to do anything and everything asked of me. How else could I make things right? How else could I atone for mucking up my parents' lives?

Relationships are a messy business.

While I did my mental walk of shame, Jason waited patiently for me to tell him more about my early morning adventure on the beach. He tucked my hand under his arm as we ambled down the sidewalk toward the restaurants that dotted the streets of Downtown Stuart.

"Yes, I found the woman who washed up on the beach. Can you believe it? That started my day on the wrong foot. I was primed for a nice walk with Jack, but after stumbling over the mermaid—"

"Mermaid?" Jason frowned as he pulled me closer so we could let other folks get by. As we walked, women's heads turned. No doubt about it, Jason was major league eye candy. His sandy blond hair was sun-streaked from surfing. His shoulders were broad and his waist tiny. Not only was he well built, but his chiseled features were well balanced.

"Mermaid. That's my private name for the woman I found. See, when I spotted her, she looked like one of those sand sculptures people leave on the beach. I didn't realize she was a real person until she moved." Trying for a light-hearted tone, I added, "Skye has been telling me I need glasses. She's probably right. Of course, it was break of dawn. The mist made things blurry."

We came to a crosswalk, and my date held my arm snuggly against his. "Cara, what were you thinking? Wandering around on a beach by yourself in the dark?"

"Don't you start! Poppy has already chewed me out. Jupiter Island is the safest community in the country. Our ratio of law enforcement officers—"

Jason interrupted. "Don't give me that baloney. You didn't have a cop escort, Cara. You could have been hurt. Seriously hurt. Someone could have overpowered you."

"So I've been told. Repeatedly."

"Promise me you won't endanger yourself like that again."

I almost snapped at him. Almost. But a tiny voice inside me said, *Your first husband couldn't have given two hoots in a handbag about your safety. But this is how real men act. They want to protect the people they love.*

Instead of getting huffy, I stopped and kissed Jason on the cheek. We had almost reached the Lyric Theatre, one of our city's loveliest sights. "I think you're going overboard. Um, excuse the pun."

Jason walked me backwards into an alcove festooned with playbills. Putting both hands on my shoulders, he gently pinned me against the wall. "Cara? Ever since I took that job up in Jacksonville, I've come to realize how much I care about you. You mean the world to me." Moving slowly, he leaned in for a kiss.

It wasn't a friend-to-friend sort of smooch. It was long and deep. Fireworks exploded throughout my body. A shower of sparks set me tingling. Even though we were standing there on a public street, I heard a moan escape my lips.

"Whoa." I pushed him away. His eyes had a gleam that could only be described as hungry. "Jason, that was, um, intense. I'm not ready for it. I mean, there's our age difference."

He tossed back his head and laughed. "Okay, Grandma." With a tug at my hand, he pulled me toward the open sidewalk. "Let's see if you can make it to the restaurant without your walker."

CHAPTER 17

The next morning I woke up when Jack licked my chin after chewing on a bully stick.

"Yuck. Your breath is disgusting," I told him. My head hurt a little, because Jason and I had shared a wonderful bottle of Malbec wine with our dinner.

In the bathroom mirror, my reflection showed whisker burns on my neck. Jason had kissed me repeatedly until my knees were as weak as overcooked spaghetti. I probably would have toppled over except that I'd been leaning against my car.

"I need to get home," I'd protested. "I have to work tomorrow." After helping me load up my pets, climb in, and buckle my seatbelt, Jason had insisted on driving me to Jupiter Island. After making sure I was safely ensconced in my house, he'd used his Uber app to get a ride back to his Porsche, which was parked behind my store.

Jason was a gentleman. He sighed and protested just a little but when the black sedan arrived from Uber, he quickly hopped in. I felt a tinge of regret as I watched them pull out of my driveway. Was I crazy, sending away such an adorable man?

All in all, Jason and I had a terrific evening. After a wonderful meal at Riverwalk Café, we'd walked around the downtown. Our stroll took us to the Eisenhower Bridge, and on a whim, we decided to take it all the way across the St. Lucie River. Thanks to the bridge's steep incline, we were both slightly winded on the way back, so we stopped to rest against the concrete buffer while we watched the lights of boats cruising up and down the waterway. The air was rich with the smell of Sargasso, mud, and salt water.

"How old is Tommy?" Jason had asked.

I guessed why he was asking. Immediately, my stomach twisted. "Eighteen. He'll be nineteen in March."

"Have you ever thought about having more kids?"

There it was, the question I'd been anticipating and dreading. As often as I'd rehearsed it in my head, I couldn't spit out a cogent sentence. "Yes. But I would be an awfully old mother. If I got pregnant today, I'd be fifty-seven by the time my child was ready to go to college. That's practically a geezer."

"Really? Look at your grandfather. He's incredibly active at seventy-nine. Honora's seventy-six, right? People are living longer than ever. You take good care of yourself, Cara. Besides, a child would keep you young."

"You say that because you've never been a parent. Babies wear you down. They are wonderful—don't get me wrong—but tiring. Exhausting. If you get one who has colic, you never get any sleep. Tommy had a mild case of it. My mother and father took turns holding him. Without them, I can't imagine…" My voice cracked. I brushed a tear from my eyes as Jason put an arm around me. "My parents were such a big help. Maybe it's not because of my age. Maybe I can't imagine having another child because I can't imagine my parents not being a part of my child's life."

"Babe," he said, as he pulled me close. I buried my face in his tee shirt, inhaling the pungent fragrance of fresh sweat that mixed with his cologne. "They wouldn't want you to forgo having a child because they've passed over. Besides, you could tell your kid about your parents. Tommy could tell his little sister or brother about them. Poppy could, too. You never met your maternal grandmother, but Poppy has told you a lot about her, right? In fact, the best way to preserve your parents' memory is to have another child, isn't it?"

I shook my head. "It wouldn't be the same."

"Of course it wouldn't. But that doesn't mean it wouldn't be wonderful." He kissed the top of my right ear. "Cara, I want a baby. I want to be a dad. And I want—"

I reached up and put my fingers over his lips to shush him. "Stop. Please. Not right now. I've had such a weird day. I'm overly emotional. Let's not ruin a wonderful evening by letting it get heavy."

He dipped his head down to kiss me tenderly. "You're right. My timing stinks. Promise me you'll think about it. Okay?"

"I will."

In the cold light of day the next morning, I did.

I thought about having a baby as Jack sprinted across my yard, as I raced to keep up with him, as I twisted my ankle in a hole in my lawn, as I limped back into the house, and as I explained the situation to Luna, my cat. She stared at me with those lemon-yellow eyes. Both animals watched me carefully as I set the kettle on my stove and turned the knob to high heat.

"I am way too old to have another baby. End of discussion."

CHAPTER 18

Once I had a cup of coffee in hand, I called Treasure Coast Memorial Hospital to see if I could get an update on my mermaid. The receptionist quickly cut me off. "No comment," she said. "The hospital administration is giving regular press briefings. You'll have to get your news that way."

"But I'm the one who found her! Come on! I'm wondering if we did the right thing by reviving her!"

"Oh," and then a pause. In a whisper, I heard: "She's still alive, but pretty messed up."

"Thanks," I said.

I slapped on a bit of makeup and hurriedly got dressed while Luna and Jack ate their breakfast. I put on a cute Lilly Pulitzer-inspired top and a khaki skirt. It was a darling outfit, but that new Lilly dress called to me like the sirens beckoned to Ulysses. Would I ever get to wear it?

"Job One is finding out whether I can keep that dress," I said as I loaded Luna and Jack in my Camry and headed north toward Stuart.

Poppy showed up at the store only minutes after I'd put on a pot of coffee, my second of the day.

"I'll go back home and pick up Sid before your doors open. I wanted to let the boy sleep in as long as possible. He was plumb tuckered out after coming to the store yesterday. He totally underestimated how banged up he is. What that boy needs is rest, rest, and more rest so he can heal."

I took two scones out of my refrigerator and pointed at them. "Heated?"

"Yes, ma'am."

After they were in the microwave, I asked, "Did you find Sid's computer?"

"Nope."

A frisson of frustration wiggled through me. "Did you get the chance to look for Sid's backpack?"

"Yup. Did it last night. Found it under his bed. But it was empty. His paycheck was missing, too."

A sinking feeling hit me. "You have to be kidding."

"Nope. I turned that there house of mine upside down. Looked high and low. Quizzed that boy good. Then I called the hospital. They said I'd have better luck if I talked to the nursing supervisor."

"We'll go do it together. I want to drop off flowers for my mermaid and get back here before the store opens."

"That can wait until after I eat one of them scones."

~*~

The nursing supervisor wore her short red curls sprayed into a helmet. She was prone to repeating everything we said. "Sid? The boy hit by the car? Are those flowers for him?"

"Actually, these are for the poor woman who washed up on Jupiter Island," I said.

"So you're the media?"

"No, sirree, young lady." Poppy gave her a wink. "My granddaughter found that poor woman yesterday morning on the sand. She's been worrying herself sick, wondering if she did the right thing, reviving her. It was a near thing, as you can imagine."

The nursing supervisor echoed, "I can imagine."

"Can I give these to her? Is she okay? I figure she's all alone, and she's had a hard time of it." I held out the flowers.

She shoved her open palm toward me. "I'll take them."

"But is my mermaid okay? Did I help or hurt by reviving her?" Responding to the woman's narrowed eyes, I added, "It's been preying on my mind."

"Mermaid? Harrumph. You gave her a chance," said the nursing supervisor as she relieved me of the flowers. But her expression didn't match her words. Her face had turned mulish. "Now it's up to God. So why are you asking about that boy if you really care about the immigrant? What are you two trying to pull?"

"Not one blessed thang," said Poppy in his best down-home twang. "That there boy, Sid, he works for Cara. You might remember that I'm the one who picked the boy up. Brought him home to live with me. But he cain't find his computer nowhere. He thinks he mighta left it here, but he ain't too sure. What with his head injuries and all. It's powerful important to him."

"I've been here every day." I remembered seeing Red Curls, even if she didn't remember seeing me. "You're always so busy."

"That's right. I remember you now," Red Curls said as she frowned. With a half-turn of her body, she blocked me out and addressed her remarks to Poppy. "You're looking for his computer, and you picked him up the day of the discharge. Didn't he have it then?"

"He thought it was still in his backpack. I didn't check when I put it in my truck. I do remember how sweet you were to him. A regular angel." Poppy gave her the smarmiest smile. I ached to poke him hard in the ribs. He was definitely shining the woman on.

"It's my job." She preened.

"No, miss, it ain't. A lot of people working here wouldn't give that kid the time of day, on account of his holes in his face and all that metal. But you was something special. He went on and on about you. Of course, I remember 'cause each time I came to visit you was taking care of him so careful like."

"Well, I try." She gave him a shy look from under her lashes. "By the way, my name is Zelda Monahan."

"He really is recovering well," I said, but no one was listening.

"Zelda. Ain't that pretty? I'm Dick Potter. This here's my grandbaby. That boy, Sid, he's been staying with me. Tires me out taking care of him, but that boy ain't got no other kin that cares about him."

"Would you like some coffee?" Zelda batted her lashes at Poppy. "I made a fresh pot."

When he mumbled, "Don't wanna put cha out," she pooh-poohed the suggestion and waved us over to where a coffee maker bubbled and dripped. All the fixings were made available to us. I went easy on the pink sweetener and heavy on the 2% milk. While Poppy doctored up his hot drink, Zelda asked Poppy a zillion questions about himself. I watched as the expensive bouquet I'd purchased in the hospital gift shop slowly wilted in her hands. Finally, a buzzing noise from her pocket rescued us. Zelda waved goodbye with a promise to be "back soon" as she wobbled off to check at the desk, where she was sure there'd be a listing of Sid's belongings.

Poppy smirked at me. "I ain't too old to work my magic with the ladies."

"TMI, too much information. What about Wilma? That friend you reconnected with over Christmas?"

"There's flirting and there's for real. This here is flirting. Zelda's got something we want. But Wilma is everything I want. I miss her, and I can't wait until she's back in town."

It surprised me to hear him speak so frankly. I wanted to ask him what his intentions were toward Wilma, but instead I held my tongue because Zelda was hurrying toward us.

"I put the flowers in water. A volunteer will take them upstairs." Zelda only had eyes for Poppy. Cocking her head with a coquettish smile, she fluttered her eyelashes at him.

"Thanks so much," I said, trying not to sound as sarcastic as I felt.

"It's right here." She underlined a section with a sparkly pink fingernail as she sidled up to my grandfather. "Sid's mother picked up his computer. See? It was the day before we discharged the boy."

Poppy's caterpillar eyebrows flew up to his hairline, and I choked on my coffee.

"Is there a problem?" Zelda pursed her lips.

"His mother?" I tried to keep the incredulity out of my voice. "She's not his mother. She's his stepmother and I thought she never visited him."

"That's what I thought, too." Poppy looked over the form, a tattered piece of paper attached to a clipboard. "She's signed in here. That's her name, all right. Amberlee Heckman."

"Is there a problem?" Zelda repeated. She was staring at me curiously. As much as she liked Poppy, she wasn't too sure about me. I needed to convince her I wasn't the enemy.

"Amberlee isn't really Sid's mother. Not biologically at least. She's his late father's second—and much, much younger—wife. I hate to sound distrustful, but I am, given what I've heard about her."

"Are you questioning me?" Zelda stuck out her jaw.

"No, miss, she ain't. Not at all. I wouldn't put up with my granddaughter speaking that way to you," said my grandfather, pushing me aside so she could take Zelda by the arm. "See, I hate to speak ill of any woman. But this Amberlee, she's a real bad egg. Couldn't be bothered to come to the ER when Sid was first brought in. According to the boy, she never dropped by to see him. Now you're telling us that out of the blue, she shows up right before he goes home and takes his computer. It's perplexing, ain't it?"

"Perhaps she couldn't get to the ER in time to see him there. Things like that happen all the time. But according to our records, she is the young man's mother," said Zelda. "Why shouldn't we have trusted her?"

"Okay, but where in tarnation is that there computer?" Poppy wondered.

Zelda's mouth sank into a deep scowl. "Please understand that I'm speaking to you only as a courtesy. I don't have to tell you anything. In fact, you two shouldn't even be on this floor. That said, Amberlee Heckman had every right to visit Sid Heckman. She is the boy's mother."

That last word was said with emphasis: MUH-ther. As if Poppy and I were non-native speakers and might not get the gist. I considered pointing out that Sid had instructed the hospital to call me immediately after he was hit. However, that probably wouldn't help the situation. In Zelda's place, I would have done exactly as she had. I would have followed the paper trail and accepted Amberlee as Sid's kin.

When you looked at it from Zelda's point of view, Poppy and I were the interlopers, not Amberlee.

I put on my most conciliatory expression. "Of course you did the right thing. It's good that Amberlee was finally able to find time to see Sid. I've always gotten the impression she doesn't care much about him."

"I just hope she don't skip out on Sid's hospital bill," Poppy said.

"That's a problem for billing to handle," said Zelda, as she softened her stance. "But I could tell she wasn't a very nice person. She looked like a tart. Skinny as a beanpole. Wearing all that fancy jewelry. When she arrived, her son was asleep. She noticed his computer hadn't been charged so she told me that she was taking it home to charge it up. I didn't think to question her motives. She's his mom, isn't she? And mothers are good people."

Most of the time. But not always.

CHAPTER 19

"What do you think happened?" I asked my grandfather.

"Durned if I know. Engines, I understand. They're logical. People? There ain't no rhyme nor reason to what happens in the human mind. Cain't imagine what old Amberlee wanted with that computer unless it was to cause mischief."

His truck bumped along the streets of downtown Stuart. He could well afford a new Toyota, but that's not on the way my grandfather spends his money. In fact, I learned the fine art of recycling from him. He's always fixed up old vehicles, even if the original owners had given up on them. "Got plenty of life left in that old jalopy," he would say right before he'd dig in. If the car or truck had been abandoned, he'd sell it to someone who needed reliable transportation but who couldn't afford car payments. Thanks to Poppy, a lot of folks on the Treasure Coast were able to keep their jobs, because they didn't have car problems.

Until that moment, I'd never recognized how his philosophy of life had affected me. Neither of my parents were into recycling, except to toss waste items into their appropriate blue bins. But Poppy was totally into reusing and refurbishing. When he wasn't fixing a car, Poppy was always repairing a broken household item. Or he'd be repurposing old stuff. Like his minnow tank. Originally, it had been a bathtub. Or his desk at the Gas E Bait. He'd attached an old door to the wall and slid file cabinets underneath. This realization (and new appreciation) came to me with a jolt, as an epiphany. But isn't that the way? We unconsciously absorb a world view and adopt it as our own, not questioning its roots.

"People are definitely more complicated," I agreed. "Of course, I don't work on motors, but I do help Skye tinker with stuff we sell."

"Yup. It's in your blood." He winked at me. "That there mother of Sid's. She's a piece of work."

"That's why I'm worried," and I told Poppy about Sid having all my financial information in his computer.

"You have to be kidding me! That's why I don't do any of my banking online. It's too risky."

My face warmed at his criticism. "Explain to me how I'd bank any other way? All my accounts are still up in St. Louis. That's where I deposited my money after I sold my house, and where the business loan is for the restaurant.

Dom lives up there, so he puts his money for Tommy—when he decides to meet his obligations—in the bank over in Illinois. Tommy is in Coral Gables. Short of driving down there to hand him spending money, I have to send him funds electronically or write him checks and trust the postal service." I would have continued, but Poppy waved my explanations away.

"I know, I know. This world is complicated, everything is caught in that big internet do-jobbie, and nobody stays put no more. Ain't there anything you can do? To keep your statements private? Lord above, Granddaughter, you could be wiped out."

"Sid assured me that he was very careful with his passwords."

"That's something at least."

I rested my head against the passenger side window. "Right."

"Drat." Poppy shook his head. "I still don't like the sound of that."

"I don't either. Why would Amberlee have taken Sid's computer? She has plenty of money to buy herself one, so why take his?"

"It don't make no sense. None at all."

"Well? What are you thinking? Come on, Poppy, tell me. You've spent more time with Sid lately than I have. What do you think is behind all this?'

"I think that woman ain't no good. I wouldn't put nothing past her. Heard tell that she runs with a fast crowd. Out drinking and bar-hopping all hours of the night. A couple of guys at the Elks Club was saying as much. I used to run into her, now and again. Jest around town. She's purely evil, as far as I can tell. So, what's behind this taking Sid's computer? I'd say it's more of her black-heartedness. Word is that she hated Sid. Jealous of how Harvey loved that boy. kin that boy's life. Speaking of which, how am I going to help Sid out when I go back to work? I been checking over at the Fill Up and Go. Looks like they got them service bays almost ready for cars."

I had to tell Poppy about my conversation with Cooper, so I began with a lengthy preamble to my bad news, explaining to Poppy how much everyone thought of his skills. I was getting around to the hard part when Poppy held up one hand, mirroring the stop sign ahead of us.

"Let me guess. They don't want me. They think I'm too old, don't they?"

I tried to respond, but the words died in my throat. Poppy is many things, but never pitiful. Until today. The ragged edge of his voice cut me to the quick.

CHAPTER 20

Poppy dropped me off behind the store and spun out of the alley so fast that I had to duck a flying piece of gravel.

MJ pulled her pink Cadillac into the space he left empty. "You look like you've lost your last friend."

"It feels that way."

She slammed her heavy car door shut. "How was your date last night? No, don't tell me! Those are whisker burns on your face. Some girls have all the luck. He's so yummy."

Her frank appraisal embarrassed me. "Actually, Jason and I hit a snag. I don't want to discuss it. Could you watch the store for me or do you have any appointments you need to visit? This day already stinks, so I might as well front-load it with garbage."

"What do you mean by, This day already stinks? It hasn't even gotten started yet." She raised a perfectly arched eyebrow as she tried to figure out what problems I might be having with Jason. MJ had an annoying habit of prying into my love life, or lack thereof.

I quickly explained what we'd learned about Sid's computer and his mother. "Amberlee must be up to something. Why take the computer? Without the password, it's of no use to anybody. Poppy talks about her like she's a demon in a dress."

"Because she likes to bar hop? If so, I'm the Devil's spawn." MJ snorted an unlady-like laugh.

"You're fine, and you know it, but according to Poppy, Amberlee is just plain wicked. It's not like him to be so negative about a person. I suspect he knows even more about her than he's letting on."

"Your grandfather knows a lot about a lot of stuff, in part because he's mastered the art of keeping his mouth shut. I'm sure he's also found all sorts of incriminating evidence in the cars he's fixed, but no one has ever accused him of being a blabbermouth. To his credit, he holds his cards close to his undershirt."

"Right." I would have pressed MJ for details, but I had a different agenda. "If your calendar is clear, I'll look up Binky Rutherford's address and take the dress over to her myself."

"Your new Lilly? Isn't that Danielle's job? She sold it to you. Possession is nine-tenths of the law, and all that."

"Danielle is in Orlando and won't be back until late tonight. I need fresh air. A drive over to the island would give me the chance to meet a neighbor. I can be sociable and tie up loose ends at the same time, can't I?"

"If you're asking my opinion, I think you should wait until Danielle gets back. She sold you the dress; it's her responsibility to figure out if Binky handed it over by mistake."

MJ could be such a black and white person, but here she was, telling me to put up with shades of gray. I wasn't in the mood.

"I either want to wear that dress or give it away. End of discussion. It's one more loose end driving me nuts."

"You can't race off. Not yet at least. Didn't you get the text message from Honora?"

"When did Honora learn how to send text messages?"

"Honestly, Cara," MJ said. "It's not like you've surrounded yourself with nitwits. Sid taught her how to do it. Honora may be old but she catches on really fast. I got a text message last night asking me to meet her here at 8:30. She wants to use the half hour before we open to present idea boards for her Creatin' Contest. I guess she and EveLynn put the boards together last night."

I opened my mouth but never had the chance to speak because EveLynn careened into the alley. With little regard for safety, she zoomed their green Subaru Forester into the space right next to MJ's Cadillac and slammed on her brakes, hard. A loud screech split the air.

Once again, I opened my mouth. This time I intended to lecture EveLynn on driving safely, especially when approaching our parking spaces. But I never got the chance. The doors on the Subaru flew open right on cue as Skye stuck her head out of the back door.

"Hello, everybody!" Skye sang out. "Good! We're all here. Can't wait to see what you've got for us, Honora. I have a nice fruit salad with a yogurt dressing chilling upstairs. There's also a plate of those bite-sized muffins."

"I'm hungry." EveLynn all but knocked Skye out of the way as she headed for the food.

Honora waved to me with a cheery smile on her face. "Yoohoo! Cara? Could you help me with these boards?"

MJ and I both went over to the passenger side. Two large pieces of gator board rested in the well behind the front seats. MJ took one and I took the other. A flap of decorative paper on each board protected the attached images.

"Be careful with those. Things might fall off." Honora was dressed in her best navy sateen dress. A navy and white ribbon belt broke up the broad expanse of dark color. On her feet were sturdy black orthopedic shoes, but at her throat were her best pearls. Instead of her usual straw boater, she wore a broad brimmed hat, white with a navy and white striped hatband. As I eased out a board, she tapped the covering with a finger. "I want to make a formal presentation, so I covered the boards until the big reveal."

"Could you do this without me?" As soon as the words were out of my mouth, I regretted them. Honora's happy grin fled her face. Her eyes lost all their sparkle.

"Yes, of course. If you have an emergency, I'll understand." But her voice quivered.

I flashed her my best smile. "No, no. It can wait. Did you happen to call Binky about that dress?"

"I did yesterday right after work. Her grandson answered the phone. He's here visiting on Spring Break. He promised to take a message, but you know how kids are. So I sent Binky a text message."

"Gee, Honora, you are one impressive lady. I wish you'd teach Poppy to text."

"Pshaw. I simply told her that there must have been a mix up. I explained that Danielle had sold you her favorite Lilly Pulitzer dress."

"And?"

"She didn't answer my text. I'm not sure why. I am positive I did it correctly."

Knowing how precise Honora can be, I figured she was right. For whatever reason, her friend had not responded. "I'll give Danielle a call and see if I can reach her. I want to get this situation settled. Either your pal Binky made a mistake or she's changed her mind. But I need to know what gives and I won't wear the dress until I find out."

"I can always depend on you," and Honora patted me on the cheek.

CHAPTER 21

While I was talking to her mother, EveLynn brushed past us, stopping only long enough to jam small muffins into her mouth. She carried in new soft goods pieces, arranged them as she wished, and left without a goodbye. That shouldn't have surprised me. EveLynn has absolutely no people skills at all. On the flip side, she's fabulous with numbers and measurements. Her talent as a seamstress is without parallel. The items she makes for my shop sell fast and bring a good profit margin. When I grouse about her lack of tact, Skye reminds me, "Every strength overused becomes a weakness. At least EveLynn doesn't waste any time. She comes in, arranges her things, and leaves. Besides, it's not her fault about the lack of skills. That's how she's wired. You might as well complain about Luna catching lizards. It's the nature of that particular beast, isn't it?"

Of course, Skye's right. When EveLynn gets under my collar, I remind myself that I make a lot of money off of her, and her mother is an absolute gem.

After we were all seated around the large table in the back, Honora showed us two concepts she'd worked up for her contest entry. One was a beach house done in khaki, cream, and shades of blue. Cute as all get out and boring as a box of sand. Soothing and charming, but dull. The second was a surf shop. Eclectic and colorful. All of us fell in love with the second concept immediately. Several of us had seen *Surfer Dude* with Matthew McConaughey, so we instantly visualized Honora's project as a knock-off of that character's house.

Skye had been brave enough to speak up. "But is this going to be a surf shop or a surfer's shack? I wouldn't imagine that a surfer's shack wouldn't be extensive enough to win any prizes."

"Definitely more of a surfer's shop," agreed Honora. "I hope to capture the spirit of the Treasure Coast. We have our own vibe, as you kids say. Very Old Florida, with a subsistence twist to it."

"What do they usually look for when they pick a winning entry?" I asked.

"I've done a bit of research as you might suspect. I think they like projects that are out of the ordinary. Of course, the entries vary from year to year, so one never knows who'll be doing what. Craftsmanship is important. I suspect that having a theme that's unique would add to the cachet."

That made sense to me and I'd said as much. We all agreed to pitch in and help in any way we could, although the entry itself would be Honora's responsibility.

"Whatever the end result, win or lose, we can promote and display the dollhouse," said MJ. "We'll have bragging rights that it was an entry in such a prestigious contest."

"Better yet," said Sid, as he hobbled in with Poppy at his side. "Honora should post her progress on her blog. That way she can let people follow along as she bashes the kit and fills the shop with merchandise."

Even sidelined and on crutches, Sid is a social media genius.

Poppy couldn't meet my eyes. I took it as a sign that he was still upset about the situation with the Fill Up and Go. I couldn't blame him. I would have been mightily disappointed, too.

"I'm off to Pumpernickel's to work my shift," said Skye, hopping up to dispense hugs. "You're looking better and moving better, Sid."

"Thanks," he said, but he didn't sound like he agreed.

"I've got to check on our Highwayman painting inventory." MJ paused before heading for the sales floor. Turning to my grandfather, she asked, "Dick, could you help me? I need to rehang several of the paintings. It goes more smoothly with two people."

"Sure thing," Poppy said.

"Sid, can you help Honora put up a post on our blog when she's ready?" I asked, while Honora put away her idea boards. "I'm not sure how that works."

"Sure, but I still need a computer. Poppy told me that you two found out how Amberlee took mine while I was in the hospital. She has no right to my computer. I'm an adult and I bought that Dell with my own money. That's theft. She out and out stole it."

"Yes, it is," I said. "But she's still your stepmother. Your father loved her. I'd think long and hard before I contacted the law."

"I've left her messages that I want it back, and that she was the last person to have it. Just so you know, I'll do whatever I have to so I get it back. She may have been married to my dad, but she's never had any use for me."

It hurt me to hear him say that, especially since he put it so plainly. The tremor in his voice told me that it had been hard for him to revisit how poorly his stepmother had treated him. When I first met Sid, I would have never guessed him to have such depth of emotion. I'd been completely thrown by the piercings, the dyed hair, and the gothic clothes he wore. As time went on, I'd come to realize this was his suit of armor, the way he girded himself against the pain he felt.

"Let's not jump to conclusions, okay? Maybe she did bring it back, and maybe somebody else took it."

"Right. And maybe global warming is a joke. Here's the good news. Amberlee could never crack my passwords," said Sid. "Not in a million years. She can't. No way. My passwords are dope."

"Dope?" Honora muttered as she pulled out the stool under her work table and got to work. "My, my."

"Dope?" Poppy rejoined us and poured himself a cup of black coffee.

"When Sid says dope, he means his passwords are terrific," I translated.

"Right...and Amberlee isn't really bright. In fact, she's pretty clueless, especially when it comes to computers. She can't even operate her television remote control without help." He plucked nervously at the edge of an adhesive band-age on his right temple. "That's what's so weird. I can't even believe she wanted my computer. She wouldn't know what to do with it, so why bother to take it?"

Hard as it was, I kept my mouth shut. I wanted to join in, bad-mouthing Amberlee, but it wasn't the right thing to do.

I stared at Sid, seeing how young and vulnerable he was, and feeling sick at heart for the additional pain this woman was causing him.

He thought I was taking the measure of his worth. "Cara, I know about security. I used good passwords. They're all up here, in my head."

"Okay," I said, trying to stay calm, because his answer had not been comforting. He had the passwords in his head? Uh-oh. Bad idea. Sid's head was not in good space. The doctors had warned Poppy that the boy might not be thinking clearly. His short-term memory had definitely suffered from the blow he'd taken. Was it possible he'd shared the passwords and forgotten about them? There didn't seem to be any reason to push the point. Not now, since I didn't have any evidence there was a problem. "Right. Well, in the meantime, you can use the computer in my office. But anything you can do to retrieve your own computer would still be a good idea."

"One hundred percent. I'm on it. I'll call her again right now."

Somehow, I doubted that would solve our problems.

"You two got this thing under control," Poppy said. "I'm going back to the house."

I nodded and tried to smile at my grandfather before kissing him goodbye. No one needed to know how worried I was. A distraction was in order. I was tired of loose ends. Time to concentrate on something I could nail down.

Something pretty and nonconsequential like a dress.

"Honora? I don't want to disturb you while you're working, but have you heard from Binky?"

"No, dear." She picked up a tiny item she was painting.

"Then I'm running next door to Vintage Threads. Maybe Danielle's assistant Claudia can tell me what's up with the dress. Be right back."

~*~

But I didn't make a beeline to Vintage Threads because I was waylaid first by customers, then a call from a vendor, and finally a panicked email from the man who was buying our family restaurant on contract. In fact, three hours flew by before I was able to go to the neighboring shop. Although the door minder buzzed loudly as I entered, Danielle's part-timer Claudia couldn't be bothered to look up from her cell phone. Other customers wandered around the store, fingering the merchandise.

Finally, I rapped on the counter and said, "Hello? Claudia? A little help, please."

"Yeah?" She cocked an over-plucked eyebrow at me. The green streaks she'd added to her hair did nothing good for her looks.

"I bought a dress from Danielle. A Lilly Pulitzer. But Honora says it has to be a mistake. She insists that she knows the original owner and says the woman would never give up that particular dress. I don't want to wear it if it needs to go back to the owner."

"What do you expect me to do about it?"

"Could you check your paperwork? Or give Danielle a call?"

"Nope. I'm busy." Claudia sighed the deep wooosh of a person being put upon. "Everyone pestering me about stupid stuff. I'm trying to take care of customers."

That was ridiculous. However, arguing with Claudia would also be ridiculous. Time to try another tactic. "Do you know anything about this dress?" I showed her a photo I'd snapped with my phone.

Claudia didn't even look at the picture. "Look, you bought the dress; it's yours, right? You got the sales receipt, don't you?"

"Yes, but if there's been a mix up—"

"Geez, this is totally annoying. People keep bugging me about everything! I don't have any answers! Like I keep saying to everybody, I am not the person in charge. You want answers, you have to talk to Danielle."

"So you don't have any records or any way to look up—"

"No, I don't. Danielle keeps everything in her head."

There seemed to be a lot of that going around.

CHAPTER 22

"Claudia is practically worthless," I said to anybody and nobody in particular, when I returned to my store.

"Claudia? From next door?" Sid hobbled out of my office. "I could have told you that. We went to high school together. She was always forgetting her assignments or saying she didn't understand what the teacher wanted from us. I think all she cares about is her social life. Did you see her thumbs? She's got callouses from text-messaging all day long. Honest."

"This is getting ridiculous. I don't know what to do about that dress," I said. "It's turning into a colossal hassle."

Honora stood over a T-square that pinned down a large piece of graph paper. Her process included sketching a project on graph paper, creating a cardboard mock-up that was to scale, making adjustments as necessary, gathering supplies, and then executing her design. Originally, it drove me nuts to watch her, because I thought she wasted a lot of time. However, over the past few months, I've come to realize that Honora's approach actually works wonderfully well. Her full-size renderings help customers visualize the end project. Alterations could then be made on the model, rather than on finished pieces, resulting in all sorts of savings.

"Binky isn't responding to my text messages or phone calls," said Honora. "I imagine her battery is dead. Happens all the time. I had to quit watching that television show *24* because Jack Bauer's phone never went dead. EveLynn got so agitated that she actually ticked down the time like a human bomb."

"Uh-huh." I tried not to laugh.

"However, I have a proposition that'll fix both your problem and mine."

"You have a problem?"

"Yes, actually I do. I've been working on a custom project for Martha Gunderson. That room box of a man's office? It's a gift for Martha's husband. EveLynn needed the car. I forgot that I promised to drop the room box off today—"

"When did we agree to start delivering room boxes?" I already paid a fortune to a delivery service that was giving me gray hairs.

"Actually, this project took a bit longer than I expected, so I told her I'd drop it off. The Gundersons live down the street from you on Jupiter Island. The Jupiter Island Bridge Club meets today. Binky is a keen bridge player. I can't imagine her missing a club meeting. One trip, and two problems solved."

I had tons of work to get done. A drive to Jupiter Island would take a big chunk out of my day. While I was debating, Honora continued, "I thought about asking EveLynn to drive over the room box, but you know how rigid she can be about schedules."

Boy, did I ever. When asked to make a change, EveLynn acted like a toddler who'd lost her favorite toy. I'd actually seen her stomp her feet and scream. We're only six months apart in age, but you'd never guess that by how juvenile she can be. Once when I rearranged her display of placemats, she actually shook with rage.

"Do you want to take my car and go by yourself?" I asked. "We could load it up for you."

"I could certainly do that, but don't you think you should meet more of your neighbors? Wouldn't you like to get this problem with the dress settled?" Honora stared at me expectantly.

"Sounds like a plan." I reminded myself we'd also be picking up a check when we dropped off Honora's project. The money would provide small comfort if I wound up giving away my new dress. Dealing with outstanding receivables is a sad fact of retail life.

"Good! I just love taking road trips." Honora untied the strings of her apron.

Life is one big circus act, and some days you wind up wearing the clown shoes.

~*~

"Amberlee still isn't answering her phone." Sid had waited until Honora and I finished our conversation. "I sent her a text message." His eyes were dark with worry.

"Keep at it. She has to respond sooner or later," I said. But I had my doubts. I just didn't trust or like Amberlee. Furthermore, I hated seeing how she was hurting Sid. My heart was in my shoes as I helped Honora carry her room box out to my car.

"First we'll meet Martha at her bridge club gathering," said Honora, as she buckled her seatbelt. "I want all her friends to see it, so I told Martha that I was running a little late finishing up the details. I volunteered to deliver the project directly to the Club."

"The Club" was short for the Jupiter Island Club, probably the largest and most expensive private club in the world, because you can't join unless you own property on the island. Places here are pricey. Poppy was selling his little cottage to me. Otherwise, no way would I be able to afford living on Jupiter Island. As it was, I would pay more in property taxes than my parents had paid monthly to buy their nice home up in St. Louis.

"Honora," I said, "it was very cunning of you to make sure that club members would see your work."

"I'm sure we'll get more orders this way." With a tiny giggle, Honora added, "But I also really do want you to meet more of your neighbors. It can't hurt for you to put names with faces. Have you been to the Club before?"

"No, actually I haven't. It's behind the golf course, right?" Traffic on Federal Highway was slow moving, but at last we turned east toward the ocean and the island. My whole body relaxed as I steered the car through the tunnel of ficus trees that transports you to another world, a place one author called "the self-imposed exile" of Jupiter Island. The dark shadows cast by trees played hide and seek with sunbeams, producing an ever-changing pattern on the pavement. Before long, I turned right at the stop sign and headed toward the south end of the golf course. Honora directed me to a sprawling set of white buildings overlooking the Intracoastal.

"It's best that we do a reconnaissance before carrying in the room box," said Honora. "If they are playing, we mustn't interrupt. We have to sit quietly until they're done. I've tried to time this correctly, but I could be off by ten or twenty minutes. I do hope you'll understand."

"You mean we need to wait until they finish a round? Or do they call it a hand?"

Her smile was patient. "No. I mean until they are finished, finished. As in, done for the day."

"What?" I thought I'd misheard her. Did she really think I had that much time to waste?

"Oh, dear. I assumed you knew how finicky these women can be. Surely Dick told you the story."

"Boy, this place has tons of legends, doesn't it?"

"Indeed it does, as does any place with such strong personalities and such a tightly knit culture. Although this particular story dates back many years ago, the tale is illustrative. Seems that one of the Jupiter Island matrons had an accident while backing out of her driveway on her way to bridge club. A worker was trimming her shrubs, you see. He was on his knees, facing away from her, with one leg stuck out behind him, and as she backed up, she ran over his foot—and kept going."

"She didn't!" I could totally imagine that happening. Every morning at eight, the island comes alive with the sounds of lawn mowers, leaf blowers, and chain saws. Keeping the place spit and polish clean takes a crew of laborers, usually Hispanics. These poor guys work in the broiling heat, where the vegetation is thick, and the bugs are merciless.

Honora's voice jolted me back to her story.

"She did, indeed. She ran right over his foot. The man's co-workers gathered around him, carried him to their truck, and drove him to the hospital. Of course, the supervisor found out and was furious. He called the Jupiter Island Department of Public Safety and reported the incident, as well as reporting the resident. The Director of Public Safety went immediately to the resident's house by himself. The maid explained that the missus was away. He asked where she'd gone, and the maid said, 'Bridge club,' so the director got in his car and drove to the club. When he walked in on the game in process and explained his mission, the perpetrator scolded him, saying, 'Young man, I'll go with you to the police station after I am finished playing bridge.'"

"You are kidding, aren't you? This is a joke, right?" I glanced over at Honora, taking my eyes from the dense shrubbery that hid homes of the rich and famous. Most were simple beach houses that had grown over the years to accommodate children and grandchildren. Very few of the homes on Jupiter Island are pretentious. In that way, it is the opposite of Palm Beach, where everything is calculated to impress. This place is a haven for the reclusive, old wealthy. People who want to go on vacation with their families and not be hassled. In Palm Beach, the goal is to mingle and be seen. On Jupiter Island, people don't want to attract attention. They come here to get away from the spotlight, not to buff up their perma-tans in the rays of harsh scrutiny.

"Unfortunately, no." Honora sighed. "And the director did not interrupt the game. Neither shall we. Instead, we will take a seat at the edge of the room and wait quietly until they are finished. When in Rome…"

"Do as the Romans do," I finished for her.

CHAPTER 23

When we arrived at the set of glass French doors that marked the entrance to the Club, Honora paused. Like a military commander, she said, "Chin up. Remember, we have to wait. Martha called ahead and told them to expect us. But don't ever forget that you're a property owner here, too."

That was good advice. I squared my shoulders and followed her as she sought out two empty chairs at the back of a room full of card tables. Fifteen women watched each other with eagle eyes. The room proved to be a battleground of clashing perfumes. Florals competed with musky and metallic tones for dominance. The crunch of peanuts and the hollow rapping of cards against the tables created a background hum to the various voices. No one seemed to be having fun, except one woman with white hair cut in a bob. Skinny to the point of scrawny, it soon became apparent that she was winning. Her cackles weighed heavily on the mood of her table.

The lingo was foreign to me. "Bid…call…trumps…" all meant nothing, but evidently it meant a lot to these people. The women dressed in ubiquitous white slacks and colorful tunic tops that I recognized as coming from a store in tiny downtown Hobe Sound. On their feet were Jack Rogers sandals, a brand associated with Palm Beach and much favored by the locals. To a person, they were tan. In fact, they'd spent decades in the sun.

None had the telltale signs of facelifts, the too tight skin or the face oddly smooth against a withered throat. These women were secure in themselves.

As the minutes droned on, having nothing else to do, I examined the cushions on our chairs. Needlepoint. Fine wool. Honora leaned over and whispered, "I bet you've never seen anything like this, have you?"

"Yes, I have." The country clubs in St. Louis sported the same handiwork. In fact, the subject matter even looked familiar.

But Honora didn't pursue the subject. I opened my phone and scanned various boards on Pinterest.

Ten minutes later, a player at the far table collected the cards. The others leaned back in their seats and chatted quietly.

Five minutes went by, and a second table finished their play. The tallest woman at that table scooped up cards with a mighty sweep of her hand. After she corralled them all, she gave Honora a tiny nod of acknowledgement. But instead of hopping up and heading for my car, Honora sat stiff as a sheet of plywood. She turned her attention to the last table. Those women still exchanged commentary and sets of cards. Despite all eyes on their backs, they played at a leisurely pace.

Time wore me down, but all I could do was wait. After all, I'd been forewarned. Tucking my phone in my pocket and leaning my head against the wall, I closed my eyes—and woke up with a jerk.

"Yes, this is your neighbor, Cara Mia Delgatto. She's Dick Potter's granddaughter." Honora's hand gripped my shoulder both to wake me up and to keep me from toppling off my chair.

A tall bridge player, who reminded me of a flamingo, stared down at me. Her large diamond stud earrings twinkled as they caught the light. "Really? Gracious."

Getting to my feet, I offered my hand and introduced myself to Mrs. Gunderson, a vision in shades of pink.

"Give me your keys, child, and I'll get a couple of servers to help me bring in the room box." Honora hurried off, leaving me to the intense scrutiny of Mrs. Gunderson and a few of her friends.

"Where do you live?" asked Jenny Martin.

I explained which house was mine, and she nodded in approval. "One of the old beach houses. I know it well. That second floor used to be an artist's studio."

That I didn't know.

"It was before everyone started tearing down the old places," said another woman, as she adjusted bifocals. "That's a gem of a lot. Are you going to knock it down?"

"Me? Heavens, no. I love that house."

"Good," said a third who'd joined us while stuffing a plastic baggie of nuts into her Vera Bradley handbag. "I hate to think we're losing places with so much character."

They peppered me with questions: "Have you lived here long? Do you have a house up north? Do you play golf? Are you married? Do you have a career?"

When I explained that I'd purchased The Treasure Chest, a few offered advice: "Scour the consignment shops. Check out that Goodwill store up in Stuart. Go to the local art shops and pick up pieces there."

As best I could, I listened and paid attention. However, they talked over each other frequently, and often two would speak at once. The pace of their advice set my head spinning. Honora's re-appearance came as a relief.

"Set it down there, please." She pointed to an empty bridge table. Two men in black slacks and crisp white shirts easily carried the room box. It was not especially heavy, but it was fragile.

"Honora!" Martha's hands flew to her mouth as she peered into the box. "You managed to capture the space perfectly. George will be astonished. Come see, everyone."

The group clustered around Martha and took turns getting a close-up inspection of the gift for her husband. Several immediately flocked to Honora so that they could ask questions about the cost. One wearing pink glasses came to me and said, "So you only sell miniatures?"

"No, we sell full-sized pieces, too. We upcycle, recycle, and repurpose as much of our stock as possible. Of course, there are a few items that are brand new, such as the soft goods created by Honora's daughter EveLynn. However, I've tried to be as 'green' as I can. We also feature local craftspeople and artists, such as Honora and the Highwaymen."

"Where is Binky? Does anybody know?" asked Honora.

The blonde with the pink glasses shrugged. "When you find out, tell her I'm terribly disappointed. We nearly had to cancel today because she was a no-show. Margrite had to rope in her daughter-in-law so we'd have a fourth."

Others chimed in, explaining they were shocked—SHOCKED in capital letters—that Binky missed her regular bridge session. As they protested, Honora gave me a look that clearly meant, "I told you something was wrong."

But one or two women didn't seem flustered.

"We're all busy. She probably got her days mixed up," said a tiny lady in periwinkle blue with bugle beads around the neckline. "The days blend into each other."

"I invite you all to come visit the store and see what Cara has," said Honora. "In fact, here are my business cards. I also brought order forms. If you order a room box or a dome scene today, I'll knock ten percent off the price."

That got everyone's attention. I was quickly inundated with questions about pricing, availability, and scheduling. While Martha Gunderson gloried in the spotlight of her friends' attention, Honora and I talked up her work. After a very draining hour, two servers were directed to carry the room box outside to Martha's car. The bridge club members went their separate ways.

"My, my," said Honora, her eyes glittering with joy. "Wasn't that fun?"

CHAPTER 24

"Turn right on Beach Road. Binky's house is farther south of us, but north of Blowing Rocks. Not far from Greg Norman's place, the beach house with the statues of lions out front."

"That's the place where President Bill Clinton fell and broke his leg?"

"The very one."

"Got it. Now I'm curious. How did your friend get a name like Binky?"

"It's short for Bianca, but her younger brother couldn't say that, so everyone started calling her 'Binky,' and it stuck. I've known her for forty years now. We used to spend more time together, but I'm ashamed to say I haven't seen her much lately. Like me, she's a widow. Binky has a daughter and a son who both live up north. I know she has a grandson who's attending University of Miami, just like Tommy. I remember that because I ran into her at Publix a few weeks ago. She had her nails painted orange and green, U of M colors."

"Ugh. I'm thrilled with Tommy's choice of school, but I'm not going to wear those colors on my fingernails. She sounds like a character."

"She definitely is that. Very patriotic. As you know, she loves to play bridge. She's a world traveler. Keen gardener. Lived here forever. Old as mud, like we all are."

"That reminds me," I said. "I'd appreciate your keeping this under your hat, but Cooper Rivers dropped by the other day. He says the financial backers behind the Fill Up and Go have decided that Poppy's too old for the job. What on earth am I going to do to keep him busy?"

"My, my, my." She shook her head and the loose folds of her neck jiggled.

This was what I had to look forward to. Loose skin. Being put out to pasture. Regular dates with my bridge club. Shoot me now.

"For right now, Poppy has his hands busy, playing nursemaid. Can you believe that Sid's mother took his computer?"

"Of course I can. You can, too. Amberlee probably sold it. For spite. She is a drug-addicted, avaricious beast."

"That's so unlike you!" I blurted out. "You usually have a kind word for everyone."

"I am only being honest. I have it on good authority that Amberlee is addicted to OxyContin. She was in a car accident a few years ago. Both she and the driver were drunk. I believe her back was injured. Harvey worried about her drug intake, because he knew she was already imbibing too much alcohol. But Amberlee found a pill-pushing doctor, and the rest is history. Lest you get the wrong idea, Amberlee always was a selfish, self-centered little princess. Harvey fell hard for her. He could never admit her faults. Not even to himself. She had him wrapped around her little finger, tighter than a tourniquet on a bleeding stump. She was the worst mistake that Harvey ever made."

"So you think I should go ahead and ask Sid to report his computer as stolen? You make it sound like you're sure she isn't going to give it back."

"Couldn't hurt. Sid doesn't have a relationship with Amberlee. I realize that's what you're trying to protect, but you can't protect something that isn't there. When a person is toxic, running the other way is an act of self-defense. I bet he'll never see his computer again."

A circular drive fronted Binky Rutherford's house. Clapboard siding ran the length and width of the exterior walls. Up close, small cracks appeared, and the hibiscus needed trimming. All in all, the place was the picture of wealthy nonchalance that comes with being part of the old rich.

In the driveway, a black Audi roadster with tinted windows and what Tommy would call "ghetto wheels" struck the wrong note entirely. Most of the locals drive more sedate vehicles. An orange and green University of Miami sticker was taped crookedly to the back bumper. Maybe the car belonged to Binky's grandson or a visitor. The car engine pinged as we walked by. Heat roiled off the motor.

"Maybe that explains why Binky didn't answer you," I said. "She must have gone for a long drive."

"That's not her car, so it has to belong to Evans."

A small portico sheltered the front door. Honora and I ambled along the paving stone walkway. A hedge of Green Island Ficus ran along the front of the house, its evergreen leaves a nice contrast to the white siding. Over my left arm, I carried the dry cleaner's bag with the dress inside. With my right hand, I rang the doorbell.

From the inside came low masculine tones. Short of pressing my ear to the door, I moved as close as I could to listen in.

"Someone is arguing inside," I reported to Honora.

"Really?" She stared at the Audi. "Cara, freshmen can't have cars on campus at U of M, can they?"

"Not unless they live off campus, and I think you can only stay off campus if you have family in town. I might be wrong about that. My mother was dying of cancer when Tommy filled out his housing application. A lot of the process flew right past me."

"I understand." She folded her hands in front of her in a ladylike gesture. "Sounds like a bit of an argument, doesn't it?"

The voices grew louder and then softer and then louder again.

Impatiently, I mashed the doorbell once more.

Heavy footsteps on the other side suggested that our presence had been noted, even though the door remained closed.

"Who is it?" a gruff voice demanded.

Honora and I exchanged looks. She shrugged.

I spoke directly to the door. "I'm one of Mrs. Rutherford's neighbors. With me is Honora McAfee. We've come to return something that belongs to Mrs. Rutherford."

Cautiously, the door opened a crack, but the chain stayed on. "Yes?"

I stared into a faded blue eye. "Hi, are you Binky Rutherford?"

Honora edged me to one side. "Binky, dear, it's me."

"Oh, my! Honora!"

"Your friends missed you at bridge. I'm glad you're all right."

"Yes, well, I've been tied up."

"Binky, dear, I'm here with my friend, Cara Mia Delgatto. Dick Potter's granddaughter."

"Really? That's wonderful. Cara, is it? Yes, be sure to tell Dick that I've been seeing Samuel Morse on the south side of the island. He'll be thrilled. Samuel Morse is an old, old friend of ours. You will give him that message, won't you dear?" Her eyes stared at me through the crack with an intensity that seemed electric. "Word for word? It's important."

But before I could respond, Honora said, "Was that your grandson who answered the door? Evans? I haven't seen him in ages."

My friend acted as if it was perfectly normal to carry on a conversation through a heavy wooden door.

"Yes, you heard Evans. Home for Spring Break at University of Miami. Took all his tests early. What brings you all the way out here?"

"Mrs. Rutherford, I believe I have something of yours. Something that you relinquished by mistake." I held up the dress, waving it the way a matador flaps his red cape at a bull.

A gnarled hand reached through the crack in the door and pulled the dress inside. But Binky still didn't ask us to come in. Honora and I exchanged looks, feeling totally awkward. If Binky had thought we were too embarrassed to stick around, she had another think coming.

"Uh, Mrs. Rutherford?" I spoke through the sliver of open space. "I bought this dress from Danielle at Vintage Threads. Honora thinks that this particular dress is really special to you. Is it possible that you handed it to Danielle Cronin by mistake?"

"Just a minute. I need to look it over in the light." Binky shut the door in our faces.

Honora and I stood there on Binky's doorstep, blinking at each other in dismay.

"What in the world?" I wondered out loud. "I realize that my neighbors value their privacy, but this is downright rude."

"I've been inside this house a thousand and one times. I can't imagine what's going on."

Masculine voices seeped through the door.

"Maybe it isn't just her grandson. Maybe she's got a boyfriend. Maybe we interrupted them while they were canoodling on her sofa."

"At our age, the comfort of a bed with a nice firm mattress is a necessity. Not a luxury. File that away for future use."

We were still giggling when the door opened a tiny bit, and my dress reappeared.

CHAPTER 25

"Something must be wrong with Binky." Honora ran her hands up and down the handle of her purse, over and over. "The way she shoved her dress at you and slammed the door in our faces isn't like her. Not at all."

"Whatever." I'd had enough. I didn't want to give back the dress, but I'd tried to do the right thing—and where had it gotten me? I'd been left standing on a doorstep like an unwanted solicitor. Binky had actually thrust the dress into my face, nearly smacking me in the nose.

Concentrating on the narrow stretch of Beach Road, I said nothing. I wanted to rail against Honora for putting me in such an embarrassing situation.

"Bianca must be in trouble." Honora's chin jutted out stubbornly. "Repeating such nonsense about dating Robert Morse."

"Samuel," I said. "Robert Morse was an actor. I think."

"Whatever. That's not like her."

"If you say so." The Lilly Pulitzer dress was still in my possession, resting comfortably on the back seat of my car. I was mightily ticked, but at least I had permission to wear my dress. Honora, however, was anything but comfortable. In fact, she was downright agitated, and her nervousness was getting to me. She was definitely raining on my parade.

I'd paid for the dress. I had forgone the pleasure of wearing it. I had made a trip back to the store to see if there'd been a mistake. I even attempted to return the dress to its original owner. And I'd had the dress shoved in my face. It was mine. End of story.

Except that I hadn't paid for it. Not yet. I still owed Danielle a check for $100. Minor details.

"I'll concede to you there might be something wrong with your friend, but maybe it's a personal matter. Maybe she's grown tired of this particular dress or it doesn't fit anymore. Could even be that Binky has a new boyfriend, and he doesn't like this dress. Any number of reasons. Point being, she gave up this dress for a second time and sent us on our way."

Honora slammed her palm against my dashboard. "No!"

The car swerved as I reacted in surprise.

"I refuse to accept those explanations. I've known Binky all my life. She would never, ever act so rudely to me. Putting aside the matter of the dress, there's something rotten in Denmark. Cara? Turn here."

Following her directions, I took a jog off of Beach Road and down a side street bordering the Country Club, of which I am not (nor will ever be) a member.

"Shortcut?" I asked in a hopeful tone, although I doubted that we were taking an alternate route back to the store.

The set of Honora's jaw had me worried. The narrowing of her eyes made me nervous.

"The Jupiter Island Department of Public Safety is up here on the right. There! That white building. Park your car."

I do not like being ordered around. I also don't like wasting my time. A glance at the in-dash clock warned me that the best part of the retail day was slipping away from me. Already I'd devoted too much time to playing weird games with friends.

There's an odd clannishness to Jupiter Island. People come here to escape the outside world. They enjoy the island's seclusion. To move here, you must be vetted, or so Poppy tells me. Once you pass the test, you're part of an exclusive group. But if you are deemed unworthy, a black cashmere sweater might be sent to your home as an anonymous gift. The message is loud and clear: You won't need a sweater down here, but you certainly will when you go up north. In other words, the sweater is code for "go away."

Perhaps Honora had overstepped her welcome, and Binky had shooed her away. I could imagine why. If you spent time with Honora, her daughter EveLynn was impossible to avoid. Since she was loud and abrasive, that tended to get old. Maybe Binky had decided to end their friendship. Maybe she was turning over a new leaf and decided to clean her closets and toss out more than a dress or two. Maybe she was cutting ties with old friends. Perhaps Honora and Lilly Pulitzer were no longer of interest to Binky.

Any or all of the above might explain our cool reception.

I gripped the steering wheel harder. "Honora, this is a fool's errand. We saw your pal. Binky didn't invite us in. Big deal. Time to back off and call it a day."

"Park over there. Turn off your engine. You're coming with me. We're going to report this to the Director of Public Safety."

"And tell him what? Hi, I bought a secondhand dress, but Honora thinks I shouldn't have it, so I tried to return it, but the original owner doesn't want it and told me so? Or how about this: Guess what? One of my neighbors decided to clean out her closet and doesn't want unannounced company so there's got to be a problem? You need to investigate her because everyone here on Jupiter Island is so incredibly friendly and welcoming that there must be a mistake?"

"I said, turn off your engine. Do it!" Honora actually shouted at me.

I did as commanded, but I sure wasn't happy about it. "Honora, you need to calm down. This can't be good for your blood pressure."

Oops.

Her look nearly withered me.

"Just because I'm an old lady doesn't mean I'm senile. I'll have you know that I do the New York Times crossword puzzle every Saturday, and that's the hardest one of the week. I'm smarter than I ever was, and a lot more 'with it' than a lot of people half my age. When I say there's a problem, you need to listen to me. I deserve a little respect, Cara."

With an indignant nod of her head, she threw open the passenger side door—and hit the police car next to us.

CHAPTER 26

"She never!" Skye said. She and MJ had been arguing when I walked through the back door, but they shut up before I heard what the problem was. In fact, if I hadn't been so eager to tell them about Honora, they might not have been on speaking terms with each other. As it was, they kept glaring at each other with sideways glances.

"She did, too," I confirmed.

"What did the cops say?" MJ asked. She pointedly turned her body so that her back was to Skye.

"Better yet, how did Honora act after she hit the cop car?" asked Skye.

"I wish I could have seen that," said MJ, before I could answer. "Usually she's so prim and proper. Very measured in all she does. Then to whack your door against the door of a cop car? Talk about losing your cool. That's so not like her."

I agreed with MJ. Skye nodded, too.

Despite the frosty atmosphere between the two of them, the three of us were enjoying a rare moment of peace. The store was quiet. Sid was sitting at my desk, using my computer.

"By the way, I'm here because I've had an upset tummy, so I asked for time off at Pumpernickel's. I figured we needed to get ready for Valentine's Day anyway." Skye continued washing off grapes to feed to Kookie. Ever since that bird joined us, Skye has babied the animal like crazy. In return, Kookie has grown more and more affectionate toward all of us.

"Good thinking. We need to get cracking on that. Changing out the display window was a great start, but we need more holiday-themed merchandise." I paused to answer my vibrating cell phone.

"I'm gonna come by to get Sid. Young fella needs a nap. Tires out awful easily," Poppy said.

"See you in a few."

"Poor Honora," Skye said as I hung up. "She must have felt like a fool after she hit that other car."

"She couldn't look me in the eyes. She complained about a headache so I took her straight home." I sighed at the memory. "I'm not mad at her, but I wasn't happy with her either. She just kept yammering on and on, saying she was certain that Binky was in trouble. Honest to Pete. Honora acted like I was questioning her intelligence or doubting her sanity—and I wasn't. But facts are facts. We had nothing to be suspicious of. Certainly we had no reason to talk to the cops."

"How'd they respond to having her damage one of their cars?" asked MJ.

"They were surprisingly nice about the whole fiasco. Mr. Fernandez assured me the department cars get dinged all the time. I promised him that Poppy would take a look at the damage and get it repaired. Mr. Fernandez laughed and gave me his business card. He knows Poppy pretty well. In fact, Mr. Fernandez was surprisingly cordial when I asked about my mermaid. I thought he'd tell me to buzz off, because I'm not family, but he seemed to think I had a perfect right to be curious."

"How is that poor woman?" asked Skye.

"Still touch-and-go. Mr. Fernandez praised me for saving her life. Even though I'm still not sure whether I helped her or not, he says I did the right thing."

"Go back to your visit to Binky's house," said MJ. "What exactly did she say when she gave you back the dress?"

"She pushed it through the opening in the door and told me to wear it in good health. Then she slammed the door in our faces."

"But she never invited you inside? Even for Jupiter Island, that's downright weird." Skye raised an incredulous eyebrow. "Who acts like that?"

"People who have more money than manners," said MJ as she crossed her arms over her bounteous chest and let her multiple bracelets clank. "They're a pretty snooty bunch over on there. But even for them, that's tacky, tacky, tacky."

I lifted one shoulder and let it drop. "Honora is totally convinced that her friend is in trouble. After all, Binky wasn't in attendance at bridge, and that's practically sacred to her. So Honora gave Mr. Fernandez an earful. As soon as Mr. Fernandez got done looking over his squad car for damage, she launched into a diatribe about Binky's special dress. She insisted that Binky would never skip bridge. Finally, she went on and on about our visit to Binky Rutherford's house. I have to give him credit: He acted like he cared. I was hoping the earth would swallow me."

"Could Honora be right?" Skye frowned. "I would know if either of you were in trouble. At least I think I would. Friends notice details because they care."

"Trust me, that woman is perfectly fine. We were face to face and she didn't say a word. Didn't even grimace! I am not giving this dress away again.

I really, really like it, and I'm obligated to pay for it. In fact, I intend to wear it tonight when I go out with Nathan Davidson."

"Might as well. That's twice Binky has tried to dump it," said MJ. "Besides, it looks great on you."

"You oughta call it the boomerang dress," said Sid, hobbling toward us. His pallor created a vivid contrast to his jet black hair. "The owner tosses it and it comes back."

"I didn't want to interrupt you while you were working, but I was wondering, have you had any luck tracking down my computer?"

"Yup."

Now that was a pleasant surprise.

"You're kidding!"

"Nope. I've been calling around, because Amberlee still hasn't returned my calls or my text messages. Turns out, she dropped it off at the trailer right before everyone moved out. Clyde—he used to be one of my roommates—told me he's been keeping it for me. He figured I'd stay with him when I was released from the hospital, but I went to live with Poppy, so he didn't know I'd been released."

Sounded pretty fishy to me, but lately I've noticed how eighteen-year-old boys resemble inert matter. They don't move until they have to, until all the forces of the universe give them a hearty push. Clyde's lack of action perfectly matched what I knew of their age group.

"This old roommate has been sitting on your computer for nearly a week? Does he know your password?"

"He would only know it if he looked over my shoulder while I was logging on. Believe me, Clyde's too lazy to pay attention to something like that."

Our conversation was suspended when two customers walked into the store. I put aside all thoughts about my financial information and did my best to ring up a sale.

At five twenty, I raced upstairs, changed into my new Lilly Pulitzer dress, and ran back down to the cash station to prepare the day's deposit.

"Where are you and Nathan planning to go tonight?" MJ asked. "That dress looks terrific on you."

Skye glared at her. Whatever they'd been arguing about, it was still a bone of contention. Skye had been working on a chest of drawers in the back, changing out the hardware while other projects dried as she prepped them for Valentine's Day. After she and I carried the piece onto the sales floor, she gave MJ a look so withering I almost burst out laughing.

"Riverwalk."

"Why? You eat there all the time."

"I eat there because I love it. You have another suggestion?"

"Caliente. It's this hot Mexican restaurant over on PGA Boulevard. Every Friday night they have mariachi bands strolling through."

Skye's jaw stuck out as she practically snarled, "Yes, but Riverwalk is always nice, and it's close by."

"Mexican sounds fun," I admitted.

"Caliente gets really, really crowded. You hate crowds," said Skye.

"But she loves music and atmosphere. Cara would love the décor, and she'd pick up new ideas for us to use for Cinco de Mayo. It would be nice to plan ahead, wouldn't it?"

"She doesn't need to go to Caliente for that!" Skye nearly shouted.

My friends glared at each other. I opened my mouth to ask why, but before I could, a *rap-tap-tap* on the front door interfered. Nathan Davidson had arrived, so I hurried to let him in. "MJ was just telling me about a Mexican place over on PGA. It's called Caliente."

"But it's such a long drive, and it's really, really noisy," volunteered Skye. "I also think it's horribly overpriced."

"No, it's not," MJ said. "They make guacamole right at your table. The salsa is to die for. Cara, you really need to go. Think of the ideas you'll get."

"Which you don't need," Skye said. "We've got enough ideas already. What if you get salsa on your dress?"

"You can always use new ideas," MJ said.

"I've spent hours on Pinterest. I have an entire file of ideas and recipes we can certainly—" Skye started.

"Those won't be enough. Besides, she's going out to eat anyway," finished MJ.

"But it's a long drive down to PGA." Skye fisted her hands on her hips and scowled.

"We can figure this out in the car," said Nathan, taking me by the elbow. His cologne was expensive, and I sniffed the air appreciatively. He'd taken care to change out of his police uniform and into his version of dressy casual clothes. Like Mitt Romney, Nathan wore his jeans with a sharp crease down the middle. Although he wasn't wearing a tie, his stiff white shirt suggested he'd be more comfortable with one. His tweed jacket looked like it was brand new.

He tugged me gently toward the door.

"Have a good time, Cara. I'll take care of your pets," MJ sang out. Her chipper attitude was totally at odds with the scowl on Skye's face.

Curious. Usually, their roles were reversed.

"Right," I said, turning my back on my friends.

CHAPTER 27

In his capacity as a captain with the Stuart Police Department, Nathan drives a police cruiser. But in his off hours, he tools around in a black Denali SUV, an incredibly macho vehicle if there ever was one. As we walked out to his car, a knot in my pocket brushed against my outer thigh. While I waited for him to open my door, I fished around in my pocket and pulled out an earring. The heft confirmed it was not a piece of costume jewelry. I held it up and examined it carefully.

"Lose an earring?" Nathan offered me a hand up as I climbed into the car.

"No," and I told Nathan about my odd visit with Binky Rutherford. "I guess I'll be making another trip to her house so I can return this earring. I could have sworn it wasn't in the pocket the first time I tried on the dress. Must have missed it. Honest to gosh, this is getting tiresome. Honora insists there's a problem, but I know there isn't. So Binky didn't invite us in. Big deal. I've never been inside MJ's place, but we're still friends."

"It's common for older people to get paranoid. There certainly are plenty of thugs who prey on them," he said. "Speaking of which, Lou told me about you finding that half-drowned woman on the beach. Cara, you really shouldn't be out walking alone at such an early hour."

"So I've been told."

"Hey, if you're accusing me of being protective, I plead guilty. I don't want anything to hurt you. I see the reports. I know what happens on our Treasure Coast beaches. Sure, there's a robust police presence on Jupiter Island, but they can't be everywhere all the time. Recently, there's been a lot of illicit activity."

"Smuggling people."

"Yes, and drugs. That woman you found was lucky to be alive. Sharks swim in our waters all the time. Jellyfish, too. Worst of all, you could have found yourself face to face with one of the creeps who takes money from undocumented immigrants and turns them into sex slaves."

I shivered. Nathan reached over and turned on the heat in the car. His hand touched mine and he intertwined our fingers. I found him very attractive because he was a guy's guy, and yes, the cliché rings true: There's something about a man in uniform. Even when they are in civilian clothes, law enforcement agents exude a command presence that's profoundly masculine.

The stress of the day melted as the world moved past us in a blur. I told him about Honora's concerns for her friend.

"Binky Rutherford?" he repeated the name.

"Yes," I said sleepily. "She's on the island. Been around forever, I guess."

"I know." He chuckled, a low bass rumble of a laugh. "I wouldn't worry about Binky. She can handle herself. A walking stick is a lethal weapon in Binky's hands."

"A lot of the Jupiter Island residents are old guard, aren't they? Accustomed to having their own way? I suspect Binky acts the same way. Doesn't suffer fools. Sharp tongue."

"It's more than that. Binky has a lot of, um, life experience. I'm sure she's fine. Like I said, you shouldn't worry about her."

"I won't." My computer had been found. Sid and Poppy would retrieve it. I'd confirmed that Binky had willingly let go of my new dress, and at last I was wearing it. Sid was safe with Poppy and getting better. My son would be calling on Sunday afternoon to touch bases, and he'd be home with me late Monday. The store seemed to be doing better, and Valentine's Day would surely mean a spike in sales. My mermaid was alive. My friends were seeing to my fur babies, Jack and Luna. All was right in my world. With those problems solved, I could relax just a little.

Nathan knew the greeter at Caliente. Otherwise, we would have stood around for an hour and a half. The place was absolutely packed. A line of waiting patrons extended out the door. Others waited in the bar area where folding glass doors opened to the outside patio. The weather was mild, so the greeter led us to a table half in and half off out of the restaurant proper. Like so many eateries in Florida, when business was good and the weather cooperated, Caliente simply expanded outdoors.

"You'll be sitting on the threshold of the doorway," she apologized. "Sorry about that. But at least you'll have a table. There are lots of people milling around the outside bar, hoping for seats, and we're really crowded. This is the best I can do."

Nathan thanked her while I admired the fabulous decorating scheme. Wrought iron tables on a plain tile floor contrasted nicely with stucco walls that had been painted with amazing images. Particularly impressive was the lavish use of the color red in a full spectrum of shades. These fiery colors worked nicely with white, black, and sunflower yellow, all appearing in accent items.

"Is this okay with you?" asked Nathan. He couldn't move his chair back very far without bumping into a knot of patrons.

"Sure," I said. I would have preferred some place quieter, but for a change, this was fine. The tantalizing odors of cooked meat, onions, and spices made me very hungry.

The waitress brought us tall glasses of water and menus emblazoned with dancing skeletons dressed in outlandish garb.

"I don't know much about this tradition of fancy skeletons. These are what they call sugar skulls, aren't they?" I looked around us.

"Right. I've been to Mexico more times than I can count," said Nathan. "As I understand it, the tradition started in Italy with sugar replicas made to adorn altars around Easter. Missionaries brought it to Mexico in the 17th century. Families order them or make them to put in their home altars or *ofrendas* on November 1 for Day of the Dead celebrations. Of course, we celebrate Halloween—"

"Nathan!" A voice from behind me interrupted him.

While he responded to the interloper, I concentrated on guiding a corn chip loaded with salsa into my mouth without spilling it on my new dress. Chewing as quickly as I could, I watched as my date half-rose out of his seat. His eyes were wide as he shook his head and raised his hands as if to fend off an intruder. I'd never seen Nathan with such an expression of horror.

"Nathan, sweetie, I haven't seen you in ages." My sister, Jodi, grabbed Nathan's face in both hands and gave him a long, deep kiss.

He struggled against Jodi's grip, but he had little choice in the matter. The crowd behind him had his chair pinned in place. Short of giving my sister a shove and sending her flying, there was little Nathan could do. He was on the back foot, and Jodi was definitely milking the situation.

After what seemed like hours but could only have been seconds, Jodi turned loose of Nathan and rubbed her lipstick into his skin. She then beamed a nasty grin at me. "Hello, little sister. Bet you didn't know that Nathan and I were close. Very, very close. In fact, we were engaged to be married for a while. I broke it off."

"Jodi? That's enough." Cooper Rivers bumped my chair as he reached around me. Although he was angling to grab Jodi by the elbow, she danced away from him too fast.

"I'm just saying hi to a very old and very intimate friend, Coop. What's your problem?" Her voice was petulant as she pouted becomingly. "What a cute dress you're wearing, Sis. Second-hand, isn't it? I've always found Lilly to be rather dowdy. But it suits you perfectly."

By contrast, she was wearing a stunning aqua silk sheath with a deep V-neck that showed a lot of tan cleavage. When she tossed her long auburn hair, large silver hoops winked from her earlobes. Matching sets of bracelets jangled on her forearms.

Emotions slapped me like angry ocean waves preceding a storm. First came chagrin, then embarrassment, followed by self-pity, and at long last, anger rose triumphant.

Nathan avoided my eyes.

When had he been planning to come clean with me? Before or after he tried to get me into his bed?

CHAPTER 28

"You did what?" MJ's eyebrows flew up to her hairline. Even though she goes out every Friday night, she shows up first thing Saturday to meet Skye and me for breakfast. It's our tradition, and I love it. The best part of moving to Florida has been the new friends I've made. MJ stared at me and said, "Repeat what you did. I could not have heard you right! This time I plan to take notes."

Skye lifted her tea cup to her mouth to cover her smirk. She'd heard my story and reveled in it the night before, after I left Nathan back at the restaurant.

"I ordered a pitcher of margaritas made with Cuervo Gold, four different appetizers, a double helping of the most expensive thing on the menu, guacamole, more chips and salsa, plus a dessert. Nathan didn't say a word, even though my portion of the bill alone would be almost two hundred bucks with tip. When the waitress walked away from the table, he seemed a bit stunned, so I went on and on about how hungry I was."

"Did he try to talk about what happened with Jodi?" MJ asked. "Tell me again how her visit to the table ended."

"I managed to smile and laugh even though she was practically sitting on Nathan's lap. Cooper acted as if he wanted to die on the spot. My sister was drunk as a skunk, and Cooper's mother is an alcoholic. Jodi's behavior must have brought back bad memories."

"Cooper's mother is dead," said Skye. "Two years ago. No, three or four actually. Died of liver failure from drinking. I remember because he came into Pumpernickel's shortly thereafter, and we talked about it."

Sadness swept through me. Cooper and I had often talked about his mother. He never knew his dad, so he and his mother had been very close, except that you can't be really close with an alcoholic. They'll always love booze more than they'll love you. But still, it being only the two of them, they had an unusually tight relationship. Even when he was young, he'd wanted to protect his mother from the inevitable result of her lethal habit.

"Jodi was drunk?" MJ asked.

"Totally. She could barely stand up. Part of it might have been play-acting to give her an excuse to hang all over Nathan, but mostly she seemed too plowed to stand up straight. Cooper kept trying to slip an arm under hers and haul her away, but she'd dodge him. No mean feat considering how little room there was around our table."

"Tell her what your sister said that almost caused the fight," Skye urged me.

Squeezing my eyes shut, I exhaled, preparing myself. When I opened them, MJ and Skye were both staring at me, expectantly. "Jodi said something about how both men—Cooper and Nathan—were getting sloppy seconds with me. She laughed and suggested they were passing me around like a bad case of...well...disease. And she was loud, broadcasting it to the entire restaurant. Fortunately, the place was noisy and hardly anyone noticed, but the men did. I thought for a moment that Nathan was going to explode. Cooper grabbed her and jerked her toward him, and she slapped him in the face. Then she started talking in this really spooky voice about how she was going to see me ruined. Cooper was trying to move her away from me, but she refused to cooperate."

"Ugh." MJ winced. "She acted even worse than I would have imagined."

"But not surprising," said Skye. "Considering the source."

"Still," said MJ. "It's good that you know about her and Nathan."

Skye gave MJ a stern look that I couldn't interpret.

"Jodi's hit a new low." MJ tapped her fingernail on the table. "Who would guess she'd be so crude? I've had other women get jealous and be catty about me, but always behind my back. Your sister has definitely crossed a line. She doesn't seem to mind letting people see what a skank she is. That surprises me. I thought she had more class than that."

"I'm not surprised. Not one bit. It galls Jodi that everyone loves Cara so much." Skye finger-combed her ponytail. "Her hatred has totally overtaken her good sense."

"What happened next?" MJ asked.

"The manager came over to our table and asked if everything was all right. Jodi settled down. Nathan told her, 'I think you had better leave, or I'll call someone and have you arrested for public intoxication,' and she laughed like a maniac. In fact, she laughed so hard that she could hardly stand up. Cooper grabbed her around the waist. The manager helped Cooper and together they sort of dragged Jodi out of the restaurant. At least, I think they left. I didn't see her again. But I didn't stick around. Maybe they took her to a booth in the back and poured hot coffee down her throat. Who knows and who cares?"

Skye shook her head. "Poor Nathan and poor Cooper."

I glared at her.

"What?" she said. "Cara, they didn't expect problems with your sister like this. Who would? She's totally gone off the deep end. I bet Cooper and Nathan were embarrassed, too."

"Whatever. I'm all out of sympathy for both men. And I'm tired of feeling like I'm walking in Jodi's footsteps. It makes me sick. It's like I'm some sort of cheap second-rate knock-off, and she's the real deal."

"That's completely wrong. You've got it turned upside down," said Skye. "You're the upgrade and she knows it."

"Did Nathan say anything? Did he apologize to you?" MJ asked.

"He tried, but I wasn't interested. I made a big deal about how the past was the past, and how we should enjoy the evening together. The waitress brought the margaritas, the appetizers, and I added a salad. I asked her to put my order in right away because I was starving," I said with a harsh laugh. "Having grown up in the restaurant business, I knew exactly how to make it impossible for Nathan to cancel all that food. Then I excused myself to go to the bathroom. When I got to the ladies', I just kept walking."

"That's when she text-messaged me. Lou and I drove to PGA to pick her up. She was hiding out in the bathroom of a gas station." Skye giggled.

"I slipped out of the back door of Caliente's, jogged through the parking lot, walked two blocks down PGA, and ducked into the first gas station I could find."

Just then, we heard pounding on the back door. I opened it to see a floral delivery person. "Miss Cara Mia Delgatto?" he asked.

"That's me."

He handed over a huge bouquet of long stemmed red roses. I thanked him, shut the door, examined the apology note, and tossed everything into the trash.

"Whoa! I'll take those home!" MJ nearly leapt from her seat.

"Suit yourself. I don't want them."

As she collected the roses, she asked, "Are these from Nathan? Didn't he try to find you?"

"Of course he did. But Lou and Skye gave me a ride here. The animals were still here, and you'd fed them, so I slept on an air mattress on the floor of my old apartment. I set my phone so that only calls from Tommy would come through."

"The way Lou hovered over you when we picked you up was so sweet," said Skye.

"Yes, and you fussed over me too, making sure I was comfortable in the apartment and then helping me get my pets settled. I don't know what I would have done without you. Either of you." I gave her a hug.

"What next? How do you plan to avoid Nathan? What's to stop him from coming to your house?" MJ turned the roses right side up and stuck them back in their vase.

"See this?" I waved a release form at her. "It's given to every resident on Jupiter Island. There's a space for listing people you want arrested if they trespass on your property. I guess it's to keep tabs on stalkers for Celine Dion and Tiger Woods, since they have homes on the island, too."

"You wouldn't do that," said MJ.

"I will, too. I plan to fill it out, scan it, and send it to Nathan's phone so he'll know I am serious. I never want to see him again."

"But Cara, what he had with Jodi is over. He has been over her for a long while." MJ threw up her hands. "Now that it's all out in the open, what difference does it make? I mean, it was only important when you didn't know, because you needed to know. In case Jodi brought it up. Uh, you're the winner, aren't you? Don't you see that? He's happier with you! And he's everything you like in a man. Now you can move forward because there are no secrets."

In that moment, it hit me. I pointed my finger at MJ. "You! You're the one who suggested that Nathan and I go to Caliente. You knew Jodi would be there. You wanted me to know he used to be involved with her."

MJ sighed. "Guilty as charged."

CHAPTER 29

I could have cheerfully wrung MJ's neck, but she's too important to my business. As it was, I counted to ten twice before I could even look her in the eyes. Even then, I was furious. I literally saw red.

"You needed to know," she said, in a matter-of-fact voice.

"What makes you say that? You date all sorts of men, surely some of them overlap."

"Right, but I don't have a sister who wants to hurt me, and I'm not you. You want to settle down. I don't. Settling down would require me to care, and I'm not interested in exposing my feelings. Never again. You aren't like that. You wear your feelings like a pashmina wrap around your shoulders. The longer you dated Nathan, the more likely you were to be hurt when you learned he was carrying on with Jodi. I just thought you should know sooner rather than later."

Skye poured hot water onto a teabag and handed me the cup with an overturned saucer functioning as a lid. "Valerian," she explained. "Nature's valium. Let it steep. You probably need a quart of it."

"You knew, too." I pointed a finger at Skye.

"But I wasn't happy about it. MJ and I argued about it," Skye said. "In the end, it was probably for the best. You were starting to get attached to Nathan. Everyone in the police department knew he and your sister were once engaged. Lou told me, and even he was worried what you'd do when you found out. You were bound to hear about it eventually."

"I thought about letting it slide, but there was an incident. It changed my mind entirely." MJ bit her bottom lip. She's not usually emotional. However, to her credit, she looked upset. Her hands shook as she twisted a paper napkin into an angry knot before saying, "I didn't know until last week that your sister goes to Caliente every Friday night. Pete, the vet, took me, and I bumped into Jodi in the ladies' room. She mentioned she'd heard you were dating Nathan Davidson. It was crystal clear that she was planning something. I wasn't sure what, but I couldn't let her get the jump on you."

My breath came in short angry huffs. My hand trembled as I lifted the saucer off the tea cup. It smelled like cooked grass clippings. Ugh. I wished I kept whiskey under the counter like my father used to do in the restaurant.

"Frankly, she scared me," MJ continued. "Jodi sounded like someone who's lost her mind. She was cackling like a witch when she talked to me about you. In fact, the entire bathroom cleared out once she opened her mouth. I've never seen such a look of pure hatred in someone's eyes. They actually glittered. And her voice? She was panting with rage. She hinted that she was going to make you pay. She said you were going down because you'd gotten the royal treatment by your parents, and now it was your turn to feel dumped on. The way she sees it, every advantage you have has come to you at her expense. And now she's going to make you sorry you were ever born."

A shiver ran up my spine.

"By the time I got back to the table, I felt physically ill. Pete took one look at me and asked if I was okay. I told him what happened. He said she's got all the symptoms of what they call borderline personality disorder, including a total inability to regulate her emotions. Cara, you have to listen to me on this one," MJ leaned closer and took my hand. "She's absolutely nuts. I wouldn't put anything past her. I talked to Lou about the conversation. You needed to know for your own protection. I don't scare easily, but she did it."

I knew that MJ doesn't scare easily. She has this weird way of seeming totally feminine and tough as tanned leather. Her direct way of talking and staring at you signals that she is not about to be cowed. By anyone.

But Jodi had gotten to her. Even recounting the incident, MJ looked nervous. My friend jiggled her leg, tapped on the table, and twitched. MJ was upset; so much so, that she was barely able to contain herself.

Pulling out the chair next to mine, Skye sank down and folded her arms around me. "How can we protect Cara?"

"I wish I knew!" said MJ. "I don't trust her. I remember when she was pulling all those pranks and now she's going to up the ante. Are you safe living all alone on Jupiter Island? Is your grandfather safe? What about Sid? He can barely get around. Are we safe here?"

"Maybe you'll want to give Nathan a call," said Skye in a whisper. "He could warn Jodi to behave."

"No way. I want nothing to do with him."

"He's a guy," said Skye. "Consider the source. They don't always use the brains God gave them."

"He's a grown man who should have known better than to try and keep something that important from me. Last night I left him with a huge dinner check, and this morning, you're suggesting I apologize?"

"That bill was punishment enough, and he's trying to apologize. He sent roses first thing! It's not just about you, Cara," said MJ. "Jodi is a whack-job. She'll take everything out on all of us. All of us. Your pets included. The store is at risk, too. You need to consider the damage she could do."

"MJ might be right," said Skye.

But I didn't say a word. My thoughts were bouncing all over the place. Could I depend on the help of the Stuart Police Department if Jodi caused havoc? How far might she go? Okay, I'd moved to Jupiter Island with its robust police presence, but Skye lived here alone in this building. Sure, Lou was here a lot, but what about when he wasn't around? And what about Poppy? And Sid? How could either of them defend themselves? MJ lived alone, too, and she wasn't particularly close to her neighbors. Were Honora and EveLynn safe? Would EveLynn recognize danger if it threatened her and her mother? Or could Honora lose her life trying to save her un-yielding daughter?

Luna wove her way through my ankles, purring and staring up at me with trusting eyes. In his crate, Jack whimpered softly. Up by the front door, Kookie began to sing a sailor's ditty in a minor key. None of the animals could protect them-selves from the wrath of Jodi.

The people and the creatures I loved would be at the mercy of my sister if she had her way.

What on earth was I going to do?

~*~

Skye bustled around, putting away the herbal tea and refilling the kettle for the next brew. MJ sat at her desk, looking over a list of local estate sales. Stacks of invoices teetered on my desk. Messages filled my Outlook in-box. Two local clubs had left phone messages requesting that I call them to set up private events after hours. There was plenty to be done, but I needed to clear my head.

"Honora will be in at noon, and I have a couple of errands to run," I told my friends. "I should be back in a couple of hours. Three at the most."

"Don't forget to make the bank deposit. It's in the safe," said MJ. "While you're gone, I'm going to brainstorm with Skye. We need to come up with a Valentine's Day promotion."

"Will do." In fact, making a deposit had been on my to-do list. So was a trip to Danielle's house to drop off the hundred bucks I owed her. A quick glance at the map on my phone suggested she lived forty-five minutes from downtown Stuart. I took that as good news. A drive would give me the chance to reconsider how I'd left things with Nathan. Windshield time was definitely a way to get my thoughts in order.

The touchscreen on the ATM machine at the bank proved stubborn. I jabbed at it repeatedly with my finger, until it gobbled down our deposit. Getting it to cash my paycheck proved nearly impossible, but I prevailed.

Pulling out onto Federal Highway, I drove north toward Port Saint Lucie. Yes, there was a lot of traffic since it was a Saturday, but after living in St. Louis, driving on the Treasure Coast was a breeze. I cranked up the radio, listened to an oldies station, and settled back to spend quality time with my car, Black Beauty. She's a good pal, this Camry of mine, despite the fact her odometer has turned over 100,000 miles. Tommy has suggested that I tint the windows. Although that makes sense, given the merciless heat of the sun, I can't bring myself to do that. It's too out of character for me. I pride myself on transparency.

Cars choked the left turn lane into the Treasure Coast Mall. Seeing parents with kids in the passenger seats reminded me of all the times I'd taken Tommy to the malls in St. Louis. Not to shop, but to meet with his friends. With a lump in my throat, I phoned my son. I was calling early for our scheduled weekly check-in, but he answered right away.

"Yo, Mom," he said.

"How are you baby boy?"

"Chill. Very chill. Studying for my midterms."

That reminded me of our conversation with Binky Rutherford. "Tommy? Can students take their tests early? Are the test dates staggered?"

"Huh?"

I explained how Binky had said her grandson was visiting after taking his spring midterms. "Evans Rutherford is a freshman, too."

"Yeah, I know him. What a jerk."

"A jerk?"

"We're in the same English 101 class. He promised to give me a ride home since he was supposed to visit his grandmother on Jupiter Island. But yesterday, he was missing from class. I called his cell phone and left a message. Late last night he sent me a text message saying he couldn't give me a ride after all."

This confused me. "But if you're in the same English 101 class, how'd he get to take his spring midterms early?"

"Beats me. The prof made a big point of saying she wasn't going to let anyone take the test early, and then she must have made an exception for

Evans."

"You're sure? Positive you have the right class and the right test?"

"One hundred percent. The test is scheduled for this Monday at eleven. No one gets to take it early. Last year some idiot got a hold of the test and passed it out to his pals. This year, we all have to suffer and take it in an auditorium."

"Weird. Do you need me to come and get you?"

"Nah. If I can't find a ride, I'll take the Tri-Rail to West Palm and you can pick me up there. Or I can use the Uber app on my phone."

"Sounds like a deal," I said.

"Yup. Hey, I've got a tutoring session on Skype for my poly-sci test that's at eight on Monday. Talk to you later?"

"Absolutely. Love you, Tommy."

"Love you too, Mom. See ya Monday after my tests."

The miles clicked by, and the traffic thinned out. North of Stuart is the small town of Jensen Beach. I pulled into the lot with the Hobby Lobby sign, just for a look-see. The next strip mall over, I did the same at JoAnn's Fabrics. Gazing at the pre-Valentine's Day offerings gave my spirits a lift. The phone reception in big box stores skips in and out. Glancing down at my phone, I saw that I'd missed a message from Nathan.

He would have to wait. I'd done a remarkable job of rehabilitating my good humor.

Twenty minutes later, the navigational system demanded I turn left. That sent me through a residential area. Danielle lived a good distance from her store. However, real estate signs suggested that property was a bargain here. The houses surprised me by being larger than those surrounding Stuart.

After a few more turns on well-tended streets, I stopped in front of a pale blue stucco with a white garage door. A chain link fence was hung with a wrap-around curtain of green woven material, giving the back yard a lot of privacy. Probably, Danielle owned a pool. That would explain her endless tan. The lawn in front had grown to ankle height, a process that takes only a couple of days here in the Sunshine State. A slight breeze brought me the cloying smell of gardenias from a glazed pot on her neighbor's porch. The clock on my phone assured me I'd arrived right on time. Five minutes before eleven. I knocked on her front door and waited for an answer.

And waited.

And waited.

After five minutes of standing in the sun, I called Danielle. Her phone went immediately to voice mail. The disembodied operator told me that her mailbox was full. Had she forgotten our agreement?

That didn't make sense given that she'd been adamant about getting the money for my dress.

One way to find out if she was home was to peep inside her garage. That necessitated walking in a clockwise direction through her overgrown grass, a process I found irritating, because no-see-ums love to munch on bare skin. They hang out in the grass and bite you so fast, you can't slap them away. Often, you don't even feel them, but the next day your skin is dotted with bite marks.

Cupping my hands over my eyes, I rested my face against her garage window. Her car, a purple Scion, sat there.

Was she in the bathroom? Taking a nap?

I trudged back the way I'd come and banged harder on the front door. No answer.

I am nothing if not tenacious, so I decided to go around back. Maybe she was sun-bathing. Before, I'd gone left, around the front of the garage, to peer in the garage window. This time, I moved right, wading through the grass, until I reached a metal gate. Standing on my tiptoes, I found the latch. With a yank, the contraption flew open and away from me with a loud clang.

Here, too, the grass was overgrown, but a sparkling blue pool beckoned, so I stayed on the concrete walkway and followed it around back.

"Danielle? Yoohoo! Hello? It's Cara." The walk curved toward the back of the house. A lanai jutted out into the yard. Although screens obscured most of the view inside, I spotted an overhead fan turning in lazy circles.

Surely Danielle was at home. Otherwise, why leave the fan on?

I listened intently. I heard a buzz. The hum of wings. I batted away one fly. Two. Three or four more. All coming from the house.

The breeze shifted. The smell changed.

I knew what I was sniffing. Sickening, sweet, cloying, and rotten. It was a smell you never forget. As fast as possible, I hurried back around the house. I threw open the door to my car, jumped inside, and locked the doors. I hit 911 and waited for the call to connect.

"I'm at 1731 Maiden Lane, Port Saint Lucie. Send help."

"Miss? Are you okay?"

"Y-y-yes. But someone needs help."

"Help?"

"I think she's dead."

CHAPTER 30

The operator asked me to stay on the phone, but I hung up on her and called Lou. He answered on the first ring. "Need another ride? Running away from another bad date?"

"S-s-she's dead."

"Who is? Can't be Skye. Can't be MJ. Or Honora. I just walked outta your store. In fact, I'm parked here out front and—" He hesitated a half a tick. "Is it your sister? You didn't do anything stupid, did you?"

"No way! It's Danielle Cronin from Vintage Threads."

"Slow down, partner. Exactly where are you?"

"Port Saint Lucie."

"Port Saint Lucie? What are you doing up there?"

I could hear him shaking his head. I could imagine him thinking all this through.

"Are you safe?" he asked.

"Y-y-yes. I'm sitting in my car in her driveway in broad daylight with the doors locked."

"Have you dialed 911?"

"Yes, and they're sending someone."

"Where did you find her body?"

"I didn't. Not exactly. I knocked on the door. She didn't come. We had an agreement for me to drop off money. I went around the house and smelled it. Her. Whatever."

"But you didn't go inside, did you?"

"No."

"So you don't know for sure that she's dead?"

"There are a lot of flies. Zillions of them." I covered my mouth and tried not to heave. When the urge passed, I said, "Lou, it smells like when you found that dead woman. Remember? I'm sure something awful has happened to Danielle. She didn't answer her phone or her door and her car is still here. The fan in her lanai is turning. Why would she leave the house and not turn it off?"

"Gotcha. Sit tight. Keep your doors locked. I'm gonna call a pal over in PSL. I'll call you right back."

It occurred to me that I could go and knock on a neighbor's door, but why? Danielle had to be dead. Why get another person involved? And what if a neighbor was the killer?

"No, no, no." I buried my face in my hands. "This cannot be happening to me."

But it was.

I turned on the ignition, turned up the A/C, and cranked up the radio full blast. At least until the authorities arrived, I could pretend my life was normal. I could enjoy the cool air and the tunes.

Lou called me right back. "My buddy at PSL will meet you at the house. Ron Cisco. I told him you're good people, except—"

"Except?"

"You're better at finding corpses than a trained cadaver dog, Cara. I swear, you need a new hobby."

"Don't I know it," I said, but I was talking to my steering wheel.

~*~

Ron Cisco was balding with a receding chin, but despite his lack of good looks, he obviously knew his business. He came roaring up, lights and sirens blazing, and arrived in advance of an ambulance and two more squad cars.

I cranked down my window to greet him and held out my driver's license.

"Stay put. Do not leave your vehicle." He trotted to the front door. Knocked and called. Trotted around to the gate and repeated the process. Then he followed my route around the house and disappeared.

In short order, Danielle's yard swarmed with people in uniforms. Lights bounced off the stucco finish of her home. The air came alive with the crackle of walkie-talkies. The activity level cranked up its volume. Cisco seemed to be the focal point, directing their activity.

I closed my eyes and tried to find my happy place. That didn't work, but I was able to calm myself.

But I sat up with a jolt when Danielle's front door swung wide open, and Cisco barked orders to a pair of arriving medics. Two men in blue EMT uniforms ran around to the back of the ambulance and unloaded a metal bier on rollers. Resting on top was a long black bag with a zipper closure. The sight of it churned my stomach. Cisco also gestured to a uniformed police woman who was carrying a camera. She followed him inside. A crime scene van rolled up and parked in front of the neighbor's house.

I closed my eyes again and wished I was anywhere but here.

"Miss Delgatto?" Ron Cisco rapped on my window, encouraging me to roll it down. "I need you to come with me to the police station. Please move your car out of the driveway. Park it next to the curb. We'll leave it here temporarily."

I did as told and locked up Black Beauty. With my purse under one arm, I climbed in the back of Ron Cisco's police cruiser and settled in for a ride to the police station.

Unfortunately, I know the drill. Too well, actually. Once there, Detective Cisco offered me a cup of coffee, brought me a bottle of water, and asked the preliminary questions to establish my identity and my details. I gave him permission to record my statement.

"In a nutshell, how did you wind up at Danielle Cronin's house?" he asked, staring down at a photocopy of my driver's license. "You live in Hobe Sound, is that right?"

"Jupiter Island. Hobe Sound is the mailing address. I stopped by Danielle's house because I owed her money. For a dress."

"That's it, that's all? It couldn't have waited? The banks close at noon."

I sipped the water and reviewed the situation. "I had given her my word that I'd bring her the money before eleven. She was planning to work on her books."

"Did anyone else know she was planning to handle money this morning?"

"I don't know."

"Ms. Cronin owns a dress shop? In Stuart?"

"Yes. She specializes in second-hand clothes. Vintage garments. She knows what I like so she keeps an eye out for vintage Lilly Pulitzer items. That's how she found a dress for me. I always keep my word, and I promised Danielle I'd get her a check for the dress so she could balance her books," and I hesitated before continuing, "but I had another reason for driving up here."

That put him on high alert. I could see his body coiling for action.

"Nothing sinister. It's just that the previous owner of the dress must have left an earring in the pocket. See? I put it in a pill bottle." I reached in my purse and withdrew an amber plastic cylinder. "Danielle or I needed to return the earring. To the previous owner, that is. A woman named Binky Rutherford. I've already made one visit to Binky's house, so I figured that this time, I would turn the problem over to Danielle. See? Here's the earring. I've been carrying it around in the pocket of my skirt. This piece of jewelry is—was—Danielle's responsibility, after all. She's the one who took the dress in on consignment. I paid for the dress, and they always say possession is nine-tenths of the law, but…"

"But that earring doesn't belong to you," said Cisco. "So you're returning it?"

"Right, and I'd promised Danielle I'd drop by with the money, so I figured I'd bring by Binky Rutherford's earring at the same time. Kill two birds with…" and I stopped because the analogy was so inappropriate and gruesome.

Fortunately Cisco didn't seem to notice. "Let's go through the timeline once more. I know this is repetitious, but indulge me. I'm still not entirely clear on why you drove up here to Ms. Cronin's house."

"I bought the dress on Thursday; it's a Lilly Pulitzer, and supposedly one of a kind. Danielle sold it to me and told me she was headed out of town. I promised to pay her on Saturday, today. But then Honora—she's my employee—said that Binky would have never given up that particular dress," I rattled on, noticing how Detective Cisco was trying to look interested. Really, he was. But clearly he didn't care about my dress. Given the gravity of the situation, I didn't either.

"Back to Ms. Cronin," he finally said. "You knew for sure she was home?"

"Uh-huh. Wait. No, I didn't know for sure. See, Danielle had told me she was coming back from her trip Friday night, last night. I didn't want to drive here for no good reason, so I ran next door—"

"Next door?"

"Danielle's shop Vintage Threads is right next to mine in Stuart."

"Ah."

"Claudia, the girl who works for Danielle, said she'd spoken to her boss first thing this morning, so she knew Danielle was at home, but she—Claudia, that is—hadn't gotten a hold of her since. I'd made a promise, and when it comes to money, your word is your bond, and there was that earring, and I needed a break from the store…" I realized I was rambling and shut up.

"Sounds like a lot of trouble for a dress and an earring." Cisco shook his head and stared at his notes.

"Believe me, it has been. A major league pain in the back-side. For me. Is she…dead? Danielle?"

"I can't answer that for sure. We did find a deceased person on the premises."

"Do you need me to—"

"No. We found her purse with her driver's license. It's definitely Danielle

Cronin. The ME will be able to match her dental records, but we know who we've got in there."

CHAPTER 31

"I counted," I told Skye when I returned to the store around four thirty. "I now know more cops on the Treasure Coast than real people. Scratch that. More cops than robbers. Uh, no. More cops than—"

"Lemon drop martini. Drink it." MJ shoved my way a tall glass with a sugared rim and a slice of lemon dangling precariously from it. "I told Honora what happened. Gee whiz, Cara, you sure know how to have a bad day."

To Skye's curious look, MJ added, "My lemon tree went absolutely nuts this last summer. I froze as many as I could. I'm pouring one for you, too. I think we all need about a pint of vodka to get over this."

"What if a customer comes in?" I wondered as I slurped the drink.

"We have enough to share," said MJ. "Or we can let Honora deal with the sales floor. She's out there right now, finishing up an order for a room box."

"I'll stick with the plain lemonade, please. Another day, another dead body. Cheers," and Skye raised her glass.

"I have become a human cadaver dog." I licked the rim of the glass. "Seriously. Forget dresses. I need to shop for a collar and leash."

"Jason would love you in one with studs. Nathan's more the military camouflage type, don't you think? And Mr. Boehner?"

Skye frowned. "Jay? He'd like you in a prim white schoolgirl collar, I bet."

MJ poured a second helping for all of us, giving Skye more plain old lemonade. "Bottoms up."

I groaned. "Not only am I a bloodhound in need of a collar, but I'm hanging out with a couple of perverts and drinking hard liquor. What a wonderful role model I am."

"Did you make one for me?" Honora pulled up a chair. "Cara, dear, you poor child. At least you found Danielle before she…lingered too long."

"Do you imbibe, Honora?" asked MJ. "This is not for the faint of heart."

"Laws, child. I not only imbibe, my generation practically invented alcoholism. Especially for stay-at-home mothers. What else did women have to do besides tie one on? My, my, but this is tasty. Good thing I don't have to drive myself home. So what do you intend to do about that earring, Cara?"

Putting my feet up on the chair across from me, I said, "Nothing. I don't give a rat's fat behind about Binky Rutherford. I am so done with her and that stupid dress, too."

"Do you still plan to return her earring?" asked Honora, as though I hadn't made my position perfectly clear.

"You think I should make another trip to Binky's house? Is that your point? That would make two home visits, one stop at Vintage Threads, and one stop at Danielle's crime scene. All for a stupid, idiotic dress that's older than I am."

"Oh, dear. I've upset you," said Honora.

"Yes, you have. Fortunately, these martinis are kicking in. I'm seeing the world in a light yellow haze that's very appealing."

"I guess this isn't the time to worry about a silly earring, is it, Cara dear? Especially considering what you found at Danielle's house. How about this. I'll call Binky's daughter BJ and see if she knows what's happening with her mother. At our age, a urinary tract infection can cause confusion. Perhaps Binky needs to see her doctor. You never know."

Not my problem. If Honora would just promise to shut up, I would agree to bundle up the earring and mail it to Binky along with a package of adult diapers. To misquote Rhett Butler, I didn't give a hang what Binky's problem was.

The rest of us watched while Honora punched buttons on her Jitterbug.

"Binky's daughter is Bianca, too, so they call her BJ. It's short for Bianca Junior." Honora took another big slurp of her cocktail as she waited for BJ to answer. I'd expected Honora to wilt under the powerful drink in her martini glass, but she hadn't. In fact, she acted as though she'd been fortified. For an old lady, she could sure hold her liquor.

"BJ? Hello. Honora MacAfee here. Yes, Honora from down in Florida. BJ, dear, I was wondering when the last time was that you talked to your mother? Oh. Right. Evans is there with her? He's out for Spring Break already? From University of Miami? Yes, I see. Has anything been bothering your mother lately? Right. I see. Nothing at all. She's fine, you say. In that case, I'll let you go. Nice to talk—"

But the frown on Honora's face suggested BJ had hung up on her.

The back door flew open and in stomped Poppy. "I got me a message from Zelda."

"Zelda?" The lemon drop martini had turned my limbs to overcooked spaghetti and my brain to mush.

"That there nurse at the hospital. She says if we hurry we can talk to your mermaid."

I jumped up. "She's awake? And talking?'

"Yup. There's a policeman outside of her door, but Zelda says he's taking an awful lot of bathroom breaks. She figures we can slip into that there immigrant's room while his back is turned. That's all you want, right? Just to see her and know she's okay?"

"Yes," I said. "I've been worried. I keep wondering if I did the right thing by resuscitating her."

Poppy put a hand on my shoulder. "Granddaughter, you did everything you could for her. I'm sure she'll be happy to thank you herself. Now if you want to go visit her, we better hurry."

~*~

"Binky Rutherford used to be sharp as a brand-new fishhook. Now she's old and forgetful, just like me," said Poppy, as he turned over the engine of his truck. "Worthless, the both of us. She used to bring her old station wagon to me before she traded it in for a newer car. We've been friends, oh, for thirty odd years. Until recently, she could take care of herself. But we're all getting on in age. Maybe I oughta go by and check up on her. No need for you to stick your nose into her business."

The alcohol made me muzzy headed. What if Poppy was acting confused? Wouldn't I want to know about it? What if Honora was right and her friend was in real trouble?

Poppy gave me a sidewise glance. "Care to tell me why you're getting schnockered in the middle of the day?"

I told him what I'd found at Danielle's house.

"And you figured right away that she was dead? Didn't go into the house, did you? Good. No need to disturb a crime scene. Woulda been something else entirely if you thought she might be incapacitated. But you were sure she was dead?"

"I smelled her. She couldn't have been dead long, but you know how it is. There was that stink. Also, there were tons and tons of flies."

"Doing their job. They're part of the dust-to-dust truth of our existence."

"Uh-huh." I stared out the window. How could we be having such a beautiful day when Danielle was dead? The birds carried on like always, squawking at a dark silhouette over-head as it soared past. The grass was still growing. My grandfather was sitting by my side. All in all, my life was terrific.

Except I'd internalized guilt the way a sponge drinks up water. Why was

Danielle dead? Why was I alive? What had happened to her? Would she still be alive if I'd arrived a little sooner?

"That's a shame." Poppy shook his head. "I remember seeing her pop in and out of your store. Awful young to die. Them cops didn't have any ideas what happened?"

"No. At least none they were sharing with me. I didn't know her well enough to even speculate, other than to wonder if it was a robbery gone wrong. She had told me she'd be at home working on her books. I assume that meant she had cash and checks at the house, although maybe not. Perhaps she went to the bank and a creep followed her home. Except..." and I paused. "There weren't any signs of forced entry. That doesn't sound like a robber, does it?"

"Nope. Of course you didn't check her windows, did ya?"

"No. Why?"

"You'd be amazed at how many crimes are opportunistic. Most bad guys don't think a lot in advance. They act on the spur of the moment, that's all. That's how come you gotta be vigilant. Don't put yourself in harm's way. What you really need, Granddaughter, is a bigger dog."

"Are we back to that?"

"Yup. A dog is a whale of a deterrent. They're unpredictable. Pretend you're a creep. You see a window open. You watch. There's only a woman living there. You decide to take advantage, but then you hear a deep bark and see a dog. A big dog. One that could go for your throat. What would you do next?"

"Move on down the road and find another house."

"Now you're using your noggin." Poppy gave me a gentle slap on the knee.

Actually, my noggin was fuzzy with the after effects of the martini, but I still understood his point.

"You're sure we can see my mermaid?" I asked, as we arrived at Treasure Coast Memorial. Poppy held me by the elbow as I climbed out of his truck, which was a very good idea because I couldn't remember the last time I had been that drunk.

"The docs told the authorities it's okay to talk to that half-drowned girl. Zelda says she is okay, but pretty quiet. That ain't surprising. If I were her, I'd keep my mouth shut, too."

"Authorities? You mean the Jupiter Island Public Safety Department? They've got jurisdiction, right?"

"No, I mean Homeland Security and the Martin County Sheriff's Office.

They got translators and people from the government who want to interview her before they send her back home."

"Translators?" Either he was mumbling or I was too drunk to hear him clearly. Or both.

"She's a native of Guatemala. The Bahamas was jest the launching point for the boat."

"What good will it do me to talk to her if she can't speak English?" My head felt woozy, and if Poppy didn't have a grip on me, I would have surely stumbled over the parking bumpers.

"Tarnation, girl. Just because you can't speak Spanish don't mean that I can't. I can also speak a smidgeon of Portuguese."

That woke me up a bit. I had never considered that Poppy might be bilingual, much less a polyglot. In fact, in a moment of embarrassing candor, I realized I considered him uneducated and unskilled. But he wasn't. He could fix a motor, he could speak other languages, and he knew how to make cranky nursing supervisors bend to his will. How easily we undervalue people who don't fit the molds we've carefully created for them. My view of "good people" or "worthwhile" people was seriously skewed toward those with a college education.

But I didn't have one.

Nor did Kiki.

Neither did Poppy.

But I put so much store by this ranking factor that I would move heaven and earth to be sure that my son finished college. How weird was that? And I'd assumed, because Poppy didn't have a four-year degree that he knew less than I did. I'd assumed he didn't speak a second language.

Shame on me.

Rather than apologize, I hurried along at my grandfather's side.

"So you've been keeping up with Zelda?"

"Ain't got much else to keep me off the streets these days. Not with Wilma out of town. Once I get Sid out the front door, I got entirely too much time on my hands. I been applying at one place after another. Been in more garages than a car with a rattle. Ain't nobody willing to hire an old man like me."

The pain in his voice dug a knife into my heart. At least, I could find comfort in the fact that I wasn't the only idiot with a set of prejudices that overwhelmed my common sense. For me, it was a college education; for many others, it was age.

Inside the hospital foyer, Poppy winked and nodded at the wrinkled lady in the pink volunteer jacket. "Hey ya, Thelma. How's tricks?"

We scooted past her and into the open elevator right before a doctor in surgical scrubs joined us. The doc took a second look when he saw Poppy.

"Dr. Mellen. How's that old Buick of yours? Still running like a top?" Poppy stuck out his hand, and the doctor responded with a hearty shake.

"She misses you, Dick. I know she does. I can tell. Where're you keeping yourself these days?"

"Nowheres special," and Poppy gave the doc a tiny salute as the man got off at another floor. When the door closed, I put my arm around my grandfather and hugged him.

"Poppy, we'll find meaningful work for you to do. I know you miss the Gas E Bait. I miss it, too. I can't imagine not having a job. You're handling it better than I would."

He planted a kiss in my hair. "Granddaughter, you make me proud."

CHAPTER 32

Zelda fluttered around Poppy like a pelican diving on a fisherman to grab his bait. "I knew you'd want to know that woman is awake," she said, speaking only to my grandfather as if I didn't exist. "They've got a guard outside of her room. She's not fully cogent, but I'm sure you want to see her with your own eyes since you saved her."

"Cara saved her." Poppy smiled gently as he corrected her.

"Right, Carla."

"Cara," I corrected the woman.

"Yes, of course, Karen. But first, could I interest you in a cup of coffee? I brought in cookies. Homemade. A plate of them? I love to bake and I'm a fabulous cook, if I do say so myself!"

"Actually, Cara's the one who wanted to see that there girl. But if the cop is a lookout, that might be tough."

"Oh, he'll be leaving his post soon enough. He's had enough coffee to float a boat," Zelda said with a giggle. "The policemen usually won't use the bathroom in a room they're guarding if it belongs to a female patient. They're funny that way. In this case, the john is right across the hall. See? Carmen can park herself at the nurses' station and take a load off while she waits for him to go tinkle."

"Cara," I said loudly.

I really did not like being referenced in the third person, but rather than voice my irritation, I acted like a good little girl. I headed in the direction that Zelda had pointed. And yes, to be honest, I badly needed to sit down because the entire floor was turning somersaults around me. The tiles took on lives of their own. Walt Disney would have been proud of their animation. Those lemon drop martinis had done a number on my head.

With an *oomph*, I sank down in a desk chair with casters and nearly toppled off the seat. Poppy's eyes went wide.

Fortunately Zelda didn't notice because she was busy batting her lashes at my grandfather. As they strode off, arm in arm, Poppy shot a wink my way. A jerk of his chin suggested that I keep watch on the man outside of the door to the room where my mermaid was staying. I offered Poppy a "thumbs up" so he'd know I was sober enough to understand his directions.

Carefully, I scooted the wheeled office chair in an arc and pointed myself at the hospital room door. Was Zelda right? Would the cop have to leave his post for a pit stop?

I propped my head up on my fists and waited, wondering what I'd say to the woman if given the chance. Glad you're alive? Have a nice trip back home? Sorry I didn't drag you into the sea oats so no one would know that you'd washed up? Of all the gin joints, why'd you happen to pick my beach?

Snoring noises echoed from the slumped figure outside the hospital room.

So much for guarding the illegal alien.

Maybe I could sneak around the cop and peek inside the room. Or make a loud noise and wake him up. If he knew I was the one who'd rescued the mermaid, perhaps he'd be—

But my thoughts were interrupted as an orderly came down the hall, pushing a meal cart. On it was a dinner tray. He paused outside the mermaid's room.

"Room 314?" he asked the cop, who was trying to act like he hadn't just been sound asleep.

"Yup. Her dinner? I didn't think she was well enough to eat."

The orderly chuckled. "Beats me. Sometimes the docs order meals just to run up the bill. Sick, ain't it?"

"Okay, look, you going to be with her? Let me run to the john while you're here." The cop stood up and hoisted his pants.

"She's in good hands." The orderly pushed his cart into the room.

As soon as the policeman disappeared inside the bathroom, I darted across the hall. The door to the mermaid's room was slightly open but it blocked my view of the bed and the woman.

So close and yet so far. Here I was outside the mermaid's room, but I still couldn't see her, couldn't reassure myself that she was okay. Poppy and Zelda would be back any minute. I wasn't sure how long Zelda would let us hang around.

After dithering a bit, I decided to stick my head around the door. All I wanted was a good look at her. I really didn't have anything much to say—and she wouldn't understand me anyway. I tiptoed to the door frame and flattened myself against the door itself so I could peep inside the room.

The orderly didn't see me, but I saw him... as he used a knife to cut through the tubing that delivered oxygen to the mermaid.

CHAPTER 33

"Stop!" I screamed. I didn't even take time to think about the fact the man was holding a knife. A big knife at that. He dropped the air tube pieces and stared at me from the far side of the bed.

"Help!" I yelled down the hall. "Poppy! Help me!"

The orderly brandished the knife in a way that suggested he knew what he was doing. The glint in his eye scared me. I sobered up fast as he came out from behind the bed.

I back-pedaled into the hallway. "No," I said, patting the air and unable to take my eyes off the silver blade.

With his one free hand, the orderly used the cart as a buffer in front of him. I was backing away from the door when it dawned on me what he was planning. Once I cleared the door, he could slam it shut and finish whatever he was doing to my mermaid.

Killing her.

Footsteps clattered behind me. I smelled Aqua Velva and knew that Poppy had my back.

"He's got a knife. He cut a tube. Her oxygen I think," I said, without looking away from the orderly.

"Move aside," said my grandfather.

But I couldn't do that. In a contest between a man with a knife and my elderly grandfather, I knew who would win. I would not lose Poppy to this madman!

The cart was the only barrier between me and the guy with a knife. Instinctively, I shoved it forward, as hard as I could. My impulsive act sent the dishes flying. Hot green beans splattered the orderly's scrubs. The air was dense with the odor of overcooked chicken, mashed potatoes, and melted butter.

"Ouch!" He jumped backwards and brushed smashed bits of green off his thighs.

"I said move!" Poppy grabbed me by the waist, spinning me around and hurling me to one side. My feet tangled up underneath me. I hit the floor hard and skidded on the tiles. In the background, Zelda screamed for help.

I was sprawled out in front of the bathroom door when it opened. The cop staggered out, fighting with the buckle on his utility belt. Slowly I rolled to my knees. My balance had been severely impaired by the vodka, but adrenaline overrode the alcohol. Teetering, I pushed myself to my feet.

The cop and I looked on in horror as my grandfather snatched up a dinner tray that had fallen to the floor. Holding it like a shield, Poppy tried to muscle his way into the hospital room. "You ain't smart enough to use that knife on me. You don't even know how to hold it right, you dope."

The cop's mouth was open in shock. Zelda's screams got louder. I could hear voices, but I couldn't tear my eyes from the scene. Poppy was crouched and totally focused on the orderly.

My grandfather acted like he knew what he was doing, but did he?

With a clang, the orderly rammed the cart into Poppy. My grandfather spun to one side, avoiding the wheeled weapon. But the cop didn't move out of the way fast enough. The cart hit the cop and brought him down. As the guy in uniform flailed the air, his long legs knocked Poppy off his feet. Both men landed in a tangled heap on the tile floor. That left me standing by myself to one side of the open doorway.

The orderly wrapped his forearm around my throat, pulling me close. I could feel his heart beating. A cold sting at my throat surprised me.

"I'll cut her open, right here, right now, if you don't back off," he said. The orderly's breath was moist against my ear. I could smell that he'd been eating garlic. I could also felt a warm trickle down my throat.

Blood. The stinging began to throb.

Poppy jumped back to his feet and held the tray in front of him like a shield. The cop was groaning as he rolled slowly to his knees. To my left, a gaggle of doctors and nurses stood at bay. Zelda's hysterical sobs echoed in the corridor.

"She's coming with me," said the orderly, as he dragged me backwards. His knees were sharp and bony as they poked the back of mine. I had no choice but to move with him. Poppy stared at me, sending me a message of sorts, but what? I couldn't tell. My assailant positioned his head directly behind mine.

"You'll have to put a bullet through her head to kill me."

I backed up with the orderly as best I could.

Poppy advanced on us. "Let her go. Be a man. Fight me instead of her, you coward!"

"Shut up, you old fart!"

The blade of the knife stung me again. The world blurred as tears filled my eyes.

"I done tole you once, now I'm telling you again. You let my granddaughter go, or I'll skin you like the squirrel you are. You'll be begging for mercy before I'm through with you." Poppy's voice had gone flat and unemotional. His eyes glittered strangely. He did not back down.

The orderly tightened his grip on me. "Clear the stairs or I'll slice her throat!"

The cold blade of the knife tickled my throat. If he took me down the stairs, I would surely die. Already blood wetted my collar. The orderly was so close that his breath warmed my skin.

That gave me an idea.

I signaled to Poppy, moving my fingers as though doing a countdown. A flicker of recognition told me he had caught my drift. My grandfather shifted his weight to the balls of his feet.

My attacker continued to move me backwards, but on the count of three, I let my knees buckle. The orderly gasped, tightened his hold around my neck, and swayed under my weight. Instinctively, my body fought the limp position. I'd inadvertently made it harder to breathe, so every cell protested loudly, but I had also managed to throw my assailant off-balance.

My thoughts flickered to Tommy. I wanted to see him grown, on his own, and married. I remembered my parents. As long as I was alive, they would be remembered. I thought of my friends. What would Skye, MJ, Honora, and Sid do for jobs? Of course, there was Poppy. He would be lost without me. And my friend Kiki Lowenstein. How often had she saved herself? What would she do in my place?

Kiki wouldn't give up. I wouldn't either. My feet dragged against the tiles. The orderly adjusted his hold around my throat.

"Don't you dare fight me, lady. You do, and they'll be picking up pieces of you all over this place! Back off, old man. I mean it. If you try anything, she's a goner." Bits of spittle landed on my head, moist and warm.

Poppy kept his focus on my assailant. I couldn't go without air much longer.

Using the fingers of my left hand, I counted down again.

Three.

Two.

One!

I rammed my head into the orderly's nose.

Crunch.

Reflexively, his hands flew up. He let go of his grip on me as he howled in pain. I dropped to the floor, tucking myself into a ball, like I'd learned in gymnastics class twenty years ago. I rolled until the wall stopped me with a jolt. Lying there, stunned, I watched as Poppy lurched forward.

Blood spurted from the orderly's nose. He cupped his hands over his face—and then wiped his nose on the back of his sleeve. With an angry curse, he waved his knife at Poppy. But he missed, slicing the air while Poppy twirled away like a ballerina.

My heart hammered in my chest. I couldn't take my eyes off my grandfather. This was not the man I knew. An odd expression changed his features. A cold glare rendered him foreign to me. He had shifted from old man to warrior. Wielding the tray like a shield in his left hand, Poppy fended off a second downward swipe of the knife. But the orderly stepped in-to a pool of blood. His feet skittered off to one side. Blinded by tears and in pain, he struggled to stay upright. My grandfather closed the distance. His right hand hooked up and caught the orderly under his chin with a loud snap.

The knife hit the floor. It spun in lazy circles, dibbling blood on the tiles in a Jackson Pollock parody. I reached for the weapon, snatching it up quickly.

Meanwhile, Poppy had the orderly by his collar. With a determined stomp of his foot, my grandfather shoved the orderly's knee backwards until it snapped. As the high-pitched wail of pain echoed off the walls, Poppy twisted the man's arm behind him. With a jerk, my grandfather pulled the creep's hand up, up, and up until we heard a loud pop.

Another screech of pain split the air. Poppy rammed the orderly face first into the wall next to me. My grandfather smacked his entire weight against my assailant. In return, the man bounced off the wall like a tennis ball hitting the side of a garage. An ominous crunch suggested broken bones. After a gurgle of pain, the man hocked up a mouthful of blood and spat it out. Broken teeth dotted the red splotch. Poppy grunted and shoved the man against the concrete block wall again.

"Poppy?" I said. "I think...I think he's under control."

My grandfather's normally placid expression had changed into a cold glare. He stared at me with an icy stillness, as if he had temporarily stepped away from his body and turned it over to a robot.

Who or what had taken over my grandfather's body?

"I think I can handle it from here," said the cop, as he hoisted his utility belt. His voice exuded authority. Poppy's vacant stare vanished and a look of pure tiredness took its place.

"Got him?" asked my grandfather.

"I do indeed," said the cop. With a practiced gesture, he snapped handcuffs on the orderly's wrists.

The knot of medical onlookers drifted away, although Zelda had recovered enough to give directions to another nurse, who hurried down the hall to check on the mermaid.

Another uniformed cop and two security guards raced toward us.

"Secure the scene here and in the hospital room," said the cop.

I heard panting and realized the noise was coming from me. Zelda helped me to my feet. I leaned on her and walked over to the nurse's station. She pulled an alcohol wipe from her pocket. My skin stung as she dabbed at my injuries. "Not very deep," she said. "More messy than dangerous. Butterfly bandages should do it. Okay, I'll wrap gauze around your throat. The bleeding has mainly stopped, but we need to get you downstairs to an ER examination room. You were so brave!"

"I didn't have much of a choice. Be brave or be dead."

Two more uniformed cops arrived to lock down the scene. One of them unrolled yellow crime scene tape. The other explained that he needed photos of me and of Poppy. We posed against a blank wall, facing front, turning to one side and then the other.

"I also need to take your statements," the cop added, but Poppy waved him quiet.

"First we need to get my grandbaby all cleaned up." He slipped an arm around me, which I appreciated. "You can take her statement later at her store. It's just four blocks from here. Send a cop over. Give this girl a break."

Someone appeared with a wheelchair, while a cop frog-marched my assailant toward the elevator bank. The creep's nose still leaked a river of blood, and his face was swelling like a balloon.

"But my mermaid?" As the seat of the wheelchair touched the back of my knees, I slowly lowered myself into the sling seat. "How is she?"

"I'll go see," said Zelda.

"Poppy, I was so scared," I said, fighting tears, as we held hands. The adrenaline ebbed from my system, leaving me with a bad case of the shakes.

"Of course you were. You had every right to be scared spitless." He gripped my hand harder. "But you got the heart of a lion, Granddaughter. You did me proud. Any other girl woulda burst into tears and been useless, but you saved us. You used your head. You figured out how to signal to me, how to use that thick skull of yours as a battering ram. If you hadn't of been so smart, this could have been curtains."

"W-w-where did you learn to fight like that?"

"My uncle taught me."

"You had an uncle?"

"Uncle Sam."

CHAPTER 34

Zelda walked toward us, pressing the palms of both hands over her mouth, as if she could contain any words that might burst free. Her tight curls swayed in response to her side to side motion. Her rolling gait reminded me of the Penguin in the Batman films. She didn't move fast. Poppy and I waited patiently for her, rather than punch the button on the elevator.

"So she's fine, right?" I brushed away tears with the back of my hand.

"No," Zelda said.

"No?" Poppy repeated as he tilted his head curiously.

"No. I'm sorry. She didn't make it."

"What?" I nearly fell out of the chair. "How?"

"He cut the tube to her oxygen tank. She was stressed and he made it worse, and I'm so, so sorry but it was too much for her. Her heart gave out."

The words tumbled around in my head.

"Dead? She died? A heart attack? That doesn't make sense." I shook my head, but that didn't clear it. The motion made me more confused than ever.

Zelda squatted, an awkward move for a bulky woman like her, but one that put us eye to eye. "When a person is drowning in salt water, the lungs become compromised. This patient developed ARDS, Acute Respiratory Distress Syndrome. As a result, the tiny blood vessels in her lungs leaked fluid. The fluid competed with the lungs' ability to transport oxygen. We hooked her up to oxygen, hoping to limit the damage, but her heart had to work very, very hard to move air around her body. Her body's response to her trauma was a stressor. You gave her a second chance, but she was hanging on by a thread. When that guy cut her oxygen, she fought him. Until that moment, she'd been balancing on a tight wire. The struggle put too much stress on her. Her heart gave out."

I choked out a sob.

Slowly rising, Zelda patted my shoulder. "That's enough for now. We need to get you down to the ER. You've had a stressful day, too."

She didn't know the half of it. With a deft signal, she waved over a male orderly to push my wheelchair.

The elevator car dinged. Poppy hovered over me as the new orderly rolled me into the metal box. After the door thunked shut, the orderly thumbed his phone in a fury of text-messaging. I said to Poppy, "Two dead people in one day. This has to be some sort of a record. For me at least. How about you?"

Cutting me a sideways glance, he said, "Not nearly. But that don't matter. How's your butt and your back after that tumble you took?"

"I have a hunch I'll be sore tomorrow."

"You won't feel it tomorrow," Poppy said. "But wait until the day after. You usually get one day of grace. Got any Epsom salt at home? No? We'll pick some up for you. Best cure for soreness God ever created. Tonight, you go home and soak in a tub of them crystals. It'll draw the soreness right out of you."

"How bad does my neck look?" I tried to see myself in the mirrored panels of the elevator car, but I couldn't make out much.

"You'll live."

"Thanks. How are you?"

"Never better." He clenched his right fist, released it, and clenched it again. "Well, pretty much. Mighta busted my pinky. Gotta admit, it's been a long time since I punched anybody that hard."

I tried to turn and talk to the orderly. "Someone needs to x-ray my grandfather's hand."

Poppy's grunts suggested me that I worried too much. But I didn't care. The orderly handed me over to a nurse who wheeled me into a curtained cubicle. With the nurse's help, I changed out of my clothes and into a hospital gown. The nurse put on a blood pressure cuff and wrote notes in a file. I tuned her out. Once snuggled under the cotton blanket, I sent Skye a message and asked her to babysit my pets for a while. I had no idea how long my exam would take, or how long it would be for them to check Poppy out thoroughly. She messaged back: Anything wrong?

I was too overwhelmed to frame a proper response, so I typed: Poppy got into a bit of a tussle. He's being checked out right now. No worries!

With my fur babies taken care of, the tension drained from my body. My head ached, and belatedly, I realized I'd hit it against the wall when I did my somersault.

"You in pain?" asked the nurse, a freckle-faced woman with frizzled strawberry blonde hair.

"Just a little headache."

"Did you hit your noggin?"

"I might have."

"We'll need to get a picture of it. Be right back," and she disappeared.

Alone in the cubicle, the full impact of my day rose up like a ghostly specter. Two women dead. Both were only barely known to me. One hadn't seemed at risk. The other seemed to be on the mend. I closed my eyes and imagined a spool of thread. At first it ran freely. Then it wrapped around an index finger. Finally it snapped. Life was like that. Danielle and my mermaid had been moving along, seemingly without snags, until fate intervened, and then they were cut free.

How could this be happening? And why was I stuck in the middle of it?

The cubicle curtains jerked to one side.

"Cara? Are you all right?" Nathan Davidson grabbed my damp hand and squeezed it so hard I gasped. "Sorry. You okay? Your neck—"

He brushed the hair back from my throat and grumbled curse words. "He'll live to regret this, I swear he will."

"It's all good. Poppy did a number on him."

"So I heard. There's plenty of fight in that old dog. They're busy patching up your attacker."

"Just so you know, I'm mad at you!" I withdrew my hand from his.

"I know you are," he said with a rueful laugh. "Boy, remind me never to tick you off again. The waitress doubled-over laughing when I realized how you'd stuck me with that ginormous bill and all that food. I brought it back to the station. Packed the refrigerator high with it." But his face changed instantly, as he added, "I would have told you. I meant to tell you about Jodi, really I did. I kept thinking the timing wasn't right, but I guess I was only postponing the inevitable. I never intended to mislead you."

"But you did."

"Cara, we weren't at that stage in a relationship where we share our pasts, were we?"

He was right, but I didn't feel much better about it.

The nurse reappeared at his elbow. "Captain Davidson? I need you to leave. We have to get this young lady's wounds dressed and check her for a concussion. Dr. Pouncer is on his way." Without waiting for Nathan's answer, she pushed him out of the cubicle and into the hall. But rather than pull the curtain shut, she held it open so a large man of Filipino descent could enter.

"What have we here?" a booming voice wondered. "A damsel in distress? Hiya. I'm Ferdinand Pouncer. Bet you're happy to see me, right? Thrilled to be in the ER? Aw, it's okay. I'm used to being everyone's least favorite doc. You might hate me now, but you're going to love me later."

His round face creased into a broad grin, as he leaned close to examine my throat. His thick fingers proved surprisingly tender and adept. He marched them over my neck as he gazed off into space.

"I think more clearly when my fingers are doing the looking for me," he explained. When he finished, he smiled down at me and said, "Geez, lady, you need to quit playing around with knives. Another half inch to the right, and you wouldn't need me."

"I could go home, right?"

"Sure, if you live in the morgue."

CHAPTER 35

Nathan insisted on driving Poppy and me back to my store in his police cruiser. I took the back seat, so Poppy could sit up front next to Nathan. A uniformed officer followed with Poppy's truck.

I wasn't ready to let Nathan off the hook, even though his apology had gone a long way toward cooling my temper. The truth was that I just didn't have the energy to stay mad at him. I was too physically and emotionally spent.

And it was only half past six.

Lou met us at the back door of The Treasure Chest. Skye peered anxiously over his shoulder. In her hands were two cups. One had valerian tea and two Advils for me. There was freshly brewed coffee for Poppy, who can drink caffeine at any time of day or night without losing any sleep. But Skye had rightly surmised that I needed to chill out. After thanking her, I swallowed the Advils and sipped my drink.

"Have MJ and Honora left for the day?"

"Yes, and MJ gave Sid a ride to Poppy's house." That was good news, because I didn't feel like talking to anyone. Well, anyone but Skye. Her hug felt like a safe haven. I was so glad to have her in my life.

"Actually, Sid wanted to stop by his friend's place to see if he could pick up his computer, but MJ put her foot down. She said, and I quote, 'I am not a taxi service. A Good Samaritan, yes; an Uber driver, no.' I think she was worried because the neighborhood is iffy. She likes to act as if she's tougher than nails, but she isn't."

"Good thinking on her part," I said. "That's definitely a job for Poppy."

Nathan rejoined us and stood directly over me. "I need to take your statement, Cara, while Lou takes a statement from Dick."

"Other way around, Captain Davidson. You can talk to Poppy; Lou can interview me."

"Come on, Cara," said Nathan. "You've got to let this whole thing with your sister drop. I said I was sorry. You're making a mountain out of a molehill."

"I can't deal with this right now." My voice broke. Skye pulled me closer and patted my back so I wouldn't have to look at Nathan.

"Don't be ridiculous. I need to be able to do my job. If you don't care about your own safety, consider the welfare of your friends and co-workers."

"Let her talk to Lou." Skye sounded fierce.

"All right, all right. Be that way," Nathan said.

Over Skye's shoulder I watched as Lou nodded, but he didn't look happy. I was putting him in a tough spot between his boss and his girlfriend. But for once I needed to take care of myself.

"Upstairs," said Lou. I followed on jittery legs. Halfway up, he turned and grabbed my hand. It wasn't like him to be physical with anyone. He rarely acted affectionate with Skye in public. So I knew he'd fought a battle within himself before deciding he should help me.

I leaned against him hard. My muscles grew stiffer with every passing minute. How I longed to take a nice hot bath! But I couldn't. For the next half an hour, while sitting on a chair in my old apartment, I relived the nightmare visit that Poppy and I had made to the hospital. Lou interrupted me only to ask clarifying questions.

When we were finished, I crossed my arms over my chest. "Done with your questions? My turn."

Lou's not a handsome man, but his face is incredibly likeable, especially when he's not angry. "Aw, Cara, that's not how it works."

"That's exactly how it works today, Lou. Who was that guy who cut my throat? I have the right to know. I live alone, remember? I might be in danger."

Lou's hands are the size of catcher mitts. Resting in his lap, palms up, they seemed to cup a world of possibilities. Or not.

"I need answers, or I'll never be able to sleep at night." My voice cracked at the end. "You can't do this to me, Lou. I've been through too much."

"Answers? I wish I had them." Scrubbing at his short haircut, Lou avoided my gaze. Finally, he hunched over so we were nearly touching foreheads. "Cara, we don't know anything about your creep. Not yet. We have to run his finger-prints through the system. You know the way this works."

"Yeah, I guess I do. So you can't tell me why he cut my mermaid's oxygen supply? What was his reason for wanting to see that poor woman dead?"

"I can hazard a guess. See, a bunch of people went overboard that day. Most of them swam away or drowned. The guy piloting the boat didn't want to be identified. Nor did the guy waiting to pick up the shipment in his truck. Your mermaid represented a problem, and she probably didn't have much value to the coyote. Both the women who washed up were in their fifties. Probably not much use in the sex trade market. Possibly destined to be household slaves."

"What? Household slaves? But you can't have slaves here."

"Not legally. But the numbers of illegals coerced into forced labor is astonishing. It's a crime that most people never realize is happening, because the slave has no way of asking for help."

"Back up. You keep using the term slave. Do you mean like a sex slave?"

"Not always. See, there's sex trafficking and labor trafficking. Florida has the third highest rate of labor trafficking. We're almost tied with Texas. California takes the top spot. Labor trafficking is defined as coercing, forcing, or tricking someone into working for you."

I found it difficult to grasp what Lou was saying. His suggestions sounded outlandish to me. After all, I'd been taught in school that slavery ended when Abraham Lincoln signed the Emancipation Proclamation. But here Lou was, looking totally serious, telling me that modern day slavery actually did exist, and my new home state was a top offender. "Wait a minute. That doesn't make sense, Lou. If you're working for someone and you don't like it, why not quit? Why not tell the authorities? Or ask for help?"

"Many of these household slaves come from countries where they've been taught to fear people in authority, particularly the police. They won't come to us because they don't trust us. Another problem is that they fear for the safety of their families back home. Of course, there are also language barriers. Some are held in isolation. If they aren't in a big city with public transportation, they have no idea how to run away, where to go for help, or how to get to a place where they can ask for help. And then, there are those who blame themselves. Maybe the whole family pitched in to pay for them to have the chance to start over, and here they are, in the land of milk and honey, only it's a prison sentence. They don't know how to get out of a bad situation, and they're too embarrassed to admit what's happened."

"Wow," I said softly. "I never realized."

"It's a big, big business. Whatever happened, these creeps couldn't allow your mermaid to be interviewed by the authorities. Killing her was a matter of tidying up loose ends."

"Just my luck to stumble onto two murder scenes in one day."

Lou shook his head. "That's one way to look at it. Another is you're lucky that you're still alive."

CHAPTER 36

When Lou and I finished, we came downstairs to find Nathan sitting on one of my kitchen chairs. He frowned at his phone while he used his thumbs to write text messages. The ping of incoming messages suggested this was a conversation. One ping in particular caused him to stop and stare. With a fierce grunt, he stood up, walked into my office, and shut the door. Normally I would have stopped anyone who presumed to take over my desk, but on this particular evening, I didn't have the energy to set boundaries.

Poppy and I took seats at the table, staring at the walls with all the energy of a pair of zombies. Skye put out place settings and warmed up Honora's Tex Mex Spaghetti Squash leftovers.

The wonderful smell of the spices perked up my appetite, but eating seemed like a chore. One I wanted to avoid. "I'm not that hungry. I think I'll grab Jack and go home."

"No you won't. You aren't going anywhere," said Nathan, as he walked out of my office. "Not until we get things under control."

It was on the tip of my tongue to say, "You're not the boss of me," but I decided against it.

"First of all, what did the ER doc say to you, Cara? Did he or she clear you to be alone?"

"I'm fine."

"That's not what I asked."

I reddened. "I'm supposed to have someone keep an eye on me."

"How do you intend to do that if you're at your house by yourself? Second, we don't know if your assailant was alone. We have to comb through the surveillance videos from inside the hospital and from the parking lot. And third, you seem to be on a roll. This is the second time you've been in close proximity to a woman who died in less than eight hours. I'm not sure how this is related, or even if it is, but I'm worried about your safety."

"I got Sid in my guest room, but you can have my room, and I'll take the sofa. You can stay at my place, Granddaughter."

"No way. That sofa of yours is old and saggy. You sleep on it and your back will be killing you. I don't want to put you out, Poppy. You're already taking care of Sid. In fact, you should go on home and make sure he's okay."

"You can stay with me," said Skye. "I changed my sheets today. You can have my bed, and I'll take the futon. The animals will be fine here, and you have extra clothes in your old apartment. I can check on you. Come on, Cara. It'll be like a pajama party. Look, the food's ready. At least have a bite or two."

With a practiced ease, she dished out helpings. Poppy stared at his plate. "What in tarnation is this mess?"

"Try it," Skye coaxed him. "It's good for you. There's spaghetti squash in there instead of wheat-based pasta."

Nathan disappeared again into my office.

"No, sirree. I didn't claw my way to the top of the food chain so's I could eat veggies I can't identify."

Lou glanced up from his notepad and chuckled. "See, Skye? I'm not the only one."

"I'm gonna grab me a burger on the way home." He stood up and gave me a kiss on the cheek. "Goodnight, Granddaughter."

"Dick, how'd you break your finger?" Skye stared at the metal sheath covering the top of Poppy's pinky.

"On a chunk of wood," said my grandfather.

"Poppy is a hero. While the cop who was guarding my mermaid took an extended vacation in the john, Poppy tangled with the turkey who cut her oxygen tube. She died, by the way."

"I know, sweetie," said Skye, wrapping her arms around me and giving me a hug. "I am so sorry."

"At least I got to break this here finger on that creep's jaw. If I'd had a few more minutes, they woulda taken that punk out in a body bag. Good riddance to trash, I say. Punk didn't know who he was messing with."

"Poppy, I didn't know who he was messing with, either. What got into you?"

"Instinct. A man does what he has to do. Besides, I couldn't let you show me up. You had him howling in pain."

"Poppy, you're full of baloney, and we both know it. You've had martial arts training or training in hand-to-hand combat. You took that kid down like he was waving around a pool noodle."

"He didn't know what he was doing. Held that there knife like a rookie does."

"Yes, but you did."

"Don't worry none about me. I got to go see about Sid. You need to go upstairs and soak them muscles of yours. Get outta them bloody clothes."

I glanced down at myself. The pretty lemon-colored polo shirt stiffened in patches where blood had dried on it. "I am never going to get this clean," I said.

"Sure you will. I'll help you. We'll douse it with Shout. Even if you don't, it doesn't matter. You're safe," Skye said.

"You done good, Granddaughter," said Poppy. "Now go take care of yourself. I won't expect you for breakfast tomorrow. You'll probably need to sleep in."

Our habit had been to meet at Harry and the Natives for breakfast on Sunday mornings. I opened my mouth to protest, but before I could, I realized how stiff I was already becoming. "Maybe you and Sid can eat there instead."

"That's an idea. After we get done, we can go round up that computer of Sid's."

"Sounds like a plan. Love you, Poppy," I said.

He grunted and left.

"Lou? You ready to get back to the station? We've got a long night ahead of us," said Nathan.

"I'll be right behind you," said Lou. "After I help Skye get Cara and the animals upstairs."

Nathan hesitated. For a tick, he leaned toward me as if to give me a kiss or a hug, but I gave him an angry look. He backed away from me. "All right then. Cara, I hope you feel better." With that, he left.

"Wow, Cara," said Lou. "That was cold."

"Listen up," I said to Lou and to Skye. "Because I want to go on record. I am sick of being second fiddle to my sister. I am also sick of problems with Binky Rutherford. I'm taking this earring back to her if I have to leave it in her mailbox. And I might drop off that dress, too. There's too much bad ju-ju swirling around me. I'm done with this."

"I'll grab the sage sticks and a white candle," said Skye.

Lou chuckled and shook his head. "You two are a real pair."

CHAPTER 37

My clothes were stiff with blood. I peeled them off while Skye ran a bath for me, liberally dousing the water with essential oils. She poured in a half a package of Epsom salt. I guess everyone in the world kept them at hand but me.

"Here, I'll take those downstairs and get the stains out." She set my wadded up things on the counter. "There's a bathrobe behind the door. Let me help you step into the tub. I'd hate for you to fall and hit your head again."

The water, salt, and the oils stung like crazy, but only for a second or two. I gasped as the water lapped at my skin, but Skye held on to my hand tightly and cooed, "It'll quit directly. Come on. Sit down. Let the water do its magic."

I hadn't realized how stiff I'd be, and her help proved invaluable. Once I was situated, she handed me a baby flannel and a plastic bottle of moisturizing body wash. She had installed a dimmer switch on the lights. With a flick of her wrist, the bathroom was softly illuminated. Putting my clothes down for a second, she lit three fat candles and set them on the counter.

"Now you relax." She closed the door behind her.

I sank down until the water reached my chin. My knees were skinned and bloodied. The tuck and roll that had saved my life had taken a toll on my body. But as the water unknotted my muscles, I puffed up with pride. I'd saved myself. Or rather, Poppy and I had saved me.

How had he learned those hand-to-hand combat skills? Were those part of regular training? Or did they hint at an education beyond what the rank and file serviceman learns? Then there was that cold glint in his eyes. The bizarre expression that had come over his face. My grandfather had morphed into a killing machine. In fact, if the cops hadn't intervened I had no doubt that Poppy would have snapped the neck on my assailant.

So who was this man, the guy I knew as my grandfather?

What arcane skills did he have—and what was he hiding?

My mind drifted back to Cooper. His business associates thought of Poppy as old and washed up, but nothing could be further from the truth. Although his diabetes could flare up and cause him to have muddled thinking, we'd brought that under control. He hadn't had a problem for months. Other than that, my grandfather was in great shape physically.

What is age but a number? Okay, people said that all the time. It was a tired cliché, but perhaps it was also a fact. My grandfather talked like an old man. He was curmudgeonly and gruff. His hair had thinned and turned gray. His skin was weathered, thanks to years in the sun, but those outside appearances meant very little when he needed to take action.

I decided to call Cooper and tell him he needed to intercede on Poppy's behalf. His investors were flat out wrong. Besides, he and I had an oral contract. When I sold him the lot for his new business, he'd agreed to give Poppy a job. If all else failed, I might threaten to take him to court. The publicity would be very bad for the new Fill Up and Go station.

My fingertips wrinkled like raisins. The water cooled. Skye tapped on the door and offered me help getting out of the tub. I took her arm gratefully. The bath had zapped the last of the adrenaline from me, and I could barely keep my eyes open. Skye had thoughtfully put out a soft tee shirt and a pair of old yoga pants for me to wear to bed. I hung up the bathrobe and slipped under the covers.

Exactly as she had committed to doing, Skye came in and checked on me to see if my concussion had worsened. I always roused as she entered the room, because Jack's tail would beat a rapid tattoo. By contrast, Luna would open one eye and go back to sleep.

"You're going to be exhausted tomorrow when you work a full shift at Pumpernickel's," I said, when she peeped in on me around two a.m. If a vote was taken, Skye would win easily as their most popular waitress. On Sundays, she hauled in more tips than most of the other wait staff did over the course of an entire week.

"Don't worry about it. I'll be okay. When I knock off at five, I'll come straight back here and take a nap."

"Geez, but you didn't have to do this. I could have gone to Poppy's house. He could nap all day." I scooted to one side, so she could take a seat on the bed. With a quick move of her feet, she lifted her legs and put her back against the head-board. Like everything in her apartment, the headboard testified to her vast creativity. Skye had purchased two teak wood grates for less than $80 from a nautical salvage shop. Since teak wood is nearly impervious to water, it is the nautical wood of choice. The grates were designed to let in light and air. The small holes were only an inch or two wide. Using metal straps, Skye attached the teak strips to a strip of cheap plywood as wide as her bed and one foot higher than the top of her mattress. Next she glued thin wood molding to three sides and framed the teak pieces. After the assembly, Skye rubbed oil into the wood to bring back its sheen. The finished headboard looked like a million dollars. I asked her to make more of them. Six people have put deposits on customized teak headboards. She's trying to keep up with the demand, but we don't have enough room for her to work on more than one headboard at a time.

"Anyway," I said sleepily, "I'm sorry to have cost you a good night's sleep."

She reached down and stroked my hair. "Getting up during the night is good practice."

"Why? Are you planning to go to med school? I've read how the doctors don't get any sleep during residency."

"Med school? No way. But I imagine I will be waking up at odd hours when the baby comes."

"Baby? But I'm not having a baby. I've decided. I plan to tell Jason when he's back in town next week. I suppose if I was really, truly, madly in love with him, I might consider it. But as much as I like him, I can't see us married. Much less as parents. He's too young for me. Really he is."

She laughed softly.

"Wait!" I sat bolt upright in her bed. "Skye? What are you saying? You weren't talking about me, were you? You didn't mean me. You meant...oh, gosh! Oh, Skye! This is wonderful! It's just grand! Does Lou know? Have you told him? When are you due?"

"Slow down. One question at a time."

"Okay, due date."

"August 21."

"And Lou?"

"He doesn't know yet."

"He is going to be so, so thrilled! He'll be over the moon!"

Her voice was as soft as the dark that surrounded us. "I hope so."

~*~

I slept and slept and slept, waking up only to eat when Skye brought me food. Losing track of time, I woke up raring to go when the sun peeped through the bedroom window. I swung my legs over the side of the bed and as I tried to stand up, I nearly toppled over, face first. Poppy had been right. I was stiff, sore, and exhausted. Had I been obligated to meet him at Harry and the Natives, I would have been in rough shape. As it was, I could barely lift my head.

Skye heard me rustling around and stuck her head in. "Hello, Sleepy Head. Are you feeling better?"

"What day is it?"

"Monday."

"Monday? I lost an entire day?"

"Don't worry. MJ and I took care of the store and your animals yesterday. How are you feeling?"

"Rested. Embarrassed. Ready to get up and be productive."

Skye loaned me undies and a loose fitting pair of velour sweatpants with a matching hooded jacket. Dressing took a lot of energy, even with Skye's help. But whenever my thoughts strayed to Danielle's death or the death of my mermaid, I distracted myself with one little word: Baby.

Skye was going to have a baby!

Her pregnancy was such wonderful news that I would have trouble keeping it to myself, but I'd promised Skye to keep my mouth shut—and I would. She had decided to wait until she was a little further along to tell Lou. After he knew what was up, she planned to tell MJ and Honora.

However, when I heard her retching in the bathroom, I wondered how long she'd be able to keep her secret. I was stripping her bed when she stuck her head inside the door. "Breakfast."

After wadding the sheets into a ball, I stepped into her small kitchen. Despite the smile on her face, she sported a sheen of perspiration from the gyrations of her tummy. "You poor kid. You shouldn't have cooked for me. I remember how the smell of food can turn your stomach."

"Phooey. After I puke, I'm good for an hour or so. Besides, I only made toast and tea. Sorry, but my cupboard is bare."

"I'm fine with toast and tea. Thanks again for taking care of me."

She lifted Jack to her lap so I could eat in peace, while she nibbled at Saltine crackers. He loves anything that goes crunch. The crackers and toast did just that, so he was a real pest.

"I'm so happy about your baby."

"So am I. I've decided that even if Lou doesn't want to be involved, I'm keeping this child. I don't have much, but I've been saving every penny on the off-chance this might happen. See, I miscarried back when I was married, thanks to a couple of swift kicks from Bucky. The doctor said I'd never be able to get pregnant, and I'd given up praying for a miracle. But now I have one."

"Do you really think that Lou won't be happy? Has he ever said he doesn't want a child? He's really nothing but a big, sweet teddy bear."

"I don't want to be disappointed, so I've steeled myself for the worst. Men can be strange when it comes to obligations. I don't want to be a burden. Or be dependent ever again. It's best not to hope, right? Lou might not want me now that I'm pregnant. You know how it is. Some men have that weird thinking about pregnant women being fat and all. So, I'm preparing myself for rejection. Just in case."

Those blue eyes had seen so much pain. I couldn't keep my opinions to myself. "But if you don't hope, if you don't trust, you lose all the joy of the moment. This is a joyful time! If you're waiting to tell him then you can't enjoy this pregnancy until you do. Don't you think this baby deserves a happy mother?"

She swallowed, her Adam's apple moving in that slender throat. A gleam told me she was near to tears. "My prayer is that my baby will have a happy mother and a happy father. But if the baby can only have one, it's up to me, right?"

I hugged her. "And you are not alone. You have friends who love you."

"What are your plans for the day?" Skye asked, as she wiped her eyes with a trembling hand. "I know Tommy is arriving later."

My response was interrupted by Jack's warning bark and a knock on her door. Skye bounced up to answer it.

"Can we move this party downstairs?" My grandfather shifted his weight from one foot to the other. "There ain't much room here, and I done brought us all a box of donuts."

"Where's Sid?" I asked.

"Sid's taking the morning off. Maybe even the whole day. He gets tired easily," said Poppy. "We went and picked up his computer yesterday after breakfast."

"How'd that go?" I started toward the stairway. Skye turned off the lights and shut her door.

Poppy shook his head. "Them slum landlords deserve to be shot. His pal's living in a dump. We didn't even go in. Sid messaged him, and he done brought the computer to the truck. When we got home, Sid spent hours checking and double-checking to see if any harm had been done."

"Had it?" I barely trusted myself to ask. Skye fell in step behind us, being patient as I slowly worked my way down the steps.

"Not that we could see. His paycheck's missing, but I told him you can replace that. Still, the other kid—Sid's friend—was awfully closed-mouthed about the whole adventure. He claims that Sid's mother and one of her friends borrowed the computer and then brought it back. Guess the two of 'em were giddy when they did. Laughing so hard he said one of them wet herself."

The stairs proved to be a challenge. I winced with each step, even though Poppy took a lot of weight off my legs by keeping one arm around my waist.

"You aren't sore?" I asked him.

"You didn't soak in them Epsom salt did you?"

"She did," said Skye.

"Poppy, Skye took wonderful care of me. Yes, I soaked in Epsom salt but I slept clear through Sunday. Don't worry. Tonight I'll have another nice, long, hot bath."

"I intend to see to it. I decided Sid and I are gonna go over to your house so we're there when Tommy comes home. Them two boys ought to get along just fine."

I didn't argue with him. I missed having a house full of young men eating pizzas, playing video games, and watching sports on TV.

A ding from the back room signaled that the dryer was finished.

"Those are your clothes, Cara," said Skye. "I think I got all the blood out. I had to run them through the wash several times." Racing around us, she flew down the steps. By the time we made it into the back room, she was whisking the clothes from the dryer. She held them up so I could see that they were, indeed, free of ugly bloodstains.

MJ threw open the back door. "Another day another dead person, hey, Cara? Your escapade at the hospital is all over the news. I heard you almost got your neck slashed. Wow. Good thing you've got lots of bandages on those cuts. The news reports brought in all sorts of customers and thrill-seekers who wanted to see 'Stuart's answer to Batman and Robin,' which I personally do not think is flattering. If the reporters called you Mrs. Peel and John Steed, I'd be thrilled, but not Batman and Robin. Not cool. Not at all."

She sounded amused, but her eyes searched mine with the sort of concern I knew she was capable of. MJ would never be warm and fuzzy, but she definitely cared about me.

Folding my things carefully, Skye patted the articles of clothes. "I can't see Emma Peel wearing Lilly Pulitzer, but maybe I'm short on imagination, hmm? Cara? I put that earring inside this empty pill bottle. I tucked it back into your pocket. The post had gotten jammed into the seam."

Poppy had chowed down on the donuts, pausing only long enough to pour himself more coffee. Now his head shot up and he looked at me thoughtfully. "What earring?"

I explained about the piece of costume jewelry I'd found in the pocket of Binky Rutherford's dress. "I could have sworn that it wasn't there when Danielle originally brought me the dress. But then it magically appeared after Honora and I tried to hand the dress back to Binky. Matter of fact, we actually did hand her the dress, before she closed the door in our faces, opened it, and gave me back the dress while I was standing on her doorstep."

"I've been thinking about that," said MJ, as she poured herself a cup of coffee. "Especially after Skye showed me the earring. Danielle delivered that dress in a Paramount Dry Cleaner's bag. Paramount is known for being meticulous, because it's the closest dry cleaner to Jupiter Island, and their customers are picky. Very picky. Good dry cleaners empty out all the pockets of a garment and put them in a small paper bag. I've gotten back dresses with a ticket stub they found. That earring is chunky. No way could they have overlooked it."

I pinched the bridge of my nose, trying to stave off the headache that threatened. "I don't understand what you are saying."

"Let me see that there piece of jewelry," said my grandfather.

Skye retrieved the pill bottle with the earring inside and handed it to Poppy.

Poppy rubbed the slender silver post between his fingers and rotated the earring to look it over. "Granddaughter, did Binky say anything to you when she handed back the dress? Anything at all?"

Closing my eyes, I went back in time. Bit by bit, the conversation came to me. "Just something stupid."

"Tell me word for word."

"She said, 'Tell Dick that I've been seeing Samuel Morse on the south end of the island.'"

"This ain't no ordinary earring," said Poppy. "It's a distress signal."

CHAPTER 38

Poppy would have lit into me, but we were interrupted when Lou knocked on the back door.

The tight expression on his face suggested that he was a man on a mission. After helping himself to coffee and a donut, he pulled up a chair.

"How're you doing, Cara? Dick?"

"Fine." Poppy sounded curt. I could tell he was miffed at me.

"No serious lasting effects? Good, because I have news."

I shot Poppy a sideways glance, wondering if he'd interrupt to share what he'd discovered about the earring, but a slight shake of his head encouraged me to wait.

"I just got a call from Ron Cisco up in Port Saint Lucie. The medical examiner confirms that Danielle Cronin was killed with a knife. The width and length of the blade might be a match for the weapon we took off the creep who attacked you two."

This took a minute to sink in. Poppy understood the correlation faster than I did.

"Then it was connected? That couldn't be a coincidence. Even if it is a commonplace type of knife. I cain't imagine two creeps prowling around this area and causing mischief. You're checking it out, right?" My grandfather's voice carried a healthy dose of urgency.

"Right. We're sending an impression from the knife up to Port Saint Lucie, along with DNA from the assailant. Also been checking the databases. He's bad news, all right. Been arrested several times down in Miami, but always managed to squeak through the system. In fact, his attorney has already been in to see him. He's going to push to get this man out on bail. And we aren't talking about some Lincoln lawyer whose car is his office. This attorney is with one of the best criminal practices in the country. I guess this creep runs with a fast set down on South Beach. Might even be connected to money being laundered through a casino."

"Danielle used to do a lot of partying down in Miami. She told me as much. I had mentioned that Tommy was going to college at U of M, and she laughed about all the good times she had before dropping out of school" I paused, thought a bit, and added, "There was a U of M bumper sticker taped onto the back of the car sitting in Binky Rutherford's driveway. I remember it seemed odd. I mean, why tape up a bumper sticker? Why not stick it to a bumper unless it's temporary? Unless you were trying to blend in on campus?" When my face creased into a frown, the contraction of my muscles caused my throat a great deal of pain. Who knew that you used your neck when you frowned? I didn't.

"Lou, it's still a little early on a Monday, and I was out late last night. What exactly are you trying to say?" MJ raised an eyebrow at him.

"Couple of things. One, this isn't your ordinary, garden-variety creep. He's connected. Got resources in Miami. Cara? You're probably right. He probably prowls the places where U of M students hang out. Two, given his background, we're thinking he was hired to do a job here. And three, there's a connection between Cara's mermaid and Danielle's murder. But I'll be doggone if I know what it is. Not yet at least."

"Yup, well, guess what? I can tell you what's you're missing," said Poppy. "The connection has something to do with that there dress of Cara's."

"What?" I nearly spit out my coffee. "A dress? You've got to be kidding me. Poppy, you can't seriously be suggesting that Danielle was killed for a dress. A vintage Lilly at that. It's not worth a ton of money."

"No, I ain't kidding." He explained to Lou how I'd tried to give the dress back to Binky, only to later find an earring in the pocket. "Binky and I go way back. I get it now. See, when Danielle went to pick up clothes from Binky, Binky knew that giving away that dress would send a signal. All her pals would realize there'd been a mistake. So she made sure the dress would come back to her—or at least that one of her friends would come by and ask about it. And that worked like a charm. When Honora and Cara showed up with that there dress in tow, Binky stuck that there earring in the dress, so she'd have yet another chance at sending up a flare. She also gave Cara a message."

He shot me a disgusted look. "A message my granddaughter didn't think to share with me, 'cause she was so all-fired sure it couldn't be important."

"A message?" Lou repeated. "Cara, you didn't tell me anything about this."

"That's because it was a bunch of nonsense. Come on. She was babbling about an old friend. Give me a break."

"What was the message, Cara? Tell me word for word," said Lou.

"She asked me to tell Poppy that she's been seeing Samuel Morse. I guess he lives on the south side of the island. Okay? It's just a bunch of hooey."

"Samuel Morse has been dead for years," said Skye.

"See?" I persisted. "Binky's mind is slipping."

Skye continued, "But before he died, he invented the Morse code."

Poppy and Lou decided they needed to speak to Police Chief Aaron Reiss, the head of the Stuart Police Department. "The problem is jurisdictional," said my grandfather as he stood to leave. "Binky is on Jupiter Island. Danielle was murdered in Port Saint Lucie. Then we got ourselves attacked here in Stuart. It's a mess."

I listened, but I was totally embarrassed. I'm a real fiend about taking and returning messages. That's one of the few business protocols that I'll get rabid about. But here I sat, face burning with shame because I'd neglected to pass along a message to my grandfather.

"I bet that if you asked a hundred people on the street who Samuel Morse was, none of them could answer." I spoke to everyone and no one, while Skye puttered around in the kitchen and MJ shuffled papers on her desk.

"Probably right," said Skye.

"How did you know?"

"I love Westerns. Someday I want to go see the desert. They always used telegraphs to send messages back then. I read up on Morse code."

"Quit pouting, Cara. It'll give you wrinkles," said MJ. "You've had a rough couple of days, and now it's out of your hands. The long arm of the law will take it from here. Besides, isn't Tommy coming home tonight? You didn't forget, did you?"

"No, I haven't forgotten."

Skye dashed past me to the restroom. The sounds of her heaving filled the small back room.

"Morning sickness. Wonder when she's due and whether Lou knows yet," said MJ in an almost bored sounding tone.

"What?" I'd been saying that a lot and mentally kicked myself. "When did you find out? How long have you known? She doesn't think you know."

"She's been up-chucking for weeks now. Don't tell me you didn't notice?"

"No, I've been a little distracted lately."

Realizing I'd been totally self-centered made me feel awful. Just horrible. And my head hurt. And my neck hurt. And I really, really missed Tommy. I sniffled back a sob and blurted out, "Cooper says his business associates don't want to hire Poppy. They've decided he's too old. That's not what I agreed to. In fact, I bought this place so that Poppy could stay in business—and, and this just isn't fair. Poppy is really depressed. Looking after Sid has been good for him, but what else will he do with his time? What happens when Sid gets well?"

MJ had this way of looking at you that made you feel about as tall as one of Honora's miniature people and every bit as capable. Rather than respond, she let that scathing glare settle over me. Meanwhile I imagined what she was thinking, and it wasn't very pleasant. Whereas, Skye goes out of her way to reassure people, MJ calls it like she sees it—and she does not wear rose-colored glasses. Nope. MJ wears safety glasses because she throws the kitchen sink at you, and she's well prepared for you tossing it right back at her.

"And that's your problem?" MJ gave a mean little laugh. "That's why you aren't paying attention to anyone or anything lately? Because you're fretting about Poppy? What is Poppy? Ten years old? Younger? Mentally challenged? Hel-lo? I think he was doing just fine before you moved down here. I imagine he can take care of himself."

I stuck out my jaw, feeling a strange combination of defiance and relief. "Of course, he can. Don't be silly."

"Silly? I'm not being silly. You, however, are being ridiculous. If you'd stop mooning over Cooper Rivers and move on with your life, you might actually notice what's going on around you. Like the fact our friend is heaving her guts out every morning. Or that Lou has practically moved in with her, but still hasn't gone totally public about being her guy. You might even notice that Sid is worried sick about his computer. Or that I've found a lump in my breast."

A silence hung there between us.

"A lump?" I found my voice. "Are you sure? Have you had it checked out?"

She swallowed twice and cleared her throat. Tears welled in her eyes. MJ is rarely emotional. To see her choked up scared me. I forced myself out of my seat and put my arms around her. After a tick, her head drooped onto my shoulder. "Of course, I'm getting it checked out. I see the doctor tomorrow at eleven. He's going over my mammogram with the radiologist first thing in the morning. My mother died of breast cancer. Who am I, if I don't have a pair of gorgeous knockers to show the world?"

I would have laughed, but I knew she wasn't kidding. Instead, I rocked her in my arms and cooed, "It's going to be all right, MJ. Knockers or no knockers. We're all here for you. What exactly did they find?"

In fits and starts, she explained that her mammogram had shown an abnormality. She'd gone back to have it redone. "Spalding, he's my ob/gyn, won't have the results until tomorrow afternoon."

"It's probably nothing."

"Yeah, but what if it's something? What if they have to cut off a boob? None of my clothes will fit right! I'll need new bras, and I've invested a mint into pretty pieces of worthless lace. And my bathing suits. They won't fit right either." A thin dribble of wetness ran down my neck and burned as it touched the cuts on my throat. That put another level of fright into me. MJ never, ever cries.

"Shhhh," I said. She was talking nonsense, and we both knew it. As random as her comments were, they illustrated her valiant attempt to keep from asking the questions that really worried us both...what if it's cancer?...and did they catch it in time?

CHAPTER 39

When Skye came out of the bathroom, MJ and I carried on like nothing was wrong—and certainly like nothing significant had been shared. Skye walked a little hesitantly and sank down gratefully in a chair. Clearly, she'd been violently ill, because spots of red were the only color in her cheeks. Resting her forehead on her crossed arms, she slumped down onto the table and moaned. MJ brewed her a cup of peppermint tea and filled a small bowl with Saltine crackers. Opening the refrigerator door, she found a plastic tube of minced ginger and stirred that into the tea.

"Just a little stomach bug," Skye said as she raised her head and smiled up at our friend.

"A stomach bug called pregnancy," said MJ.

"Did Cara tell you?" Skye pouted at me.

"I wasn't born yesterday, Skye," said MJ. "You've been puking for the past six weeks. Your boobs are bigger, and you look terrible. Hello? Meanwhile, your apartment reeks of Lou's cologne. I might not be Agatha Christie, but I'm not stupid."

Skye let her head roll onto the back of her chair. "Cara? Will this ever get better?"

"Yes," I said. "Have you talked to your ob/gyn? Does he or she know how sick you're getting? Are you losing weight rather than gaining it?"

"Only five pounds."

"Gaining five pounds isn't much. Your blood volume increases by 40 to 50 percent. That's probably the bulk of the weight gain. But that usually happens over time," I explained.

"Lost it. I lost five pounds," she murmured.

"What?" MJ used my new favorite word. "Skye, are you kidding? You've lost five pounds? And you haven't talked to your doctor? In how long? That's not good."

Skye shook her head. "I've been meaning to, but between work and the store, I haven't had the chance. Besides, this is what they call a self-limiting condition isn't it? It'll run its course."

"Not if you let it sap all your energy." I got up, grabbed the landline phone, and handed it to her. "Make the call. Do it now."

With a groan, Skye punched in a number. MJ and I listened while she explained to the receptionist what her problem was. After the recitation, she didn't say a word. Not for the rest of the call until she said, "Thank you. Goodbye."

MJ slammed herself into the chair next to Skye. "Excuse me? Did she fob you off?"

"Skye, please tell us that the receptionist told you to come in so they could check you. Please?"

She traced a pattern on the table top with her index finger. "Not exactly. She told me to drink a lot of water. To switch to Pedialyte if I needed to. Although I tried that and couldn't choke it down. Oh, and to drink soup."

"That's all?" asked MJ, grabbing the phone. Her fingers flew on the number pad.

"Elizabeth? MJ Austin here. Put Spalding on the line. Right now. Immediately."

Skye's face reflected the shock in my own. I would never, ever talk to a receptionist like that. I treat them like they're the Swiss guards in front of the Vatican. But truth to tell, it's harder to get past a receptionist in a doctor's office than to connect with the president of my bank. He'll answer my call any day. But my doctor? No way. I have to beg and plead with his receptionist Martha to get a message to Dr. Simmons. When I do, he usually doesn't call until the next day. More than once, I've wound up in the ER or at a doc-in-the-box because I couldn't get in touch with my own GP.

But MJ knew exactly what she was doing. In short order, she was connected to a man who sounded completely at her disposal. "Spalding? It's me. No, I'll see you tomorrow. I'm fine, but a friend needs help. She has morning sickness. Lost five pounds in six weeks. I know; how crazy is that? Her doc's a fool. When can you see her? This afternoon? Right. At two? We'll be there. Gatorade? Ginger ale? Got it. Will do. See ya."

And that was that.

Skye insisted on working her shift at Pumpernickel's. "Babies are expensive," she said as she headed for the front door. At least she left with her pockets stuffed full of soda crackers.

The store wouldn't open for another half an hour, and there was no point to wasting time. I put on the clothes Skye had washed for me and set up the machine for a second pot of coffee. "MJ? Let's brainstorm what we can do for Valentine's Day," I said. "It'll take our minds off..." and I caught myself.

MJ gave me a terse look. "Take our minds off all these distractions. Boy, let me loan you a scarf, Cara. Your neck looks awful."

"Thanks," I said as I wound the soft fabric around my throat.

We'd no more than pulled up a few ideas on Pinterest when we heard car doors slam outside. A happy Honora showed up with EveLynn two inches behind her. EveLynn has no sense of personal space, so she's usually tailgating her mother. Honora handles her daughter's deficits with grace, but it can't be easy. Being around EveLynn tires me out. Living with her would drive me insane.

"Cara, I heard about your close call at the hospital. So you and Dick are heroes! Are you all right?"

"Mainly. I'm a bit sore." I tried to smile. "Thanks for working the store yesterday."

"You're welcome. Epsom salt. That's the ticket. Be sure to soak in it. Remember our visit to the bridge club, Cara?" Honora chirped like a little bird in her naturally high-pitched and crisp voice. "You'll recall that I handed out those order forms? So far I've gotten six of them back. Can you believe that? Six custom orders. I took one while the customer was standing here in the shop. That makes seven. Sid's not here, is he? Not yet? Oh, dear, then MJ, will you input them? We don't want to let any grass grow under our feet, even if it is miniature carpeting. Once we get the deposits, I'll get them started. Isn't that glorious?"

Her sunny mood contrasted with the somber concern MJ and I had about Skye's weight loss.

As for MJ, I had promised to keep her condition a secret. Maybe there would be good news tomorrow, after the specialist had taken another look at her mammogram. At least she was under a doctor's care. Sure, I could worry, but what good would it do? In the face of Honora's good news, I did my best to act appropriately pleased and not as fractious as I felt.

EveLynn helped herself to a can of cola from our refrigerator and snarfed down the last two donuts left in the box that Poppy had brought. I didn't care. She was welcome to them.

When Kookie screeched from his perch on the sales floor, it dawned on me that I hadn't flipped the sign to read OPEN. Hustling to do so, I discovered four people waiting to get inside. I couldn't believe I'd been so negligent. Kookie couldn't either. "Bad Cara," he said.

I have no idea where he learned that phrase, and I'm not sure I want to know either. Instead, I jingled his toy bell. That distracted him and the huge white cockatoo set about the serious work of playing.

I greeted all the shoppers, but I was especially happy to see Jessie

Dimovski. I knew she'd been born in Bombay, India, but grown up in Pennsylvania. Whenever possible, she came down here to take long walks on the beach and collect sea glass. Usually she and Skye would put their heads together and come up with new ideas for displaying the pitted pieces that washed up in the surf. We were lingering over the display of our coconut scented bath products, when Claudia came running in as if being chased by a pack of wild badgers. "Cara, catch! It's the key to Vintage Threads."

A silver blur flew through the air. I caught it rather than let it drop onto the floor. "Excuse me? I missed something. Why are you giving me this? Are you ducking out and you need me to unlock the shop? What's up?"

"I'm leaving. Gone. Outta here. Gassed up my car and I'm leaving town."

"But why? With Danielle gone…" I kept my voice low so as not to alert my customers to a problem. I knew Jessie was a keen reader of mysteries, so it wouldn't spook her, but the others might decide to leave immediately.

"That's the point." Claudia pulled me to one side and whispered urgently in my ear. "I just found out that the dude who knifed Danielle was a Miami hit man. See, he came into the shop and asked for Danielle on Saturday. About an hour before you showed up. I wasn't going to tell him where she lived, but he…" and her voice trailed off. Covering her head with her arms, she wailed. The keening noise caused my shoppers to turn and stare at us. Even Jessie looked shocked. I took Claudia by one hand, peeling her arm away from her head, and hustled her upstairs. After we ducked into my old apartment, I sat her down in a folding chair.

"You told him where Danielle lived?" I couldn't believe what I was hearing. "Why on earth would you share personal information like that?"

"H-h-he already knew she lived in Port Saint Lucie, but not where, and I, uh, I was busy on my phone. See, Emma's boyfriend Dallas broke up with her and they've been going together since—" She stopped to sniffle. "And Emma really, really needed to talk to me because we're best friends, and she thinks that Dallas was—"

"Focus, Claudia. What exactly did you tell the man who was asking about Danielle?"

"Nothing. I mean, not much. See, at first I told him no, I wouldn't share her address, but he kept asking. I wanted him to go away and quit bothering me. He was a real pest—and we had customers. Lots and lots of customers. How would I know he wanted to hurt her? He looked like someone she would have the hots for! He was her kind of guy."

Mascara dripped down her face, leaving inky trails and gray smudges. For all her stupidity, her grief was genuine. Without the thick face paint, I could see she was younger than I'd guessed. Early twenties at most. I forced myself not to respond, to think, rather than let my feelings take the lead, because my first impulse was to smack her hard. I'd witnessed her slavish devotion to her cell phone. I knew she was trying to excuse the fact she hadn't wanted to be bothered. She'd told the man what he wanted to know because she'd been eager to get back to her cell phone.

But a hard slap wouldn't bring Danielle back.

"Did you tell the police about his visit? Claudia, this is important."

"No. I lied to them. Told them you were the only person who asked about Danielle. I was scared."

"And how do you know he's from Miami?"

"He said so. He said that he and Danielle used to go clubbing together."

Wow. My head hurt and I was having trouble keeping track of what Claudia was saying. I pressed my fingers to my temples and tried to focus. "Claudia, listen to me. You have to tell the police about this. They don't know for sure if the man who killed Danielle is the same person who cut me up, but they think so. And yes, they think the guy is from Miami. But here's the really bad part. Whoever he is, he's connected. He's got an attorney trying to get him out on bail. For your own safety, you need to tell the police exactly what you know. Maybe they can keep him off the streets."

"No way. I'm out of here. Not my problem." She darted to my left and then to my right, trying to get around me so she could run downstairs.

I grabbed her by the shoulders. "Claudia, listen to me. Do you know why he killed Danielle? Did he say anything else? Do you know what he was after?"

"It was that dress," she said. "That stupid, stupid dress."

I tried to hold her in place, but she fought me. Claudia kept sending pitiful glances at the stairs. Meanwhile, I did my best to reason with her.

"Why on earth would a guy care about my stupid dress?"

"He asked me where Danielle got that dress you had. I told him I didn't know—and I didn't. Because I don't! See, Danielle was really sneaky about her clients. She didn't share names with me, because she once had this clerk who went and opened her own shop over in Salerno. But he kept after me. He said he was just curious. I asked him why he cared. And he said there'd been a mistake concerning the dress, and he needed to see Danielle to get things straightened out. And that they used to be friends back in Miami. So I told him where she lived. Big deal! He could have gotten it off the internet. It isn't my fault that he killed her!"

Wrenching herself free of my grasp, Claudia tore away. Before I could stop her, she was galloping down the stairs. I did my best to follow, but on my stiff legs, I needed to grip the railing and hobble my way along. That slowed me down. I was halfway down the staircase when I heard the front door slam. Rather than try to follow Claudia, I turned around and went back to my apartment. Sure enough, from the window there, I could see Claudia running across the street.

I couldn't chase after her. Shoot. I could barely walk at a snail's pace. It was hopeless.

There in the privacy of my old apartment, I phoned Lou. He listened while I explained what happened.

"Do you happen to have this Claudia's last name?"

"No." Boy, did I feel dumb. The simplest piece of information, and I'd neglected to ask for it.

"It might be better in the long haul for her to leave town," he said. "We've got the guy, for the time being. But who knows what he's said to his pals? And we don't really know why he killed Danielle yet. Why murder someone over a dress? We're missing one of the pieces. This is a puzzle that doesn't make sense."

After hanging up, I moved slowly down the stairs. My muscles screamed in protest, but I gritted my teeth. The store was teaming with customers, all fingering the merchandise, picking it up and showing it to each other. Jessie had left. I was really disappointed that I hadn't had the chance to chat longer with her.

MJ was busy talking to a couple who wanted to buy a Highwayman painting. Honora carefully stacked more of her daughter's table runners on an old ladder we used to display the soft goods. When Honora noticed me, she toddled over.

"Cara darling, I am worried about Skye. She's been suffering terribly from morning sickness. We need to keep an eye on her. She's lost a lot of weight."

Really?

I considered Skye my best friend, next to Kiki Lowenstein, who lived up in St. Louis. Yet I was the only person in our little tribe who hadn't noticed that Skye was going to have a baby.

Some pal I was.

CHAPTER 40

Poppy called. "What time is Tommy gonna arrive?"

"I'm not sure. Sometime after his tests. He was going to use his Uber app or take the train. I'm expecting a text from him."

"Tell you what. I'll text Tommy and see what his ETA is. Then we'll meet him over at your house. I'll order pizza for the boys. Maybe even take them fishing. You can take your time closing up the store. That'll give me some time with them boys."

"Sounds like a plan." I texted Tommy to tell him what Poppy had proposed. He sent me back a one-word message: *Gr8.*

Tommy had been close to my father, his namesake, and I knew he missed my dad terribly. Poppy would have big shoes to fill, but both he and my son needed each other. I was glad that Poppy was making an effort.

An hour passed and we had a lull in foot traffic. I dug around in the recycling bin and found the dry cleaner's bag. I planned to return the dress exactly as I found it. Okay, so I'd worn it once. Big deal. That would be Binky's problem.

How odd it is that we imbue inanimate objects with power. Perhaps it is a testament to our lack of humility as a species, because certainly we are not gods. We cannot create life and spirit and will where there is none. Yet we do. I had had such high hopes for this dress. I'd planned to wear it and feel beautiful and sexy. My sister had ruined my vision of myself when she told me the dress turned me into a dowdy old woman. Jodi would know. Almost every man I'd dated had fallen for her.

Whatever.

I tucked the dress into the bag and ducked into the downstairs bathroom where we kept a big bottle of Advil. My head felt like I was playing hostess to a garage band. After chugging water from the faucet and swallowing the pills, I pressed a damp washcloth to my eyes. Leaning against the wall, I felt my phone vibrating in my skirt pocket.

I expected it to be Tommy, telling me he'd finished his tests and was on his way. With fumbling fingers, I answered my phone.

"Cara? Doug Fogarty here from First Midwestern Bank. How are you?"

I could count on one hand the number of times the president of the bank we used back in St. Louis has called me. Doug and I went to high school together. His father and mine had been good friends. Dad believed in doing business with people you knew. Douglas, as the senior Fogarty had been called, often came to the restaurant via the back door. He'd sit on a stool in the kitchen and talk to my father as he cooked. His son, Douglas Junior or Doug, had followed in his father's footsteps.

"How nice to hear from you, Doug," I said.

"Glad you think so," his voice warmed up as he spoke. "Because I'm troubled, Cara. Deeply concerned. What have we done to offend you?"

This caught me off guard. I dropped the washcloth, bent to retrieve it, and noticed my puzzled face in the bathroom mirror. "Pardon? I'm not sure I follow. Could you give me more information, Doug?"

My father had taught me that before answering an important question, you should always know exactly what is being asked. That line—"Can you give me more information?"—proved to be a powerful tool. Without it, I had a tendency to formulate a response before fully understanding what had been asked of me.

"I won't beat around the bush. I'm calling to verify this ACH. Usually we let things like this go through, but this is such an abnormally large amount, I thought I should give you a jingle."

"Come again?" Gently lowering the toilet seat, I sat on top of it, turning the small bathroom into my temporary office. Doug's comments totally bewildered me. "Doug, I don't know what you are talking about."

He proceeded to scare the dickens out of me by explaining that they'd received a request for an ACH transfer. "It's almost all the money you have in your account, so I thought I'd better ask. To make sure you approve of this, and to make sure you're okay. As a friend. An old family friend and schoolmate."

For a moment, I thought I'd faint, because tiny stars danced before my eyes as my field of vision turned black. Instead, I pressed the washcloth to the back of my neck.

"But you stopped the transfer? Please tell me you did?"

"I had the day off yesterday. I came in and saw this transaction. Are you saying you don't want it to go through?"

"Right. I do not want the money taken out of my account. I did not authorize any such transaction."

"Okay, then I better get off the phone and see if I can stop this."

The line went dead.

A full-blown panic sucked me down into a black hole. But I couldn't stay in the bathroom for long. Not in the middle of the day. Especially since I'd been AWOL all of Sunday.

A new clutch of customers kept me busy for the next half hour. They left and more customers wandered in. Sweat trickled down my back as I took sneaky looks at the clock on my phone. Thirty minutes. Forty. Forty-five. Finally an hour had passed.

My phone rang and I answered it on the first ring, excusing myself from the woman who'd spent a hundred bucks on one of Skye's driftwood holiday trees.

"I managed to reverse the transaction," Doug said. "The funds hadn't cleared our bank yet. But I'm totally confused. According to Beth Landis, who was processing the transfer, you two were on the phone yesterday—and you insisted that she move the money immediately."

"I never made that call, Doug. I didn't authorize any money to come out of my account. How could this have happened?" On shaking legs, I walked past customers, past Honora, and into the back room.

"It's actually remarkably simple. If you own a business and if you don't have specific controls on your account to require authorization, and someone makes an ACH request, the money just comes out of your account. If you don't catch it in the first 48 hours, you have very little legal recourse as a business. The rules are more protective for individuals and provide you more time to dispute incorrect charges."

Reaching into the refrigerator, I grabbed a Diet Dr Pepper and popped the top. At my friend Kiki Lowenstein's store, she kept a stash of Dr Pepper. It became the "go to" drink for any crisis. Tasting the bubbling brew brought me a sense of camaraderie, as though Kiki was standing right there beside me with one hand on my shoulder. The sweet taste made me feel marginally better. I drained the can in nothing flat and tossed it into the recycling bin. It landed with a clatter.

"I was afraid something like this might happen," I told Doug. "Recently my computer guy, Sid, had his computer stolen, but he's assured me that he has everything password protected. I figured that if people couldn't get into the computer, I was safe."

"Look. This isn't because of his computer. All the information a person would need would be on a paycheck or a bank statement."

"Oh, my gosh. Sid had just gotten paid. His paycheck was in his backpack. He told me it was missing, but I didn't realize!"

"There's more to this. The person who called—pretending to be you—had more information than that. Whoever did this was someone with access to your personal information. Date of birth. Where you were born. All of that. One of us should call the police. They might be able to trace the person through phone records."

"How about if you initiate it? And let me know what you find out?"

"Will do."

"Okay, what do we need to do so this never happens again?"

He walked me through a series of steps. I ended the call after thanking him profusely. Using the extra makeup in the bathroom that we keep there just for such purposes, I fixed my face. Squaring my shoulders, I went back out onto the sales floor.

Honora didn't ask me what was wrong. She took a long look, hugged me and said, "You'll survive, dear girl. Whatever it was. Whatever it is. You'll survive."

"You've got that right," I said.

Amberlee was going down.

CHAPTER 41

I told MJ and Honora about the ACH. "Had Doug called twenty-four hours later, I would have been toast."

"What does ACH stand for?" asked Honora.

"Automated Clearing House. It's an electronic network for processing financial transactions."

"You're sure it's Amberlee behind all this?" wondered MJ as she frowned at a chipped red fingernail. "My impression has always been that she isn't very bright. I don't think she's ever had a real job. How would she know enough to pull this off?"

Honora eased off her stool. "You don't want to jump to conclusions, Cara."

I swallowed a sharp retort. Sure, I now knew that there'd been a back door to my bank account. With Doug's help, there would never be another ACH transfer without my knowledge. But I didn't know what I didn't know. What if there was yet another sneaky way to siphon off my funds? What if this time I couldn't reverse the damage in time? A momentary wave of panic swept through me.

"Who else could have done this? Sid's pal who was holding his computer?" I shrugged, trying not to seem as frightened as I was. "Could be, but doubtful. There was an adult woman behind this, and Amberlee took Sid's computer. Doesn't take a rocket scientist to figure this out."

"Actually, I dated a rocket scientist. They aren't all that smart." MJ fished around in her purse, grabbed a bottle of nail polish and fixed the chip. "You should tell Nathan about this."

"No. I don't want Nathan more involved in my business." I paused when her expression turned sour. "It's nothing personal. He's fine. Honest, he is. But I don't need his help. Not yet. He has more important things to attend to. I need to wait to hear back from Doug. He's initiating things on his end."

"Then talk to Lou," said Skye as she walked into the back room. "He was still eating his lunch when I left the deli."

"Did you tell him about the baby?" MJ asked.

"No. I couldn't. I feel beaten down," admitted Skye. "Getting sick has really taken a toll on me."

"You need to stay strong for your baby's sake," I said, as I patted my friend on the back. Usually Skye's a bit taller than I, but today the weight of her worries stooped her shoulders as if she was trying to curl into a ball.

"Cara is absolutely right," said Honora.

"I'm afraid my first doc will be angry with me. I called him to say I was getting a second opinion, and his nurse chewed me out."

"Those people have a lot of nerve," I said.

"You have to do what's best for your health and the health of your baby. Remember that your doctor has hundreds of other patients, but you only have one baby to worry about." Honora took Skye by the hand and squeezed it.

"You're right, Honora," Skye said as she lifted her chin. "I hadn't thought of it that way. If my old ob/gyn is angry, that's his problem not mine. My baby is my first priority."

"Keep repeating that," suggested MJ as she dangled her keys. "Your baby, your first priority. She or he will never have a better advocate than you."

"Well said." I wanted to consider the matter finished, but then a thought sprang into my mind. "But even so. Skye, why didn't you tell Lou where you were going when you left the deli? Seems like an ideal situation."

"Because I miscarried before. It could happen again. No need to tell him until I know for sure that I get to keep this baby." But Skye didn't look us in the eyes.

"You shouldn't lose it unless you get kicked in the tummy again," MJ said.

Trust her to be blunt to the point of hurtful.

Skye lifted one shoulder and let it drop. "Okay, I'll say it: I'm scared. I'm worried about Lou's reaction. I didn't mention the pregnancy when he was at Pumpernickel's because I didn't want him going all weird on me out in public."

"He might get weird, but eventually, he's going to be thrilled," said MJ. "Maybe not at first, because most men aren't thrilled at first. Promise me you won't let his first reaction ruin this for both of you. Because he will be happy. Sooner or later. Although not right away. Just give it time. Men are much more delicate than we are. Much more prone to worrying and feeling skittish."

Skye refused to look at us, and that made me more worried. Did she have a valid reason to think Lou would be unhappy? Or was she simply feeling hormonal? Was it something as simple as the normal nervous jitters every woman gets with a first baby?

"I need to use the restroom before we go to the doctor's," said Skye. "Be right back."

"Your advice about Lou getting weird was perfect," I said to MJ. "That was very wise of you."

"Wisdom born of pain," said MJ. "It's the kind of smarts you'd rather not have, believe me. Experience is a cruel teacher."

"I didn't know you'd ever been pregnant." The words were out of my mouth before I had a chance to stop them. Honora quickly turned away, pretending not to have overhead. The toilet flushed and Skye rejoined us.

MJ's eyes skewered me and her voice was cold. "Just because I don't have a child doesn't mean I wasn't ever pregnant."

~*~

At closing time, Skye and MJ still hadn't returned. A red sunset burned up the horizon, reducing a nearby palm tree to a black silhouette. My mind got hooked on that old saying, "Red sky at night; Sailors delight. Red sky in the morning; Sailors take warning." But it didn't seem correct. Not tonight. Especially given how ominous the atmosphere had turned. The natural world was churning, twisting, and gearing up for a big change. Splatters of rain tapped on the display window. The wind picked up, blowing loose palm fronds end over end down the street. A thin plastic grocery bag did a slow waltz until it caught in the mandevilla bushes in the glazed pots at the store's front door. Before I flipped the sign to CLOSED I reached down and grabbed the bag.

"I wish that they were back from the ob/gyn's office," I said to Honora.

"I'm sure that if there was a problem, MJ would have phoned." Honora unfurled her plastic rain bonnet. With great care, she tucked it over her straw boater. "Don't fret so, Cara dear. There's EveLynn. I'm off. Have a good evening, dear."

I followed our usual closing routine, but as I covered Kookie's cage, he said, "Kookie loves Skye. Where is Skye? Kookie loves her."

A lump formed in my throat. When we adopted Kookie, the big white cockatoo had been in mourning for his original mistress. Pete, the vet, hadn't expected Kookie to recover from his grief, but the bird had, thanks to Skye's loving ministrations. I'd never heard Kookie call out to Skye. It touched me that the bird was worried about his new mistress. I'm still afraid of birds—it's a leftover reaction from a childhood trauma—but Kookie and I have signed a peace treaty. As he called out for my friend, he bowed his head, a sign he wanted me to rub it. Warily, I extended my hand and did as the bird requested. He muttered happy silly endearments as I told him, "Skye is coming back. Skye loves Kookie. It's okay, big guy."

The bird's plaintive cry echoed in my head all the way to Jupiter Island. The sound of the rain, the howl of the wind, the gray of the sky compounded my worries. Hanging behind me was the brightly colored Lilly Pulitzer dress, swaying inside the plastic drycleaner's bag.

Despite the rain, Jack beelined past Poppy's truck and pranced to my front door. Luna allowed me to tuck her under my blouse to keep her head dry.

The odd voices of a video game greeted me before I even turned the key. So did the pungent smell of fish. A frying pan, dirty dishes, half-filled glasses, empty cola cans, and various pieces of cutlery littered my kitchen counter. Living alone, I'd become unaccustomed to messes like this, but I reminded myself this was actually more normal than my usual tidiness. In the living room, Sid and Tommy shouted encouragements to Poppy as he attempted to navigate his character through a fight with a baron.

"Mom! We're playing League of Legends. Poppy is catching on pretty good for an old geezer." Tommy popped up to give me a quick peck on the cheek.

Empty Domino's Pizza boxes littered my makeshift coffee table of two wine boxes turned upside down. Sid beamed a happy smile toward me, the first I'd seen in a long while. After a quick change into jeans and a "Life Is Good" tee, I fed Jack. The jeers in the next room suggested that Poppy's character had died. He ambled into the kitchen. "Sorry about the mess. We was down at the beach and having a good time until that there rain drenched us."

That meant that Sid was managing his crutches better. A good sign indeed. While Jack gobbled down a dish of food, I told Poppy about my afternoon.

"Thank goodness that banker knew you."

I agreed. "Let's face it: There's no substitute for personal relationships. Even in this age of computer connections. But the weirdest part of my day was Claudia's visit."

I told him what Claudia had said.

"I figured that Danielle musta told Binky that she wanted that dress for my granddaughter. When she heard who you were, Binky must have been hoping you'd take a message to me, and that I'd figure out what's what. And I woulda a lot faster if—"

"Okay. All right. Could we just move on?"

"Your dog need to go out? It's almost dark. I was planning to drive to the south end of the island and watch for a signal."

"If you really think she's in danger, why not call the island police?"

"It ain't Binky that I'm worried about. She can take care of herself." He stopped himself, as he searched for the right words. "Binky has had special training."

"In what? Bridge?" I hooted with laughter.

"Granddaughter, don't you know anything? The CIA was born on Jupiter Island. Binky and her husband were two of their first recruits."

CHAPTER 42

For a place only a half-mile wide and less than ten miles long, this island harbors more than its share of secrets. At first, I thought that Poppy was kidding me about Jupiter Island being the birthplace of the CIA. Rather than contradict my grandfather, I grabbed my dog and his leash. The boys scarcely looked up when I told them that Poppy and I were going for a quick drive.

"Okay, you have a lot of explaining to do," I said as my grandfather pulled out of my driveway. The rain had slowed to a drizzle. My lightweight waterproof jacket rested on my lap, but I was loathe to put it on. In the closed quarters of the truck, the coat would function like a sauna. "How on earth is it remotely possible that the CIA started here? It's a government agency. By definition, one might surmise it would have been born in Washington, D.C."

"Yup, and one might be wrong. Back in 1931, the Reed family owned the whole island. Joseph and Parmelia Pryor Reed were friends with Prescott Bush, George Walker, Robert Lovett, and the Harriman family. A bunch of 'em had been members of Yale's Skull and Bones Society. All of 'em came here to visit or had residences nearby. After the war—"

"Which war?"

"What do you mean, Which war?"

"There's World War I, World War II, Korea, Vietnam, Iraq, and—"

"We'll never learn, will we? After World War II," said my grandfather with a sniff of derision, "Lovett testified about how useful the FBI had been in creating false documents. What they'd done had been important. He argued that we ought, as a nation, to pick up where we'd left off with the OSS."

"And what is the OSS?"

"The Office of Strategic Services. Only, the military didn't like that idea one bit. General Douglas MacArthur gave it a big thumbs down, but then he and Truman didn't always see eye-to-eye, so maybe his opinion just gave Lovett's brain-child a good push down the birth canal. His pal Averill Harriman was also a resident on the island, and Harriman was 'ambassador at large' to Europe at the time. Harriman, like a lot of us, wondered if psychological defense was an area we needed to understand better as a nation. After all, how did a bunch of jackbooted thugs take over a civilized culture like the Germans? It surely had to be all that psychological mumbo-jumbo, because it defied common decency and good sense. Of course, Harriman and Lovett played golf with Prescott Bush, who employed Joseph Reed. Reed had been a specialist during the war in codes and espionage, so it ain't surprising he was right there agreeing how we needed a secret agency inside our government. That's Bush, the father of George H. W. Bush. When they weren't on the golf course, they were—"

"Poppy, you've totally lost me."

"Might be for the best. What you don't know can't hurt you if you're attending some swanky event here on the island," he said, taking a quick right onto Laurel before bumping us over the railroad tracks. After we turned the corner at Old Dixie, he pulled his truck onto the side of the road.

I couldn't imagine attending a "swanky event on the island," but I was happy for Poppy to stop yammering on about people whose names I could barely recall from history class. The fine mist turned the black asphalt into an imprecise re-flection of our surroundings. I found it difficult to see, and I figured that Poppy did, too.

"I hope you realized that we passed the turn for Binky's place awhile back."

"I know that. Remember, how Binky said that Samuel was on the south end of the island? She was telling me to come this-a way. Yonder is the highest spot on the south side. Good thing you got your legs covered, because there ain't no clear pathway. Put on that windbreaker of yours. We need to scramble up this hill and wait."

"In the rain?"

"You afraid you'll melt?"

"Not hardly."

"Then quit acting like you're some delicate flower."

"What about Jack?" I held my little buddy tightly.

"It'll be a fine adventure for him. I'll stuff him inside my shirt."

Jack was surprisingly amenable to the arrangement. Poppy buttoned up, pulled on a waxed jacket that zipped up. Only the Chihuahua's head stuck out. As I watched, Poppy pulled two ultra-thin silver squares from under the driver's seat. "Space age technology. Jack knew what he was doing."

"Jack? My Jack?"

"Kennedy."

Climbing at a 45-degree angle isn't easy in daylight. Climbing it in the dark with a light rain falling is not something I'd do for fun. A full moon lit up the ground now and then, when the cloud cover shifted. Otherwise, I might not have made it. Poppy reached back to help me several times.

"Ouch!" I yelled as I set my hand palm side down on a cactus plant. Poppy held the beam of a small flashlight toward my skin while I extracted two large thorns. *Opuntias,* or prickly pears, are native to Florida. I'd actually transplanted a few small ones into containers on my porch. There I admired their beautiful oval shapes and yellow blossoms. Here, under my skin, I didn't think much of them. The thorns stung like crazy.

At the top, our efforts were rewarded by the view, which took my breath away. Silver moonbeams glinted on the Intracoastal, sending a tinsel strand our way. Smaller dimples of light winked as the water rippled. The muffled clanging of boats against the docks drifted our way, as did the rumble of sporadic car tires traveling along Old Dixie. In the distance, a dog barked.

"What now?" I asked.

"We wait." Poppy handed me Jack and unfurled one of the silver blankets. The thin square covered a surprising amount of ground. After we plonked down on it, he opened up the second square and tossed it over our heads to form a makeshift tent.

"Come here, young un." Poppy slung an arm around my shoulders so I could lean into him. In the silence and the dark, secure in the watchful presence of my grandfather, a sense of peace came over me.

I dozed off with my head resting against Poppy's shoulder. Jack curled up in my lap. I probably only had been sleeping for twenty minutes when a sudden movement of his body jerked me into consciousness. He rose to his feet with surprising nimbleness. Jack stared out into the darkness and whimpered.

"There she blows," Poppy said.

The flashes seemed indistinct to me, but my grandfather watched intently.

"That's a message?"

"You bet your bippy, it is. Like riding a bike. Reading and sending Morse code comes right back to you."

We stood there. The mist and rain had turned into a fog that expanded the halo of the streetlights. During my brief nap, the world had become more phantasmagoric, more indistinct and unreal. The scent of wet cotton drifted up from my jeans. It mingled with the fragrance of greenery we had crushed under our feet, causing it to die with a small gasp of sadness at being trampled.

Was it possible I was dreaming? How on earth had I wound up standing here with my grandfather on the top of a hill in Hobe Sound watching for a coded message? Any minute, I expected him to slap me on the back and say, "Just fooling with you."

But one glance told me he was deadly serious. His jaw was set hard as he took a tiny pair of binoculars from his back pocket. My grandfather had a knack for whipping out the most unusual equipment at the exact right moment. Was there a Q in his life?

That thought propelled me down a dark rabbit hole of intrigue.

If there was a Q, did that make my grandfather an elderly James Bond?

A brisk shake of my head helped me clear my thinking. Such a scenario simply wasn't possible. My grandfather was a grouchy, prickly, mechanic who had diabetes.

After a long sequence of flashing lights, Poppy handed me the binoculars. Pulling that tiny flashlight from yet another pocket, he used his free hand to cover and uncover the beam repeatedly.

That brought on a second spate of flashes. I picked up Jack and tucked him inside my windbreaker.

"Are you two really, like, talking to each other?"

"Well, I ain't sharing my grocery list. Of course we are. What the blazes do you think we're doing out here if we ain't communicating?"

I adjusted the dog inside my jacket. Jack had been a surprisingly good trooper about this whole ordeal, probably because it had tired him out. Jack crawls into my bed at eight and that's it, that's all for him. He's a very sound sleeper. "If you're communicating, what is she saying? Is that her sending the messages?"

"Of course it is. Who else would it be? The rest of her bridge club? She done told me there were two hostiles. Now only one. He's holding her and her grandson hostage. Waiting for a shipment of humans. Slaves. Some for the sex trade, some for domestics."

I whipped out my phone and punched in 911, but before the operator answered, my grandfather grabbed the gizmo away from me.

"Are you out of your cotton-picking mind?"

"No, are you? We need to call the cops and get them to her house fast!" I lunged for the phone, but Poppy has incredibly long arms. To keep the iPhone out of my grasp, he held it over his head.

"Don't be stupid, girl!"

"Me, stupid? Thanks heaps, Poppy. She's calling for help, and you're just standing here in the middle of nowhere, but I'm stupid?"

His sigh suggested I was dumber than yesterday's toast. "Calm down, missy. Let me finish talking with her and then I'll explain it to you."

I fumed while he played with his flashlight. "What if you get her message wrong?"

"I won't." A few more exchanges passed between Binky and Poppy. My legs ached from the climb. The damp wicked into my clothes. When dialing 911, I'd felt a lightning bolt of energy, but now I slowly succumbed to exhaustion.

"Come on," said my grandfather, putting an arm around my waist. "Let's get back to the truck, and I'll fill you in on the details."

CHAPTER 43

"Binky ain't worried about herself," Poppy said. "She's fine. But Evans, her grandson, has asthma. He's scared witless. She wants him out of the middle of this." My grandfather shifted into drive and pulled gently onto Old Dixie.

"Evans was supposed to give Tommy a ride here, but he left campus early," I said.

"Yup. He's got asthma, so Binky's a little nervous about him."

"Then are you sure we shouldn't call the cops? Someone has to rescue that boy! What if he has an asthma attack?"

"Sending in the cavalry right now would blow any chance of rounding up them smugglers and putting them behind bars. See, if the cops swarm Binky's house, they'll take down the ringleader. When they do that, he'll miss a check-in, and the smugglers will know their cover has been compromised. They won't land here. If they don't land here, their human cargo won't get rescued—and those creeps'll probably go free. But if we can wait until they land, and surround them the minute that boat pulls up to the dock, there's a better than decent chance they'll squeal on everyone involved. That would give us a chance to shut down an entire ring of human traffickers." He glanced at me. "Them's the two hardest decisions you got to make when doing intelligence work. Whether to shut down an operation early and lose valuable intel or wait too late and cause too much damage."

I didn't know what to say because I was shocked. My grandfather sounded like he knew exactly what he was doing. How was that even possible?

The rain kicked up again. Small gusts of wind rocked Poppy's truck. No one would be traveling on the ocean in this weather. Correction: No one should be traveling on the ocean in this weather. I could hear the roar of the waves, slapping the shoreline in the face. Although I've visited several coastlines, I've never been anywhere with a surf as loud as this. The Anastasia reef breaks up the natural path of the water, multiplying the force of the crashing waves coming off of the Gulf Stream. This one-two punch—a natural current and a rocky reef—has caused many ships to wreck along our shoreline. Thus, we had earned the nickname, the Treasure Coast, when those vessels spilled their precious cargo up and down the sandy beaches of our state.

I appreciated the security of Poppy's truck. He noticed me shivering and turned on the heat. The warmth felt wonderful. "But what about Evans?

Shouldn't I call the police because of him? He's not safe. Can you really gamble on his health?"

Poppy raised a caterpillar-shaped eyebrow at me. "That's where I gotta trust Binky. If she says they can hold out, I gotta believe her. That's how come we call people like her 'assets.' They got experience and smarts, and they aren't just warm bodies. They're experts. A human asset to the intelligence community."

My head was beginning to hurt, and the wet fabric of my jeans chaffed my skin. "I'm not sure that's your decision to make. Or hers. As a mother, I can't imagine putting my child at risk. Sure, you say that Binky has it covered, but what if she's wrong?"

"She ain't."

Then it struck me. "Wait a minute. You said that the boat was going to pull up to the dock. What dock? There aren't any piers on the beach. Not here, at least."

Again Poppy gave me a look that made me feel smaller than the dog in my arms. "Don't you know anything about this here island? Not one blasted thing? All the lots used to run the entire width of Jupiter Island. Binky's got oceanfront on the east and Intracoastal access on the west. Bridge Road divides her property in half, but it's still all hers. There's the Indian River between this here island and the mainland. Makes it perfect for what these fellows got in mind."

"So the smugglers are planning to swing around the island on the south side? Down by Jupiter Inlet. And then turn north and go along the Intracoastal until they come to the yacht club. Is that it?"

"Uh-huh. I got my own sources. They tell me that the smugglers are tired of losing money when the immigrants jump overboard at the sight of land. If they pull up at a dock, there's a better chance they can keep control over their cargo—and deliver more warm bodies to buyers."

~*~

Like a nightlight in the bedroom, the warm glow from my house reached out to us as we pulled into my driveway. The boys were happily engrossed in their video games. Their hoots of laughter and cries of warnings rang loudly through my small cottage. After putting Jack down and watching him run to Tommy's lap, I ducked into my bathroom where I exchanged my soggy jeans for a pair of warm and dry drawstring pants. What I needed was a hot cup of tea to take off the chill.

Poppy poured himself a cup of coffee, left over in the carafe in my refrigerator. It heated up in my microwave while I put on the kettle.

"Mom, is there anything to eat around here?" Tommy shouted over one shoulder. He didn't take his eyes off the TV screen. Despite his size and deep voice, he was still my little boy in so many wonderful ways. One of which was his expectation that I could miraculously produce food at the snap of two fingers.

"There's peanut butter, bread, and cherry jam. Cans of soup. Carrot sticks," I recited the contents of my kitchen.

"Nope. We ate all that. Ate all your cereal and two bowls of popcorn."

Tommy and Sid gave each other a high five.

"I've got coupons for a place that does Stromboli and pasta. They'll deliver it to the island. But if you want snacks, here are a couple of convenience stores open, even if the grocery stores aren't." After pouring hot water into my cup and watching the tea bag float to the top, I moved closer to the boys. Sid looked happier, more relaxed than he'd been since getting out of the hospital. Whatever they were playing, the action proved totally engrossing.

Digging around in my purse, I extracted my wallet and my keys. "Here are two twenty dollar bills, Tommy. If you decide to go get food, use the money to pay for it. The car keys are here, too."

"Uh-huh." He barely skipped a beat.

"Granddaughter, you got a computer I can use?" asked Poppy. "I promised Wilma I'd keep in touch now that Sid's taught me to email."

"The old hard drive that came with the store is in the guest bedroom. You can't miss it. The monitor is on top of that table from Ikea."

Sid piped up. "Geez, that monster is slow and clunky. But if you need something, Dick, it'll work. I got it running for Cara. It's hooked up to the internet, too."

Poppy grunted.

"That's it for me, boys. I'm going to bed. Come on, Jack." I scooped up the small dog and left the boys to their games. By the time my head hit my pillow, I was as unresponsive as a blown out lightbulb. Through the miasma of my dreams, I heard the boys and Poppy speaking in urgent voices. Barely, I registered a clanking sound and the metallic *thunk* that signified the setting of a lock. In all likelihood, I would have slept until morning, but the cup of tea went right through me. Around midnight, I woke up needing to use the bathroom. After that, I wanted a glass of water. I walked into the kitchen and looked around. I poked my head into the living room. I checked the upstairs, the spare room, and the tiny laundry room.

Except for Jack and me, the house was totally empty.

The coupons for pizza and my money hadn't been touched. That didn't surprise me. The McDonald's at the corner of Bridge Road and Federal Highway was open twenty-four hours. What did surprise me was seeing Tommy's cell phone sitting on the coffee table. Usually he keeps it on his person. Thinking I'd do him a favor, I picked it up to plug it into the charger in my kitchen. While doing so, it vibrated in my hand.

The text came from someone who called herself Sleepy Cat: Really? Tom Terrific to the rescue. Wow. Aren't you scared?

I chuckled. When Tommy was growing up, my father nicknamed him "Tom Terrific" after the cartoon character. Obviously, my son had shared his moniker with this girl.

As I plugged Tommy's phone in, I remembered that my phone needed a charge, too. After grabbing it from my bedside table, I carried it into the spare bedroom where I'd installed a power strip for all my electrical needs and promptly discovered that the big, clunky hard drive was MIA. I rubbed my eyes. Where could it have gone? Why would the boys and Poppy unhook the hard drive in the middle of the night and haul it away?

I dialed Sid's cell phone. It went immediately to voice mail.

Same with Poppy's.

The truck was missing.

The boys were gone.

The hard drive had been unhooked and taken.

The food coupons and money were where I'd left them.

The rain had let up. I pressed my face to the window in my kitchen. That big, bright moon seemed far away. As I watched, clouds floated past, but for the most part, the sky was clear. The round sea grape leaves barely moved, which meant the wind had died down.

All was quiet, as though the world was holding its breath.

When I realized exactly where the guys had gone. I thought my legs would give away. If I hadn't been leaning over my kitchen counter, I would have collapsed on the ground. I knew what had happened as surely as I knew my own name.

Poppy, Tommy, and Sid had gone to Binky Rutherford's house.

CHAPTER 44

My son was out there, at risk, thanks to the stupid maneuvers of my crazy grandfather. Fury blinded me to all but the mission at hand. I shoved poor Jack into his crate, pulled on a pair of tennis shoes, grabbed my car keys, jumped into the Camry, and raced out of my driveway. Halfway down the street I remembered that I was braless, but I didn't care.

Think this through, Cara.

Why would they have unhooked the hard drive? Where were the boys? And why did Poppy take them with him?

Poppy had told me Binky would be okay, but she and he both were worried about Evans. A distraction. That's what my grandfather had wanted. My son was the same age as Evans. Was it remotely possible that Poppy had decided to use Tommy as a decoy? If so, what was the purpose of the hard drive? It didn't make any sense.

"Jupiter Island Department of Public Safety," answered a chipper female voice.

"This is Cara Mia Delgatto on Beach Road. I'm worried about my son," but that's all I managed because the call dropped. I slammed my palm against my steering wheel. Of all the times not to get reception!

Blue reflectors marking the lanes of Bridge Road winked at me as I sped by. Surprisingly, the road was dry-ish. The weather had cleared up. Was it possible the boat would arrive tonight? I hadn't checked the forecast. Maybe that had been the plan all along. If so…

Evans and Binky would be expendable. They only had value until the boat landed. Binky's house had offered a hideout for the person on the receiving end. The smuggler had needed a place to hang out until the shipment arrived, a spot that wouldn't arouse any suspicions, but one that would also allow him to monitor activity on the island. Binky's house—with access to both coastal and Intracoastal—would have been ideal.

I didn't worry about exceeding the posted speed limit, even though the JI cops were known to hand out tickets like a kindly widow shares candy with trick-or-treaters. My heart crowded my throat, making it nearly impossible to swallow. I heard the *thump-thump-thump* of my own heartbeat in my head as the motor strained in my car. There's a slight curve, a bend in Bridge Road where it meets Gomez. At the Y-shaped intersection, an antique cannon serves to remind drivers that the Spanish Fleet sank right off our coast.

Approaching Binky's house, I was forced to slow down. A Jupiter Island Department of Public Safety car blocked the street.

"You'll have to turn around, miss," said the clean-cut young man in uniform.

I responded with a curse word that shocked him. "My son's in there!"

"For your safety and his, you need to turn around, everything's under control." One of his hands rested on the roof of my car. The other caressed the handle of a big black gun in his utility belt.

I've seen enough cell phone videos to be rightly worried. This cop meant business. He might be here to serve and protect, but the clamping down of his face suggested he'd serve and protect me from the back of his cruiser.

"Please, please, listen to me. My grandfather has some crazy scheme to rescue Binky Rutherford and her grandson. My son Tommy is missing, so he must be involved too. Sir, you have to let me past. I have to get my son out of this!"

"For the last time, miss, turn around. Go home."

My three-point turn looked more like an octagonal stop sign, but I did point my car the other way. At the cannon, I veered left, rather than right, and pulled my car into the nearest driveway marked, "Service."

Using my phone as a flashlight, I jogged back the way I'd come. When I spotted the reflectors on the cruiser, I turned off the app. Too scared to walk upright, I hunched over and shuffled along as quietly as possible. The cop who'd stopped me was talking into a handheld receiver that crackled in the still night air. A row of Australian pines muscled the shoulder of Bridge Road. These marked the edge of Binky's property. Like the Indians in a bad western, I moved from tree to tree, keeping the broad trunks between me and the cop. A root tripped me, but as I went down, I managed to protect my phone. Once on all fours, I crawled forward, praying that I wouldn't encounter any snakes.

What drove me was the love of my son—and a deep desire to throttle my grandfather. I turned the flashlight app and shielded the beam with my palms. I needed to get my bearings. Where exactly was I? Then I spotted clusters of orange blossoms and knew exactly where I was.

A thick hedge of Ixora paralleled the driveway on Binky's property. Tucking the phone into my back pocket, I used both hands to guide myself to a spot where the branches thinned out. I scrambled through the small hole in the hedge. Panting, partially from exertion and a lot from fear, I hesitated and looked around.

ALL WASHED UP 179

The Audi was in the same spot as last time, but now Poppy's truck sat in the driveway, between the Audi and the house. The engine on the Toyota purred quietly. Sid waited in the driver's seat of my grandfather's truck, with his head turned toward the house, watching intently. He couldn't see me, although I could make out the glimmer of the silver hoop in his right eyebrow. I dropped flat and crawled on my belly, moving past the truck and inching toward the Audi. My goal was a clear view of the stoop. As I moved, I counted my lucky stars that my tee shirt was dark gray and my pants were black. I blended in with the night and the paint job on the Audi. Eventually, I flattened myself against the front bumper of the car. That put me nearly parallel with Poppy's front bumper. There I stopped. My position gave me a good vantage point. I could see the entire doorway, illuminated by an overhead light.

Tommy was standing there, waiting for the door to swing open. When it did, I heard him say, "Hi, Evans!"

Instinct nearly trumped good sense. I longed to race to Tommy's side. However, a sixth sense warned me not to interfere. Instead, I stayed motionless.

"Dude, I managed to fix that old hard drive of yours," said Tommy in a rush of words. His voice sounded higher than usual. I could detect the stress, but no one else would probably recognize it. "But I need help getting it out of the truck. That thing is heavy."

Evans face might naturally be pale in any circumstances, but it appeared ghostly as he stood in the doorway. Glancing behind him, his body hesitated, as if asking for approval. I saw him give an answering nod to someone deeper inside the home. Tommy took one step to the right to let Evans join him on the sidewalk.

I held my breath. Where was Poppy? I knew he was involved in this. Somehow. Somewhere.

The Jupiter Island police also knew something was up. But where were they? I had to assume Tommy was protected, but how?

I had to do the hardest thing I've ever done in my entire life: I had to trust other people with my son's life.

CHAPTER 45

Evans was six inches shorter than my son. Tommy adjusted his stride to keep Evans immediately to his right, herding him toward the truck, the way a sheepdog moved cattle. Although the pairing looked awkward, Tommy chatted to Evans in a conversational way. My son's body language seemed relaxed and loose. But then I noticed his left hand was balled into a knot. He talked with his right hand waving, but I couldn't hear what he was saying over the hum of the truck's engine. Evans held himself like a fine cut-glass vase that might break at any minute. Sid's expression was alert, focused on the other two boys, but not betraying any tension. His eyes never wavered as he watched his friends approach.

From my vantage point, I couldn't see much. I could, however, hear my son.

"It'll take two of us to lift this old beast of a hard drive," Tommy said loudly. "Grab a corner. On my count. One, two, three."

Tommy and Evans both ducked down, ostensibly to lift up the hard drive from the floorboard of the Toyota truck. A loud oomph followed, and both heads disappeared. Tommy must have shoved Evans inside and scrambled over him. The movement was quick, practiced, and successful.

"Hey!" yelled a voice inside the house.

With a squeal of tires, Sid threw the vehicle into reverse. A crack and a ding told me that a bullet had hit the truck. I stood up long enough to see Sid duck down. He gave the steering wheel a hard turn to the right. Another crack filled the night air. Sid was driving blindly. All three boys were shielded by the body of the truck as it bumped over Binky's lawn, veering widely to the right, racing down Beach Road, and sliding to a stop a football field away.

"You little—" A voice roared from the house. A man came running outside. There was a crack of a gun. The shot came from a tall Australian pine directly across the street. A flash of light and a second crack followed the first.

The man on the sidewalk folded like a paper napkin. From the far side of Binky's lawn, a dark figure in a bulletproof vest raced to the grunting guy on the ground. "Got him," he yelled. A flash of silver and the metal clank of handcuffs followed. "Suspect under control," he said, speaking directly in-to a microphone clipped to his shoulder.

But my attention turned to Binky's foyer. Indistinct scuffling and grunts suggested a tussle.

"Don't shoot!"

The voice was Poppy's—and it came from inside Binky's house.

"He's got a gun on us," my grandfather continued. "We're coming out."

"Hold your fire," screamed a disembodied voice from across the street.

Poppy staggered forward with his hands behind his head. Pausing in the doorway, he glanced over at the restrained kidnapper. As he shuffled a few steps, another person appeared behind him. Binky Rutherford wobbled along, leaning heavily on a cane. The interior lights of her home lit up a pair of pink cotton pajamas with some sort of tiny darker red print on them. I stayed low and hidden behind the Audi's bumper.

"He's got a gun on us!" Binky cried out. "A big, big gun."

"I know you cops are out there! One wrong move and I'll blast them both to Kingdom come." The voice was gruff and no-nonsense.

Scooting toward the walkway, I cautiously raised my head. Poppy's eyes flickered my way. I nodded.

"You ain't going to get away with this," Poppy called back over his shoulder.

A distraction.

The assailant said, "If I go down, you go down. You shouldn't have tried to sneak in the back way, old man."

As he spoke, I slipped into the low hedge of Green Island Ficus that bordered the front of Binky's house. In the pale glimmer of her security light, I could see a flicker along her jawline that suggested she had noticed me. But otherwise, she never betrayed my existence. Instead, she moved her feet more slowly, scuffing her fuzzy pink house slippers.

"Hurry up," demanded the creep.

"If you'd put down that big old rifle," started Poppy, as I crept closer to the door, "I could help my friend."

"Shut your yap, old man."

That had been Poppy's way of warning me. I nodded. Now he moved past me, and Binky was teetering on the threshold of the doorframe.

"Move it!" the bad guy barked. "Cops? Listen up. I've got both these old geezers in my crosshairs. Tell you how this is going to work. We're going to go for a ride, the three of us."

As he spoke, I flattened myself against the clapboard siding. My arms were outstretched. My right hand was nearly even with the doorbell.

"Don't be stupid!" spat out Poppy. "You'll never get away with this."

"Oh, yes, I will," said the creep. "I've got a boat waiting for me at the

Intracoastal, and two hostages to secure my passage. You're the one who's stupid."

A *beep-beep* signaled that the assailant had used his keys to remotely unlock the doors on the Audi. That gave me enough cover to move freely. My fingers inched up to the doorbell button.

Binky hesitated inside the foyer. She shot a glance my way.

I pushed the doorbell, holding it down with all my might. The chimes boomed loudly. As I'd predicted, the sudden noise started the gunman.

Without hesitation, Binky and Poppy threw themselves to the ground. A shot rang out. Another one. The glint of a rifle barrel appeared in the doorway.

Using my arm as a club, I brought it down on the rifle...hard.

The barrel dipped down, but I hadn't knocked the weapon out of the assailant's grasp. I raised my hand to slap at the gun again.

But Binky was faster than I was. She rolled to her feet and jumped up. Using her cane as a weapon, she swept the gunman's feet out from under him. With a fluid motion, she produced a small dagger from handle of the walking stick. In a flash, she was on top of the assailant and holding a knife blade to the man's throat.

Cops swarmed around us, shouting orders.

Poppy grabbed me and turned me around. "You okay, Granddaughter?"

"Never better. Except the side of my hand stings a little."

"We need to get ice on it," he said.

Binky backed away and let the police handcuff the assailant. "Evans? Where is he? Honey?" She shaded her eyes and scanned the darkness.

"Over here, Granny!" came a voice from the opposite side of the road.

"He's fine," Poppy said. "They all are. Binky, you okay?"

"Right as rain," she said. "Just like the old days, hey, Dick?"

"Yup." He chortled.

"Mom! Mom!" Tommy yelled at me from the side of the road. He, Sid, and Evans stood by the Toyota truck and waved at us.

My prayers had been answered. My son was safe.

CHAPTER 46

The next morning, I awakened in my own comfy bed. The air was rich with the smell of pancakes and bacon. Every muscle complained about moving. A bass drum thumped around in my head. Tommy brought me a pain pill and water, before offering to serve me breakfast in bed. While I swallowed the tablet, he put a mug of coffee on my bedside table.

"I think I'd rather sit in the living room, please. I don't want to spill the coffee in my lap."

Tommy helped me to the sofa, before racing back to grab the coffee.

"How's your arm?" asked Sid.

The ulna, that part of your forearm that becomes the bump at the base of your wrist, had cracked when I brought it down on the gun. Fortunately, the fracture wasn't a true break, so the hospital had sent me home with splint, pain-killers, and instructions on icing my injury. Tommy, Sid, and Poppy promised to make sure I followed directions. There wasn't much for them to do, as the combination of my exhaustion and the painkillers totally knocked me out. A hazy memory floated around, the sense that Poppy had helped me to the bathroom during the night.

"It hurts."

"Not surprising. You hit that gun barrel hard," said Sid.

"Speaking of hard, you sure did some fancy stunt driving, Sid," I said.

He beamed. "Yeah. Tommy says I'll be a natural at GTA."

"GTA?"

"Grand Theft Auto," explained my son. "Skye is on her way over to help you dress. Just so you know, MJ's taking care of the store. Honora's there, too. I was thinking, Mom. You and MJ and Skye, you're like the Three Musketeers, aren't you?"

"Speaking of friends, where is Jack?" I asked, as Luna rubbed her whiskers against my face. I stroked her head and tried to steer her clear of my bacon.

"Poppy is out taking him for a walk. Sid and I were getting ready to watch the news. We're sure you're going to be front and center."

"Sid? You've got the remote? Turn up the TV, will you?"

The screen graphics announced: Human traffickers foiled at Jupiter Island. A pretty-boy announcer swept his hand toward the Intracoastal. "This quiet waterway swarmed with law enforcement agents last night. They formed a landing party, of sorts, surrounding a boat full of undocumented immigrants being smuggled into the country."

The camera switched to a man in a business suit and tie. His title, Deputy Director of US Immigration and Customs Enforcement, flashed along the bottom of the screen. "This human trafficking ring has operated with impunity for several years. Thanks to cooperation with local citizens, we were able to arrest several key figures last night."

He went on to explain that twenty-seven people on the boat had agreed to be, what amounted to, indentured servants. "For the promise of a better life, they signed away their freedom to these predators. They didn't realize that they'd never be able to pay off their so-called debts. That's how these human traffickers work. They prey on people's hopes for a better life."

Shoving a microphone closer to the deputy director's face, a reporter asked, "Is anyone on Jupiter Island involved?"

"That's still under investigation."

My fork froze half-way to my mouth with a syrup covered piece of blueberry pancake dangling precariously. "Really? They don't mean Binky, do they?"

"No," Sid said. "Poppy thinks someone who has ties to the island was helping the smugglers and quit. That's one reason your bad guy wanted to use Binky's house as a hideaway."

"Fewer than eight hundred residents live here at the peak of Season, and less than half that number live here full time," said a reporter. "That leaves a lot of empty houses. Big houses. Many with guest houses and garages where a person could hang out and not be discovered for weeks. Officials think that human traffickers took advantage of the vacancies and Jupiter Island's no lights policy designed to protect sea turtles."

Once the juicy soundbites had been delivered, the news shifted to a weather report.

"How're Binky and Evans? Do we know?" I asked.

"They're fine," Tommy said. "Evans and his grandmother went to the hospital because his asthma had flared up. We saw them while we waited for the doc to fit you with that splint. Evans needed a breathing treatment. I guess they checked out his grandmother, too. She was a little dehydrated, but otherwise okay. Did you know that she used to be a spy? Or something like that. Evans told us that she wasn't worried at all about that bad guy in her home. He felt awful about bringing that creep into his grandmother's house, but he really didn't have a choice in the matter."

"Whoa. Back up. Evans brought the trafficker to his grandmother's house? How on earth did Evans get involved with a smuggler? How did all this start?"

"Evans is a poker player," explained Tommy.

"But not a very good one," added Sid.

"Someone let him into a private game in a swanky penthouse on South Shore, and he lost a bunch of money. So he told the dude he owed that he'd borrow it from his grandmother who lived on Jupiter Island. That's when Haiger, the guy with the knife, got involved. He was instructed to keep an eye on Evans, because he was an 'investment.' Haiger was told to drive Evans up here to pick up the dough. That was Haiger's Audi in the driveway of Binky's house. But Haiger had a better idea. They had lost money on the last shipment of immigrants when they bailed out. He talked to his boss about changing things up and using the Intracoastal side of the island."

"Most of the smugglers don't care whether their cargo make it here alive," said Sid. "But this new shipment of people was destined to be domestic servants and sex slaves. Buyers were waiting for them."

"Once he got to Binky's house," said Tommy, "Haiger pulled a knife on Evans and told Binky he'd carve up her grandson if she didn't behave. Haiger planned to hang out at Binky's place until the next shipment left the Bahamas and then meet the ship himself."

"But why did Haiger let Danielle into the house?" That made no sense to me.

"Binky explained to Haiger that if she didn't carry through with the appointment, it would raise a red flag," said Sid. "Haiger tied Evans up in a guest bedroom to make sure Binky was on her best behavior."

Tommy nodded his agreement. "Evans told me that Binky would have been fine, but his asthma started acting up because of the stress. That's why Binky gave Danielle the dress. Danielle noticed it in the closet. She said you'd buy it in a heartbeat. That's why Binky sold it to Danielle. Her idea was to get you involved so she—Binky—could get a message to Poppy. Can you believe that Poppy was, like, James Bond? Back in the day?"

Rather than blurt out, "Yes, I've seen him in action," I shook my head as if to marvel at my grandfather. Frowning, I wondered, "Why did Haiger let Danielle walk away only to kill her later?"

"On her way out the door, Danielle recognized Haiger from partying on South Beach, and that would have been cool," Tommy explained. "But Danielle couldn't leave it alone. After she drove away, she started calling people. People who got nervous. They sent down a reinforcement who told

Haiger to clean up his mess. That was the guy the cops took down first."

"Too bad I didn't understand that Binky was sending a message. She told me what to say to Poppy, but I ignored it because I didn't think it was important."

"Uh-huh," said Tommy. "Binky was totally frustrated with you. She even put an earring in the dress so she'd get another crack at you if you messed up again. Evans was totally impressed by how sneaky she was. Especially for an old lady."

"Poppy told Evans he needs to take poker lessons," Sid said.

"From his grandmother," added Tommy.

That made me laugh.

CHAPTER 47

Poppy returned with Jack, who promptly jumped into my lap and tried to steal my bacon.

"We need to talk," I said to my grandfather.

"Yup. But it can wait a day or day, can't it? Let me have a little time to enjoy my grandson."

I realized he was right and opened my mouth to say as much, right as Skye rapped at the front door. Tommy jumped up to let her in. Her face was blotchy as if she'd just had a good cry. Her swollen eyes refused to look at me, in that way of saying, "Don't ask."

"What can I get you to eat, Skye?" Tommy asked, politely. "We've got all sorts of stuff here for breakfast. I'd be happy to make you a stack of blueberry pancakes."

If he noticed her red-rimmed eyes, he didn't say anything. Instead, Tommy kept plying her with food. In that way, he was definitely my father's grandson, because my dad believed that most of life's problems can be solved with a good, hot meal.

In the end, Skye only nibbled at a piece of toast and sipped a cup of tea. Her silence told me she was upset, but I knew better than to push. I sent up a prayer that her baby was okay, because any other problem we could solve.

After I finished my breakfast, she and I went into my bedroom and shut the door. I knew Skye well enough to know that she was not ready to talk about whatever caused her tears, so instead of asking, I let her set the pace.

"I picked up two containers of Epsom salt on my way here." She fluttered around me, helping me undress. The splint was bulky, and my sore muscles limited my mobility.

"Good," I said. "We don't want to incur the wrath of Poppy."

"How're you feeling?" she asked as she poured Epsom salt in and stirred them until they dissolved.

"Like I was run over by a truck."

"No doubt. You're quite the hero. Or is it heroine? Anyway, you did a remarkable thing, saving your grandfather and Binky."

After wrapping my arm in a plastic trash bag, she helped me into the tub. My arm dangled off the side.

"You probably want your privacy." She started to leave, but I stopped her.

"After giving birth, I gave up on modesty. Have a seat and we'll chat."

"Let me get my tea."

"Are you okay?" I asked when she returned. "You seem a little pale. I haven't had the chance to talk with you since you went to see Spalding."

"He's calling in a prescription for me. I'm trying to take it easy until the nausea subsides. But they called me into work at the last minute. I usually don't wait tables at night, as you know, but another girl called off so they asked me to fill in."

"So you're tired? Otherwise all right?"

She stared down into her cup. "No. Not exactly. A customer ordered liver and onions. The smell sent me running to the ladies' room. I was sick for a long time. When I came out, Zed, the manager, wanted to know what the problem was. 'If you've got the flu, you shouldn't be here,' were his exact words. I caved in and told him I'm pregnant. He had a complete melt-down. Called me all sorts of names."

I felt my mouth drop open. "Names? That's ridiculous. What on earth?"

"You would have thought that I was his wife, and I'd cheated on him. It was totally bizarre. Zed yelled so loud that everyone in Pumpernickel's heard. According to him, I'm nothing more than a slut, and he's disgusted. He fired me on the spot."

"What?" I was back to my one word vocabulary.

"Didn't even give me two weeks' notice. Said my morals weren't compatible with the family dining business. Zed even suggested that keeping me would cause harm to Pumpernickel's reputation. Oh, and he's sure the owner will back him up."

"That's utterly ridiculous, and stupid, business-wise. You're the best waitress he has. The most popular by far."

"That's what I thought, and what I've always been told, but I guess that doesn't count for much when you're pregnant and not married."

I remembered being pregnant and married to a man my parents didn't trust. My father had cried for hours when I told him I was expecting. "I can't trust a man who ran off with my daughter. Especially one who knows how much she means to me, and who cheated me out of the chance to be at her wedding. But here's what I can tell you, Cara. I've got your back. Whatever Dominic Petrcelli does or doesn't do as your baby's father, know that your child has a grandfather who'll be there for him."

Thinking back on my father's pledge, I drew strength from the memory. My dad had said exactly what I needed to hear. His promise had been the best gift he'd ever given me. I could do the same now for Skye.

"Well, I'm certainly not going to fire you. In fact, maybe it's for the best that you're leaving Pumpernickel's," I said. "Now you can work at The Treasure Chest full time."

"Can you afford to pay me?"

"Absolutely. I was planning on asking you anyway." This wasn't strictly true. We were still several months away from being able to afford Skye as a full-time employee. However, I would not leave my friend in the lurch. No way. I'd scrimp on some other cost to make sure that Skye and her baby were taken care of.

"That means the world to me. You're so good to me, Cara." Mopping her eyes with the back of her hand, she said, "That's enough moping around. I came here to take care of you, and look at me. I'm being silly."

"No, you're being a realist. Besides, all your hormones are probably going nuts right now." I hesitated. I wanted to ask her if she'd talked to Lou yet, but I decided to give her time.

"I've told you my latest tragedy. Tell me all about what happened last night."

I brought her up-to-date on the events of the night before. Considering her relationship with Lou, she seemed surprisingly unaware of what had happened. This confused me, because usually they share everything. Sometimes even too much because little bits of my personal life are brought up in conversation. I kept giving her openings for mentioning him. Finally, I couldn't take the suspense.

"Skye, didn't Lou tell you about what went down? I'm sure he's aware. It was such a big sting. Didn't they call on the Stuart police for help?"

She stared at the back of my bathroom door. Finally, she said, "Y-yes. He came over after everything went down. When he arrived, I was sick again. He got it into his head that he should take me to the hospital because I've been puking so much."

"So you told him?"

"Since everyone knew at Pumpernickel's, it seemed like a moot point."

"Hurrah!" I couldn't keep the thrill out of my voice. This was going to be so freaking cool! I could just imagine Lou bouncing a baby on one knee. I splashed the water with glee, but she just kept staring at bathroom door.

"Come on!" I said. "Tell me everything. How did he react? What did he say?"

"He asked me if I was sure that he was the father."

CHAPTER 48

I rarely cuss. My dad taught me that if you start cussing the words will sneak up on you and you'll embarrass yourself. "History is filled with moments when important men showed their true colors by cursing when they thought they wouldn't be heard. The best habit is one that doesn't fail you in a pinch. It's better not to allow those words to take up residency inside your head, so you don't let them escape in a moment of forgetfulness."

But I had a lot of choice words to say about Lou. He had danced around his relationship with Skye for months. Being coy, never openly proclaiming her his sweetheart. Once when MJ asked him if he was going to buy Skye a diamond for Christmas, he got all huffy and told her to mind her own business. Another time, when Sid called her "your girlfriend" to his face, the big cop had glared at the boy.

I hauled myself out of my tub and let fly with the sort of language my parents would have never approved of. Skye handed me a towel and pivoted to rest her hands on the countertop. Between sobs, she choked out, "It's okay. I still want this baby. No matter what Lou says or thinks. Financially it'll be a struggle, but I'll manage. To be fair, I guess the pregnancy took him by surprise."

I bit back a snarky comment. Why is it that when women get pregnant after having sex with a man, the man claims to be "surprised?" It's like this bizarre variation on NIMBY, not in my back yard. Oh yeah, other men get women pregnant, but not me.

"What's wrong with him? How dumb can he be?"

Maybe Lou slept through Human Biology 101. Or flunked it. More likely, he willfully ignored it, as many of us try to do. Point being: If you have sex, you run the risk of a pregnancy occurring. No matter how much you aren't expecting a baby as an outcome, it's still a possibility. To pretend otherwise is wishful thinking. Scratch that. Delusional thinking.

"Maybe I'm being unfair to him," said Skye. "He never made a commitment."

"Uh, when you go to bed with someone, you're making a commitment."

"That's your Roman Catholic upbringing."

"Maybe. Possibly. Okay, yes."

I was furious with Lou. I wanted to march right into the Stuart Police Station and throttle him. Instead, I toweled off quickly, walked into my bedroom, and tried to pull on a pair of jeans. Not the wisest move. Forgetting my messed up arm, I lurched to one side and fell on my bed with my pants around my ankles. In response, my mattress and box springs groaned.

"Mom? You okay in there?" Tommy yelled through the closed door.

"Never better!" My weird position—supported on my good elbow, pants half on and half off—gave Skye a case of the giggles.

"Were you really planning to go commando? You've always struck me as a panties and bra type of girl."

"No. I was too angry to think," I said as she hauled me to my feet. Between us, we managed to get me dressed. "What am I going to do without you, Skye? I can't even get my clothes on!"

"How about if I move in for a while? I can sleep upstairs." She shivered. "In fact, I really don't want to be alone in my apartment right now."

"You don't think Lou would come and yell at you, do you?" The thought horrified me.

"No, but I don't need to look out my window and see customers coming from Pumpernickel's or deal with Lou. If he ever shows up at my door. Which he won't. He'll probably act like he doesn't know me."

"That jerk."

She sighed. "At least he didn't hit me."

We'd no sooner gotten the bathroom picked up, when my cell phone rang. I recognized the number as being a call from Honora.

"Cara, dear, how are you? We heard about the kerfuffle you were involved in last night." Although she spoke deliberately, there was a certain breathlessness to her voice. Was it just because she was worried about me? Or was there more to it? I wasn't in the mood for problems. Especially at the store.

"My arm's a mess, but I'm okay," I said, not even trying to sugarcoat it. "Fortunately Skye came over to help me take a bath and get dressed. Thanks for holding down the fort. It's not too busy there, is it? I hope not. I really don't think I can handle working today."

"No one expects you to, dear girl. It's actually pretty quiet. EveLynn is here, but I'm keeping her in the back so she doesn't bother customers. You know how she gets."

I did indeed. "Any word from Binky?"

"Only a quick conversation. She's fine. Evans is, too, and she's singing your praises. Yours and Dick's."

"Where's MJ?"

"She said she had a doctor's appointment."

"Oh, no. I totally forgot! Okay, got to go. Call me if you need anything." And I ended the call without waiting for her response.

Skye had been watching me. "What's wrong?"

"It's MJ. We have to go. To her doctor. The one she took you to. Spalding. We need to leave. Now. Come on," and I grabbed my purse. Before Skye could ask any questions, I told Tommy and Sid, "I'm on my way out the door. I'll call you later to see what you might want from the grocery store, okay? If MJ phones, tell her I'm on my way."

"I'll pull up my car." Skye tucked her purse under her arm and headed outside.

Jack realized something was up. He came rip-roaring after me, nipping at my heels. "Tommy! Come grab him!"

"Mom, what's the rush?" My son scooped up the Chihuahua.

"MJ needs my help. Our help," I amended my comment, as I slammed the door in his face.

On the way to Spalding's office, I shared MJ's secret with Skye. "I know she won't want you to know, but I don't see any way around it. Not right now. After all, it's not like I can drive myself to her appointment. I don't even know where Spalding's office is. Gosh, I don't even know if Spalding is his first name or his last."

"His last name, but everyone calls him just that. Spalding. How long have you known about this?" Even under pressure, Skye drove carefully. I liked that about her.

"Not long. She's totally panicked. Her mother died of breast cancer. Besides, she sees herself as all alone."

"Join the club," said Skye, under her breath, but I still heard her.

CHAPTER 49

Spalding's office turned out to be in Greenwich, a professional office complex off of Military Trail in Jupiter. The length of the drive had me squirming in my seat. "If we've missed her, I'll just…"

"Apologize and move on," Skye completed the sentence for me.

"Or not."

"We'll get there. He's often running late. He was for my visit. Getting upset won't help any of us." She slowed and turned carefully onto Chimney Sweep Court. I have no idea what bright spark thought up the English-sounding names for this stretch of Military Trail. Must have been a true Anglophile. The spot's surrounded by seaworthy and coastal references, and then—bam—suddenly we're visiting the British Isles.

As with most professional complexes, this one seemed deliberately designed to be difficult to navigate. A prominent round-about sent us spiraling in a circle. The building numbers were confusing. At last Skye found an empty space, threw her Mustang into park, and we both bailed out at the same time. As we trotted toward the entrance, we passed MJ's pink Cadillac, looking anachronistic and oddly feminine among a sea of SUVs and Land Rovers, the new favorite choices of the Treasure Coast elite.

We must have looked a sight. Me with my arm in a sling. Her with a pair of red-from-crying eyes. The elevator couldn't come quickly enough for us, so when it opened and we discovered we'd called the freight car, we shrugged and hurried inside. Leaning against the padded walls, I crossed my fingers and said a prayer that we'd arrive in time. In my mind's eye, I saw MJ as she'd been that day when she told me about her mother. For the most part, MJ managed to be unfailingly resolute. Occasionally abrasive. Often brusque. Totally opinionated. But all this covered up a soft spot that she took great care to protect. The possibility she'd have to have a mastectomy had peeled away her carapace. When people work that hard to be tough, it can be exhausting to get past their defenses. Usually, they've been hurt before—and they aren't certain they'll survive if it happens again.

I didn't want MJ to fall apart.

Selfishly, we needed her at the store.

Unselfishly, I cared about her.

If being tough was the only way she could survive, then I would put up with her stepping on my feelings and offering opinions I'd rather not hear. I could suffer through her rough handling if that's what she needed to function.

And what if the news was bad? Would she totally come undone?

My mother had handled cancer by pretending it wasn't happening. She had refused to slow down. She only went to the doctor, because my father insisted. I never saw her cry, although Poppy told me that she did...to him. I never knew whether she was being tough because she thought it would save us (Dad and me) grief, or because she hoped to keep herself from falling to pieces. In the year and a half since she had died, I'd come to the conclusion that I didn't want to leave this world the way she had. I wouldn't spend my last days lying and faking people out. Mom's pretense kept me from talking with her honestly. I couldn't help her because I couldn't reach her, and she couldn't help me because she refused to acknowledge the truth. If she'd been more forthcoming, perhaps we could have found a halfway point, a spot midway between sorrow and love, where we could have drawn strength from each other and moved toward the end together, rather than watching the distance between us grow.

What would MJ choose?

Or would she have any choices?

~*~

A solid walnut door stood between us and our friend. Theoretically at least. I wasn't sure if MJ was still in the doctor's office or if she'd be willing to see us.

"Ready?" I asked Skye.

"You bet."

We instinctively squared our shoulders, preparing for the challenge ahead. But when the door swung open, we stared into an empty waiting area. Soft music flowed in from invisible speakers. The aqua and grey tones instantly soothed us. Comfortable seating abounded, as did current copies of popular magazines. In one corner, a trendy coffee maker offered a pleasing selection of brews. The scent of coffee and hazelnut filled the air. A textured glass window blocked the view of the inner workings of the office, although we could make out the shapes of heads bobbing around. A clipboard was attached to a narrow ledge, and it bore a simple directive: Sign In.

But no MJ.

"You don't think we missed her, do you?" I asked Skye.

"No. I don't think so."

"There was only that one bank of elevators."

"Right."

I rapped on the glass. When the window slid open, I explained to a young woman in dreadlocks, "We're friends of MJ Austin's. I promised her I'd come to this appointment with her, but I was unavoidably detained."

To underscore my point, I displayed my bandaged arm. The dark skinned woman raised an eyebrow but otherwise didn't act impressed. Just thoughtful. As if she was considering what to tell us.

"See, MJ was expecting us. Even though we're running late. Could we join her now?" I tried not to whine, but my voice did sound pitiful. My face flushed as I realized that I had lied. MJ was not expecting Skye. However, I didn't care. Without Skye I couldn't have made the trip. Besides, Skye was a part of our team, and she needed to know whatever MJ was going through. In addition, hadn't MJ brought Skye here—and heard about her medical concerns? Wasn't turnabout fair play?

The thoughtful brown eyes on the other side of the window regarded me suspiciously. Her stern expression seemed totally at odds with the pattern of tumbling kittens on her pink scrubs.

Skye gently moved me to one side. "Elizabeth? It's me. Skye. From yesterday. Remember? I was here with MJ? We don't want her to go through this alone. I know Dr. Spalding is going to talk to her about her mammogram results, and what's going to happen next. We're only here to support her. Can you help us?"

Elizabeth's protective stance softened. "Hey, girl. Yeah, maybe. Let me check and see if it's okay. Be right back."

Although Elizabeth slid the glass shut in my face, I didn't care. We were finally making progress. Sort of. I sure hoped that MJ would be okay. It would have been awful if she thought I'd deserted her when she needed me.

Skye's hand patted my shoulder. "Don't worry. Elizabeth will take care of it. She's a sweetheart. Protective of the doc, but a real sweetie."

I hoped so.

When footsteps marked her return, and the window opened, Elizabeth's face reappeared. "I'm coming around to get you and take you back to the doctor's office. It's good that you came when you did. You're just in time."

~*~

Words tumbled past me as the doctor explained the radiologist had found a mass in one of MJ's breasts. I heard: "Biopsy. Alternative treatments. Lymph nodes. History of cancer. Density. Biopsy. Stage One. Mastectomy. Reconstruction. Radiation. Chemo."

Very little of what we heard made any sense. Skye nodded and asked good questions, while I tried to sound like an intelligent person. Between the pain in my arm and my exhaustion, I was having trouble concentrating. Fortunately, MJ didn't notice that I wasn't myself.

She sat frozen, perched on the edge of her chair. Her face was blank. Her eyes unfocused.

"MJ? Have you heard anything I've said?" Dr. Spalding asked. As we waited for a response, our friend blinked.

"MJ?" I put a hand on her forearm.

"What am I going to do?" She turned wide eyes on me. "Who will take care of me? No one will want me. No man. I'll be a freak."

This response brought a swift rebuttal from Dr. Spalding "MJ, don't be ridiculous. We've known each other for years. We've even dated! Did you think I was only interested in a handful of flesh? For crying out loud. You're probably the sexiest woman I know, and even if you were wearing a tent dress, you'd turn heads."

"But I'm sexy because I feel sexy. And I won't. Not when my hair falls out and I've got a big ugly scar where I had a beautiful...girl." She raised both hands to her chest.

"Didn't you hear about the reconstruction?" Skye slid an arm around MJ's shoulders. "As for your hair, it might not fall out. You could always wear a wig. That might be fun."

"Have you lost your mind?" MJ snarled at Skye. "There's nothing sexy about a wig."

"That depends on who's wearing it," said Skye. "And what the wig looks like."

"You supply the sex appeal," I said. "It's not your hair or your clothes. MJ, this is a shock. Give yourself time. You don't need to fret over every detail."

"I'd hardly call one of my breasts a detail."

Now I was ticked. Maybe it was cumulative. I'd had a rough couple of days. Sure, MJ had received devastating news, but there was hope on her horizon. My mother had been diagnosed as Stage 4 cancer, and she never had a chance. But MJ did. She had more than a fighting chance, and she was wasting her energy by fighting with us.

I could not keep my mouth shut, so I said, "How about this? The surgeon can remove your breast, we'll take it to a taxidermist and have it mounted?"

"Better yet, we can put it in a frame. No, on second thought, mounted is best because you can hang it on a wall." Skye put a finger to her cheek as she thought this through.

"Right. You can show it off to any prospective dates? That'll give the men a chance to preview coming events. Or they can climb up on a ladder and take your boob for a test drive. Most guys can only concentrate on one at a time anyway," I said this with a total deadpan delivery.

MJ looked at me with horror. But only for a tick. Then she burst out laughing, and so did we.

"You want that on a mahogany plaque or a maple one?" asked Skye.

"What should the personalization read? MJ's left? Or what's left of MJ?"

"You know most surgeons charge extra for staying within the lines when they cut. Maybe if you use a Magic Marker and draw a guideline, Dr. Hershowitz can just trim around the edges." Dr. Spalding chortled with laughter, too.

With a shaking hand, MJ wiped her eyes. I took the opportunity to grab her fingers and twine mine through hers.

"Last night Tommy told me that we reminded him of the Three Musketeers. I think he's absolutely spot on. I know this won't be easy, and I understand you're devastated. You have every right to be. Or a left to be, under the circumstances. But we're here for you. You're going to get through this."

"I'd been wanting a boob lift anyway," she said with a long sigh. "At least insurance will pay for half the job, right?"

"Right," said Skye. "Group hug."

"All for one and one for all."

CHAPTER 50

The three of us went to lunch at Berry Fresh Café. I had my second stack of pancakes of the day. This time I indulged in lemon ricotta pancakes, MJ had French toast with Nutella, and Skye had C'est Si Bon Hash, with asparagus, pickled beets, spinach and goat cheese on a bed of potatoes and covered with scrambled eggs. She took a pass on the Hollandaise sauce as a topping.

Skye told MJ about Lou's reaction to the news that she was pregnant.

To our shock, MJ answered with a shrug. "He's a guy. They always react that way. It's in their nature. No, honestly, it's true. They've been conditioned by other guys to think the woman is pulling one over on them. Give him time. He loves you. Worships you. But he's scared. You are too, but he's facing a theoretical change, fatherhood, and you have tangible evidence of change with your body's reactions."

I wondered how much of this was directly from personal experience, but I didn't have the emotional energy to ask. Fortunately, MJ took the conversation and steered it.

"How are you doing, Cara? I heard you blew the lid off that smuggling ring last night. It was all over the news this morning. How badly is your arm broken?"

"Could have been a lot worse. It's just cracked. I need help getting dressed, of course. Skye volunteered to move in with me short term." I didn't want this to blindside MJ. If she heard about it second hand, she might feel left out.

"Makes sense for both of you."

"But remember, I have a pull-out sleeper sofa in my living room. If you want, you can come and stay over, too," I said.

"Maybe. But I think my six cats would miss me. Still, they can get along without me for a couple of days, so if I start feeling blue or—"

"After your surgery."

"After my surgery, I'll definitely take you up on that." She paused with a spoon in her hand. As it dripped coffee onto her placemat, the liquid in her cup swirled in a circle. "You really mean it, don't you?"

"Mean what?"

"That we're in this together."

"Of course I mean it. I wouldn't have said it if I didn't. Look, you two have been my family since I moved here. Without you, I couldn't run the store. Yes, Honora and Sid are included, but they're on different trajectories.

Honora has EveLynn. Sid is growing up, and eventually he'll probably move on. Poppy is, and will always be, my grandfather, but I can't see sharing details of my life with him. That's not the relationship I have, or that I want to have, with him."

"But he needs you, just like we do. Maybe more. They won't be using him at the new Fill Up and Go, will they? That's so unfair. Totally wrong. Right now, he's a big help to Sid, but that won't last forever. If Dick doesn't have a reason to get up in the morning, he'll lay down and die. He won't take care of himself. We've seen him spiral down in the past," Skye said.

I'd been chewing on a piece of parsley I'd swiped from the edge of Skye's plate. "That's true. I've been worried about it."

"I appreciate the fact you'll let me work full time at the store. I'll need to."

"Why?" asked MJ. "I bet you'll double your tips at Pumpernickel's when you start showing."

That led to a heated discussion about the legalities of the manager at Pumpernickel's firing a pregnant employee. Finally I said, "To tackle that, we need an attorney's advice. However, even if Skye has a case, this won't get solved quickly. So we need a Plan B, even though we're agreed that the jerk at Pumpernickel's is a total loser."

"Cara's right. I don't know whether I can fight this or not, but even if I can, he's not going to roll over and give up fast. If we can come up with enough work for me to do at The Treasure Chest, that would be ideal. But I won't be helpful to the business if I don't have items to get gussied up for the sales floor. That's the special value I bring to the table. We need more raw materials, and we need them prepped for me to work on."

"Why not hire Dick to do the prep work?" asked MJ. "He's already doing some of it. What if you brought him on full time? He can strip the varnish, reglue pieces, take off the hardware, sand surfaces, put down the initial coat of primer—and leave the finishing touches to you, Skye."

Skye sipped her tea and nodded in agreement. "That certainly would maximize our talents and time. But where would Poppy do all this? We don't have enough space as it is."

"She's right," MJ said.

"I know." I signaled the waitress, and she set the folio in front of me along with a pen. It was hot pink, lime, and orange. That reminded me of Lilly Pulitzer. And that reminded me of Danielle. And that made me realize—

"Danielle's store."

"Right." MJ agreed with a hand slap to the table. "It'll be empty won't it? I mean, I assume her family won't take over the business. That was a pretty specialized undertaking."

"And Claudia's flown the coop," said Skye. "She won't be coming back."

"Then that's the plan. I'll ask around and find out who she was renting from. I'll see if I can take over her space. Poppy can use it as a workshop, if he's willing. He can prep pieces. Skye can do the finishing work."

"And I can sell them," said MJ. "I don't know why I didn't think of this before. I'd been asking Essie Feldman to find us a warehouse space for years and years. Right up until she died. But I'd put that notion aside when you took over. I guess I didn't worry about it, because at first we didn't sell as much furniture as we do now."

"It doesn't matter." I smiled at my friends. "What's really important is that we've brainstormed the challenges ahead and figured out a way forward. Sure, it's a business problem, but point being, we all contributed, and now we'll all benefit. And that's how it's going to be. The three of us. I know you have my back, and I won't let either of you down."

CHAPTER 51

Two days later, we'd settled into a new normal. I was learning to work around the problems with my arm, thanks in part to Skye. She'd moved in, camping out on an inflatable mattress in the upstairs room, the one that had once been an artist's studio. Tommy was enjoying his break, sleeping a lot and playing video games. Sid and Poppy had found a comfortable rhythm. In many ways, they suited each other well as housemates. I suggested that Sid take more time off from work. That way he could heal, and Tommy had a friend his own age to pal around with.

In a surprise move, Dom gave our son a ticket to St. Louis, supposedly so Tommy could visit with his old friends. This was Dom's way of hurting me. What college freshman would rather hang around with his mom than chill with his pals? There was a hunger in me to mother my boy, to cook for him, and simply bask in his presence. But Dom was nothing if not cruel, and I couldn't—wouldn't—make Tommy feel bad about flying up to St. Louis. So I kept my mouth shut even though that was really hard.

After talking to Doug up in St. Louis, I paid a visit to the Stuart Police Department and made a statement to Detective Ollie Anderson regarding what had happened regarding the funds being moved out of my business account.

"Sid's computer went missing for a few days. His stepmother, Amberlee, came and claimed it at the hospital. She has to be involved in the ACH transfer." I wanted to go into a rant about how Amberlee didn't really care about the boy, but Ollie was already aware of the situation.

"I'll see what I can track down. Do you know of anyone who would want to do this? Steal from you and hurt your business?" he asked as he brushed a crumb from his tie. To sweeten my visit, I'd brought biscotti. Food is the universal currency of goodwill.

Of course, my sister popped into my head instantly, but that didn't make a bit of sense.

"I can't think of anyone specifically." I cleared my throat. "Amberlee has to be behind all this. I don't think she harbors any grudges against me. If she does, that's a surprise. Maybe she's not happy that I've taken such an interest in Sid. For some reason, she has a real hatred for that boy. I guess because her late husband loved his son."

"Some people are hard to figure. When it comes to kids, people can have pretty messed up notions."

I wondered if he was talking about Amberlee or about Lou. The big cop still hadn't apologized to Skye. I'd expected to see a bouquet of roses and a penitent man show up at the back door of The Treasure Chest, but so far, nada. That made me wonder if all of us had gotten him wrong. Since Ollie and I were alone in the interview room, I figured I'd take advantage of the privacy.

"Ollie, what's up with Lou? You know about Skye being pregnant, right? Why would he act like such an idiot?"

Ollie used two thick fingers to smooth down his tie. After repeating the gesture several times, he realized the bunched up fabric was hopelessly scrunched. Next he drummed his fingers on the table. I waited. I had all day. Maybe he did, too.

"I wish I knew. He loves her. Right now, he's totally miserable. Captain Davidson raked him over the coals for acting so weird lately. Have you seen him? Lou's walking around like a zombie. Or worse. He can't be sleeping. He bit off the dispatcher's head about something petty. I tried to talk to him, but he tuned me out."

"He doesn't seriously think she was cheating on him, does he?"

Ollie rolled his eyes. "Who knows what's bubbling in that thick brain of his. Of course, it's his kid. Honest to Pete, you'd think he'd be the happiest guy on earth. He's been head over heels in love with Skye ever since he first saw her. Visited her for a long time while she was in jail. She's the only girl for Lou, and that's the truth."

We sat silently studying the table top and thinking our separate thoughts.

"I'll see what I can find out," said Ollie.

I didn't know if he was talking about the unauthorized withdrawal of money from my business account or about Lou's messed up mental processes.

And I decided not to ask.

~*~

As I pulled up to the airport in West Palm, Tommy leaned over and gave me a kiss. He said, "Mom, are you ever planning to have a home again? I miss the way you used to decorate. I know you're busy at the store, but still..."

"You miss our house? Up in Missouri?"

"Yeah. No. Sort of. I miss it because you loved it. You made it comfortable. I won't ask Dad to drive me past it when I'm up there, but I kinda wish this place was like that, too. I teased you about the pillows everywhere back when we lived in St. Louis, and the way you had everything arranged, but I liked it. My friends did, too."

That struck a chord in my heart. It never occurred to me that my son actually cared about such minor details. Then again, maybe they weren't minor details. Tommy had picked up on the love I'd poured into our house. Although I adored Seaspray, I had just moved in. Even at the old apartment, I had lived like a squatter does.

And Tommy had noticed.

"I'll see what I can do, honey," I'd said as I reached up to give him a hug. With a quick smile, he jumped out of the car and headed for the sliding doors into the terminal.

Pulling away, I held back the tears until the exit ramp dumped me onto 95. At the next exit, I pulled off, found a gas station, and gave myself over to tears. The attendant rapped on my window, asking if I was okay. "Fine. Dropped my son off at the airport. Hard."

"Sure is. But birdies got to fly, right?"

"Right," I said, and I moved the car out of Park and into Drive.

Back at Seaspray, I did a slow tour of the place, taking in my empty house. Essentially I had a blank canvas. The renters before me had banged up the walls and left the floor scuzzy. The outside needed a coat of paint. The screens over the vents in the eaves had rotted out. As a consequence, rats had taken up residence in the attic. A pest control company had made short work of them. But to move in, I'd had to scrub the place thoroughly and spackle the walls. Next came a coat of neutral paint. Since my outdoor environment was so blessedly colorful, I liked the idea of a neutral interior that opened my eyes to the glorious views around the house. I could do anything I wanted with this place. Where to start?

Jack cocked his ears at the sound of a car on the gravel. He barked like a wild thing. I hadn't heard the black Escalade pull up, but I recognized the car and its owner, Cooper. In one hand he loosely held a leash. Gerard, the Bahamian Potcake dog, strained to sniff at me and wag his tail at Jack.

"Hi." I ushered them inside. "What brings you two here?"

Gerard ran right past me and helped himself to Jack's toys.

"Stop! No!" Cooper lunged to grab a chew treat. Jack barked at the big dog. Gerard was eager to play, and the two of them chased each other in circles.

"It's okay about the chewie. Jack won't miss it. Come here, Gerard. How are you, buddy?" I patted Gerard as he looked up at me with pleading eyes. He seemed relieved that I wasn't going to yank the chewie out of his mouth. When I sank down onto my sofa, he jumped up and snuggled next to me.

"Bad dog," said Cooper, as he struggled to drag the yellow creature onto the floor.

"No. It's okay. Everything here can be washed." I grabbed the other side of Gerard's collar. That left Cooper and me performing an odd tug-of-war with the dog in the middle.

Throwing up his hands, Cooper pulled up one of the two plastic chairs I'd added for the comfort of my guests. "You sure you don't mind?"

"Absolutely. I'm a big believer in dog-friendly décor. Can I get you anything? Water? Iced tea? Hibiscus tea? What brings you here? News about the Fill Up and Go station?" I figured it was best to take the lead in the conversation. At best, I felt awkward. At worst, his presence always rattled me.

"That and other things. They definitely won't budge when it comes to hiring Dick." Cooper rubbed his jaw. The motion caused his jet black hair to sway. He was an incredibly handsome man, partially because of his Native American blood.

"Okay." I couldn't think of a more suitable response. I didn't want to let him off the hook. He'd promised me that Poppy had a job—and he'd promised as much to Poppy before I'd become involved. Why was it that every time I met with Cooper, I wound up feeling let down?

Momentarily I considered bringing up what happened at Caliente.

Then I decided, Why bother?

"I dropped by because I think I have a partial solution. Or at least an idea that might work. I have a garage where we keep construction equipment. With a little work, it could be transformed into a space your grandfather could use. I've already contracted with a company that'll add a lift. We've installed shop lights. The zoning is fine. I've added extra electrical sockets for any power tools he'll need."

"And the rent?"

"It's free. I'd hope he'd reduce the amount he charges me to fix my vehicles, but that's entirely up to him. I told him that he'd have a job as a mechanic, and I'm trying to make good on my word."

"Have you talked to him?"

"No. I came to you first. I might not have enough time to talk to him and you both. I dropped off an envelope at your store. Inside are details, like the name of the company installing the lift, and so on. There's also a form explaining that Dick has the rights to one-third of the space, rent-free, as long as he wishes. I'll even continue to pay the utilities."

That part about "might not have enough time" raised my curiosity, but I decided not to make life easy for Cooper. Instead of suggesting that he explain himself, I waited.

"Okay," Cooper got to his feet. "That's basically it."

"Basically it," I repeated.

"Except for one more thing. I never meant to hurt you. I'll always love you." His eyes were direct and his voice broke. Obviously, he was sincere. But the endearment came out of the blue. I wasn't sure what to make of it.

"What's this all about, Cooper? You aren't planning to do something rash, are you? Like committing suicide?"

He scoffed. "Not hardly. Certainly not rash. I've been working this through for months. After I drop off Gerard at the pound, I'm turning myself in. You were right. I've been involved in bid-rigging. There's no doubt I'll lose my license as an architect. After the dust settles, I'll probably be able to eke out a living doing construction. At least I hope I will. I don't know whether I'll have to serve any prison time."

My mouth went suddenly dry. How odd it is that we want to be right, but then when we are, we often discover that being wrong would be so much better. I'd guessed at Cooper's crime, and I had a hunch it was the hold my sister had over him, but in the bald light of day, my sleuthing wasn't much of a comfort. While a part of me felt sorry for him, another part decided he was a total fool. How on earth had he gotten involved in something so crooked? And why had he figured he could get away with it?

We stared at each other for a long, long time.

"I'm not the guy you thought I was. I really, really screwed up. So it's time to pay the piper."

"What about my sister?"

His laugh was hollow. "She will probably dump me faster than you can say, 'Keep the ring.' I won't have any more value to her, and she won't have anything more to hold over my head. So we'll both walk away. At least, that's what I imagine. It wasn't like she loved me for myself. I was a trophy, and a valuable one because I represented her getting the better of you. Besides, she'll have her hands full. The little plot she hatched with Amberlee to rob you of your money backfired."

I felt my mouth flop open, but I was too shocked to say anything. That was good, because Cooper continued to talk.

"Amberlee has already phoned Jodi to say the cops up in St. Louis have been questioning her—and she doesn't like the scrutiny. Not one bit. There's no reason for Amberlee to keep Jodi's involvement a secret. Knowing your sister the way I do, she'll find a way to wiggle out of any charges. She's got this very well-developed sense of self-preservation that makes her absolutely ruthless."

I was searching for something to say when he tugged at Gerard's leash. "Okay, I've cleaned up all my outstanding messes. Except for you, buddy."

The dog hopped off the sofa and leaned against Cooper's leg.

"What did you mean when you mentioned taking Gerard to the pound?" I reached over to pat the animal's head. Gerard turned to stare up at me, and then he licked my hand.

"Jodi absolutely had to have this dog when we were in the Bahamas. I suspected then that she was showing off for the other couples. Proving what a compassionate person she is, and all that. But now she's fed up. He sheds. He needs to go out. He chewed on a pair of her shoes. Dog stuff. After I leave here, I'm dropping Gerard off at the animal shelter. I hope he'll find a good home."

"No you don't. I'll take him." I reached out and grabbed the leash before Cooper could say another word.

Gerard stood next to me as I watched the Escalade pull out of my driveway. When the shiny black vehicle disappeared, I gathered the dog into my arms and started to cry.

~The End~

A Note from the Author…

This has been one of my favorite books to write. I've lived on the Treasure Coast of Florida for nearly five years now, and my hope is that I can transport you here as well through my work. If you can feel the sand between your toes, I've done my job.

As usual, I've started planning Book #4 while putting the finishing touches on this one. ***Cast Off*** will visit another Treasure Coast legend, the famous Queen's Jewels that were scattered up and down our shores when the 1715 Fleet (the Spanish Armada) sank.

Meanwhile, if you see a woman walking the beach and picking up seashells, come on over and say hello!

I have chosen to write books about women, who are creative, passionate, and spunky. If you like Cara Mia and her friends, you'll probably like my Kiki Lowenstein Mystery Series. If you like courageous women and history, check out my series featuring Jane Eyre as an amateur sleuth. You'll find a complete list of my works on my author page, http://tinyurl.com/JoannaSlan

Bonus Materials Just for You!

Send me an email and we'll automatically send you a file with recipes and craft projects. Here's the address for the file: AWUBonus@JoannaSlan.com

In addition to adding you to my mailing list at no charge, you'll receive recipes (including MJ's Lemon Drop Martinis and and Honora's Tex Mex Spaghetti Squash) and two craft tutorials.

On occasion I find out that my mystery author friends have discounted books and free reads, when they do, I'll email you!

Thanks so much for your interest!

Hugs and kisses,

Joanna

One of My Readers...

Appears in this book, thanks to a contest she won. Jessie Dimovski. If you sign up for my newsletter, you might see YOUR name in an upcoming Cara Mia or Kiki book. To sign up, just send an email to Sally Lippert, my assistant, at SALFL27@att.net

Talk to Me!

I love hearing from readers. I learn so much from you! So let me know what you think of my characters, my books, and whatever's on your mind. You can email me at JCSlan@JoannaSlan.com. Or you can contact my assistant, Sally Lippert, at SALFL@att.net

Let's Get Social—

List of Joanna's Works -- http://tinyurl.com/JoannaSlan

Joanna's Website -- http://www.JoannaSlan.com

Facebook -- http://www.Facebook.com/JoannaCampbellSlan

Blog -- http://www.JoannaSlan.blogspot.com

Twitter -- http://www.twitter.com/JoannaSlan

LinkedIn -- www.LinkedIn.com/in/JoannaSlan

Goodreads -- https://www.goodreads.com/JoannaCampbellSlan

Amazon Author Page – http://tinyurl.com/JoannaSlan

Pinterest -- https://www.pinterest.com/joannaslan/

Mistakes? I've Made a Few –

Okay, more than a few. We've had this book proofread repeatedly, but you'll probably find something we've missed. Or something I've gotten COMPLETELY wrong. If so, send an email to my assistant, Sally Lippert. She'll come up with a suitable way to thank you—and to break the bad news to me. Sally's email is SALFL27@att.net

~*~

Did You Like the Book?

You have tremendous power as a reader these days! And your opinion really counts, thanks to the magic of algorithms. (The math is beyond me, but the concept isn't.) Your support makes all the difference to me. Here are a few ways you can help me:

1. Leave a review on Amazon, Barnes and Noble, or Goodreads.
2. Buy a copy of this book for a friend.
3. Discuss this book at a book club event. (Let me know and I'll do what I can to provide questions, bookmarks, and even "show up" by phone or Skype.)
4. Ask your local library to carry my books.
5. Mention this book on Facebook.
6. "Like" my page on Facebook.

Thank you in advance!

~*~

How Much of This is True?

I was shocked to learn that there are 20.9 million people enslaved throughout the world, and that Florida is a hub for human trafficking. In one month twenty individuals washed up on the shores of Jupiter Island—all were undocumented immigrants. The prime launching spot for these desperate journeys are the Bahamas.

As for the background of the CIA, I am relying on my research as verification.

There is, indeed, a Museum of Lifestyle and Fashion in Boynton Beach. Their Lilly Pulitzer presentation inspired me.

Also, yes, there is a Creatin' Contest and I, personally, entered Big Wave Dave's Surf Shop—and got an honorable mention! You can view Big Wave Dave's here: https://www.pinterest.com/joannaslan/big-wave-daves-surf-shop-a-miniature-contest-entry/

As for Bahamian Potcake dogs, I recently made the acquaintance of a lovely pooch named Gracie. She's just a joy! You can read more about this unique breed here: http://www.potcake.org/2.html

~*~

Made in the USA
Lexington, KY
22 August 2017